THE ENDURANCE OF
MOSES WILSON

THE LAREDO SERIES BOOK 2

LEE ANN SONTHEIMER MURPHY

World Castle Publishing, LLC
Pensacola, Florida
Copyright © 2024 Lee Ann Sontheimer Murphy
Paperback ISBN: 9798891262300
eBook ISBN: 9798891262317
First Edition World Castle Publishing, LLC, July 29, 2024
http://www.worldcastlepublishing.com

Licensing Notes

Cover: Cover Designs by Karen
Cover-designs-by-karen.com
Editor: Karen Fuller

CHAPTER ONE

Moses Wilson took to Texas life as if he'd been born there and not in faraway Kentucky. He liked the life of a cowboy and ranch hand, comfortable in the saddle. It suited him more than being a farmer back home, although sometimes he missed his folks there. Still, he liked the Double B Ranch very well, and he had two of his brothers there. The youngest of them all, Ezekiel, had grown up into a fine young man who bunked alongside him in the bunkhouse. His oldest brother, Boone, served as top hand and lived with his growing family on one side of a dog trot cabin. Boone had been the reason he came to Texas in the first place. After first hearing the news Boone had been shot and would die, then that he would be hanged for a murder he didn't commit, Moses hightailed it to Texas. He had figured he might find Boone dead and buried, but his brother beat the odds as well as the murder charge. Moses had come to love Boone's wife, Rachel, as a sister, and his brother's two young ones were as dear to him as if they'd been his own children. Jemima, named after their mother, at three, almost four was beautiful and sassy. They called her "Mima." Their boy, Robert, was named after their long-dead father, but everyone called him Rob. If Moses wasn't mistaken, Rachel had been breeding again when he left.

He'd just returned from trailing cattle to Abilene, Kansas. When he'd left in the spring, after round-up, Texas had delighted him with the soft green grasses. Even the mesquite, pesky and prickly as it was, had leafed out. Moses first arrived in Texas in stark winter, and spring was always welcome. In South Texas, it didn't always get as cold or as snowy as back in the Kentucky hills, but he savored the warmth of spring. He'd first come to the ranch in the spring with his brothers at a time of jubilation. It remained the best season, Moses thought. Summer could be very hot and often dry, winter cold and fall wet. Although it rained in spring, that seemed better than the fall rains, which were often chill.

July heat bore down as hot and heavy as a wool blanket as he rode with the other dozen cowboys who'd made the trek, Ezekiel among them. Moses rode lead along with Mac, a Scotsman who had served with Boone in the war and been a cowboy since. Deke – short for Deacon – was the trail boss or point man now, although he understood that Boone had once held the position. Zeke had long since graduated from riding drag at the rear of the herd. Moses craved a long drink of the ranch's cool well water, his throat as caked with dust as his clothes. Over the more than three months on the trail, he'd grown lean. With any luck, Rachel might cook a feast for their return, and if not, Cookie would provide decent grub at the bunkhouse. Liam's wife, Maggie, also laid a tasty table, but he'd eaten there less times than he could count on one hand.

If Maggie wasn't married to his boss, who'd also become a friend, Moses would have fancied her. He admired her dainty German prettiness, with blonde hair and blue eyes. But she was taken, and he'd never poach on another man's woman, especially not Liam's. He'd often wished she had a sister closer to his age, but he'd never heard anything about her family except that Liam met her in San Antonio.

"We're nearly home," Ezekiel shouted as he rode up beside him. "Ain't far at all now."

"I'm glad," Moses replied. He'd get a good wash, some

decent grub not cooked over a campfire, and tonight, he'd sleep in a bed, not on the ground. Most of the time, he didn't mind the trail, relishing the change of scenery and the comradeship around the evening fire. What he didn't like was the endless dust, the frequent storms, dangerous lightning, the chance for a stampede, the possibility of rustlers, illness, or the plentiful rattlesnakes. They'd lost a man on the trail this time to bee stings, of all things. Ol' Matt had been stung multiple times, swollen up, and died. They'd buried him along the trail, but a death was always a somber moment that made a man think about his own mortality.

"Reckon Boone knows we're coming home?"

Moses gazed ahead, his hand shading his face. "I believe that's him just ahead," he told his brother. "Let's ride to meet him!"

The few cattle, almost all bulls that they brought home wouldn't be as likely to stampede as a full herd, so Moses kicked his horse, Gypsy, forward. Ezekiel followed suit, removing his hat and waving it above his head as he whooped with delight. Riding at full gallop, they reached Boone, who remained stationary, waiting.

His brother wore a lazy grin and had a lit smoke in one hand.

"'Bout time you got back. I been lookin' out for you about a week now."

Boone would never admit it but he'd likely been worried. After their pa died, Boone had done his best to fill their father's shoes even though he'd been very young. Having ridden the trail for years, he knew the dangers all too well.

"Weather held us back," Moses said. "I'm over the moon to get here, though. Trail seemed long this time out."

"You both look well," Boone remarked.

"We had a round of the back door trots, though," Ezekiel

added. "Didn't last long."

Boone narrowed his eyes as he looked them both over with a sharp gaze. "Dysentery? You're all right now, though?"

"Right as rain," Moses said. "How's the family?"

His brother's grin faded. "We had a bit of a rough patch, but it's all good now."

"What happened?"

"Let's ride on, and I'll tell you everything going on at the ranch."

Hours later, once the horses had been tended and stabled, after Moses and Zeke had cleaned up and then put on fresh clothing, Boone told them all the news.

"Rachel was with child," he said, eyes sad and voice deep with emotion. "But she lost it, and I thought for a while I might lose her too."

Moses knew full well how much Boone loved his wife and could imagine how concerned he'd been. "I wish I'd been here for you. Is she well now?"

Boone nodded. "She is, but I think it near broke her heart. She was awful quiet for a few weeks, but she's perked up some. Having both of you back will likely help. Don't let on I told you, though, or she might get sad again."

"I won't," Moses said. They were sitting outside under a tall shade tree. "Mima and Rob are doing fine, I suppose."

"They're my pride and joy, though they devil me something awful." Boone's grin was back. "My baby girl talks as much as Ma ever did. Little Rob is chattering, too. I can even understand him about half the time."

Moses laughed. "I wonder if she even recollects me."

"That child? I'm sure she does, Moses."

Ezekiel sprawled out in the grass. He'd be chigger bitten, but Moses didn't say a word. The kid was old enough to know better, and he'd itch if he didn't.

"Any news from Ma and the rest back home?" Zeke asked. As the youngest, he might be the most partial to their mother, although Moses missed her more than he would say. After Boone left, first for the war, then for Texas, he'd become his Ma's right hand. His other brothers, save Garrett, were all married.

"Not awful much," Boone said. "Ma's hankering to see us, she writes."

Moses digested the information. "Is Ma wanting us home to kill a fatted calf?"

Ezekiel sat up and brushed off dry grass. "Oh, snap, is she?"

Boone shook his head. "Naw, she's thinking about coming down here one of these days."

"Horsefeathers!" Moses exclaimed. "Ma couldn't make that long trip. She's not much on horseback as it is."

"I imagine she could manage on the Iron Horse," Boone said, referencing the train. "Railroads are getting closer all the time, and she's stubborn enough she just might up and do it."

"I don't reckon Ma's ready for Texas," he said. Boone laughed.

"More like Texas ain't prepared for Ma," he said. "That's the news from Kentucky."

"Did we miss anything on the ranch?"

"Liam bought a few new horses up around Austin way and Maggie's in the family way. He's looking for a boy this time around, and so is she. He's sticking closer to home these days – baby's going to be born come late August, he says. She's some frazzled and so he got her some help."

"Did he hire a gal from Laredo?" Zeke asked. "Maybe she can make tamales."

"Doubtful," Boone said. "He sent for one of her sisters up to San Antonio. She got here not long after y'all headed up the trail. Name's Matilda, but they call her "Mattie. You can ride into

Laredo for tamales now that you're back."

"I can," the youngest Wilson brother said. "And I likely will once I get my wages."

"I'm 'bout ready to mop up a plate of anything, even whistle berries," Moses said. "We ate cold biscuits for breakfast this morning to head out for home."

"I'd ask you to supper, but Rachel wasn't expecting company, so I doubt there's enough," Boone said. "But come with me and visit with her a spell before Cookie rings the dinner bell."

The dog trot cabin sat beneath some tall trees within view of the main ranch house. For now, Boone and his brood lived on one side, and the other remained empty. As they approached, a very small girl rose to her feet on the porch and dashed down the steps.

"Daddy, Daddy," she cried, her feet flying below her calico dress. She rushed toward Boone, who scooped her up into his arms as she giggled. Then she saw Moses. "Mo-Mo, it's Mo-Mo."

The nickname pleased him and he grinned as she held out her hands to him.

"Told you she ain't forgot you," Boone said as he handed his girl over. "Not Zeke, neither."

Mima hugged his neck tight, then showered his cheeks with sloppy, wet kisses. Moses knew the moment she saw Ezekiel because she began chanting, "It's Z, too! Z came back, too."

Zeke cuddled his niece with the same affection she had for him.

Moses had loved his niece since she was born, but almost two years ago, he'd stayed at Boone's because both his brother and Rachel had been down sick with a bad case of influenza. No hand at nursing, Moses had offered to tend young Jemima. Raised in a large family, he couldn't remember a time when there weren't little ones trailing around. He rocked her, sang some of the songs he remembered Ma had sung, and made up stories. As little as she'd been, Mima remembered.

The day Rob was born, a year ago, back in January, both he and Ezekiel had entertained the girl. They had taken her for a short visit to the bunkhouse and then to Maggie's.

"You're as purdy as your mama," he told her now. "And near grown up too."

Mima giggled. "I'm a little gal, Mo-Mo."

"Could have fooled me." He raised her high into the air, then spun her about till she screeched with delight. He put her down because his head was spinning, too. As Moses waited for the world to stop so he could get his bearings, Rachel came out onto the porch with the baby.

Rob must be two years old now, he reckoned. The kid had Boone's brown hair but it surrounded his face with a curly mop. He rode his mama's hip and gazed at Moses without any recognition. Rachel, however, offered him a small smile.

She looked haggard, he thought, and skinnier than he'd ever seen her. But the welcome in her eyes was genuine, and when she handed her son over to Boone, the look they exchanged warmed his heart. Rachel still loved his brother, he noted, and it was mutual. She hurried down the steps and hugged him, then Ezekiel.

"Welcome home, both of you," she said. "I don't have near enough cooked for you to join us...."

"They'll come for supper tomorrow," Boone told her. "We can have beefsteak with beans, maybe biscuits."

Moses laughed at the joke since the fare they'd eaten for months on the trail was the same.

"No, we won't," Rachel said. "I'll kill a couple chickens and fry them."

"You don't have to go to all that fuss," Moses replied, although the idea of fried chicken made his mouth water. "We ain't picky."

"Pshaw," she said with a light laugh. "You both missed the Fourth of July, still out there. I'm happy to cook. I'm glad you're both back safe. I worry when you're out on the trail."

Boone joined his wife, and with his son tucked in one arm, he slung the other around her shoulders. "You worry all of the time, honey, about everyone."

Rachel rolled her eyes. "You give me good reason, Boone Wilson."

They made casual talk until Mima hung on her mama's skirts, and the baby began to fuss with hunger. Realizing it was likely supper time, Moses made his excuses and headed back toward the bunkhouse with Ezekiel in tow. Midway there, he stopped.

"I think I'll go swap howdys with Liam," he told his younger brother. "Then I'm beat. I'll be heading for some grub and bed."

"I'm hungry enough to eat my boots," the kid said. "I'll see you there."

Moses ambled toward the ranch house, eager to share a few trail stories with Liam. Deke, as trail boss, would have already made a report, but he'd like to embellish it a little.

When the slender blonde woman exited the house and headed for a small, well-tended garden nearby, he thought it was Maggie, but when he caught a glimpse of her face, Moses realized it wasn't. *Must be the sister,* he thought, *named Maddie or Mattie or some such.*

Her soft yellow hair had been braided, then wrapped about her head to resemble a crown. Moses had seen many hairstyles with braids, but he favored this one above all others. The woman moved with a soft grace that made him think of elegant swans swimming across a placid lake. Back home, one of the richest families in the region had a lovely lake in front of their mansion, with swans and he had long admired their beauty. She wore a simple calico dress, but it suited her. The dark blue pattern contrasted with her ivory skin as she sauntered into the garden with a basket on one arm.

Moses watched as she picked leaf lettuce, then pulled a few carrots and a few herbs. As she moved, her position changed so that she faced him, and he gained a full view of her lovely face. Her eyes were a deep blue, framed by golden lashes darker than her hair. Her small nose turned up on one end, and her lips were the pink of spring roses, full and curved. He thought he'd never seen a prettier woman, as dainty and delicate as a china doll on a store shelf.

Once she'd filled her basket, adding new potatoes she dug from the ground, green beans from the bush, and more carrots, she hefted it higher on her arm. It appeared to be heavy, and without thinking, Moses stepped forward.

"Let me carry that for you."

She halted and stared at him, scrutinizing his face. "I don't know you, cowboy," she said finally, her voice touched with the same light accent Maggie had. "I thought you were Boone Wilson, but I see you're not."

Moses swept his hat from his head and bowed. "I'm his brother, ma'am, Moses Wilson."

Her blue eyes didn't waver as she met his. "I've not had the pleasure. Are you new on the ranch?"

"No, ma'am, but we just got back from the trail," he said. "I reckon you arrived on the ranch whilst I was away."

Her head dipped toward her chin in a quick nod. "I came here in late May to help my sister, Mrs. Rafferty."

"Maggie."

"You're familiar?"

"We all know Liam's wife," Moses said. "Here, let me carry that basket."

He took it from her, careful not to spill the contents, wishing she'd tell him her name. He figured he knew from what Boone had told him, but he'd like to hear it from her lips.

"*Danke,*" she said, then blushed. "Thank you. It was a bit heavy."

It wasn't, not to him, but he carried it as she strolled back toward the ranch house. As they reached it, Liam emerged onto the porch and grinned. "Maggie's looking for you, Matilda. Thought you'd got lost in that little ol' garden. Moses, you're a sight for those sore old eyes. Good to see you back, man."

"Always glad to be home," Moses replied. In the short years he'd been on the ranch, it had become that and more.

"Come in, join us for supper," Liam said. "It's near ready, and it's some kind of German beef concoction, but I can vow it's tasty."

"It's *rouladen,*" Matilda said. "With fried potatoes and that cornbread that you Texas folk like so very much. There is plenty."

"Then I'm much obliged, and thank you kindly," Moses replied. "Maggie's a fine cook."

The pretty blonde he'd just met gazed at him, eyes glinting with pride. "My sister is, that's true, but I prepared the meal."

"I reckon it'll be right good, then."

Moses placed the laden basket where Matilda directed him and sat down at the large round table with Liam's family. He greeted Maggie, who was very pregnant but still pretty, and bowed his head for the blessing. Matilda served the food, and at his first bite of the unfamiliar dish, Moses sighed with pleasure. *Rouladen* turned out to be beef steak pounded then, filled with carrots, onions, and bacon, and then wrapped into a bundle. The meat was tender and delicious. He couldn't complain about the taters or the cornbread, either.

Although Liam had already been briefed about the drive by Deacon Lee, he asked about the trail, and Moses replied, adding a few stories to liven the conversation. When he told about the five-foot-long rattler he'd killed at a watering hole, both women shuddered, but Liam grinned.

"I hope you ate it."

"We did," Moses said, although at the time, he hadn't relished it a bit. "Cook boned it, cut it into chunks, and fried it. Wasn't half bad."

"I hate snakes," Matilda said. "I don't think I'd care to eat one."

Moses smiled at her. "If it's up to me, you won't never have to, Miss Matilda."

"I'll hold you to that," she told him with a pert smile. "Call me Mattie."

For the first time since he'd come across her in the garden, she offered him a full smile, and he realized he was smitten. Moses didn't taste the rest of the meal or remember much of the discussion, focused on the lovely young woman. When he left, he tripped over his own feet on the way out but managed to make it to the bunkhouse.

"You look addled," Zeke said when he fell into bed. "You alright?"

"Never been better."

"Where'd you go anyhow? I thought you were right behind me."

"Liam asked me to take supper with his family," he said. "And I think I met an angel."

Ezekiel snorted and rolled over to sleep, snoring within minutes, but Moses lay awake, hands folded under his head, and thought about Mattie.

CHAPTER TWO

She had always vowed she'd never get tangled up with a cowboy, and when she first learned her parents wanted her to spend the summer months at the ranch to help her sister, Mattie balked. Town raised in San Antonio as the daughter of German immigrants, Hans and Isle Baumann, she considered herself very American. Although German had been her first language, and she spoke it well, she preferred to speak English. She'd attended the German-English School through the eighth grade and had considered becoming a schoolteacher, but instead, she'd been tasked with helping at home with her younger siblings. Mattie dreamed big, hoping to become the wife of a prosperous merchant. She wanted a nice house built from brick or stone on Madison or East Guenther Street, one with parquet floors, solid furniture, and room for the children she hoped one day to have.

Mattie enjoyed shopping in the stores on the plaza, strolling past the Menger Hotel to exchange a glance or two with the gentleman who stayed there. She'd walk past the Alamo to smile at the soldiers stationed at the quartermaster's post. Her parents wanted her to marry a good German man, and they had several on a short list, all older, most at least 40, and all established craftsmen. Their favorite was a brewer, Christoph Voight, a heavy-set widower with three children between the ages of three and seven. Mattie turned up her pert nose at him and dreamed.

After her sister wed Irish Liam Rafferty, the Baumann

parents became more determined to make sure their other children wed to someone with a German heritage. It didn't matter that Liam had managed to build a successful ranch, had read law before the war, and supported Maggie with a solid living or sent money back home. He wasn't German, and that would never change.

Maggie married for love, and Mattie hoped to do the same. And, although she'd given more than a passing glance to the cowboys who frequented San Antonio as they embarked on cattle drives or raised a little hell, Mattie didn't think she could marry one. Raised in a fastidious German home, the cowboys seemed too dirty, too rough, too rugged, and too loud. She couldn't imagine one of them settling down to a sedate life with a wife and babies. So, she ignored them when they whistled at her or called after her, or said she was beautiful.

Whatever plans for the summer she might have had ended when her father all but ordered her to go stay with Magdalena at the Ranch. Mattie had sulked and fussed, but she went. Of the siblings, she was the obvious choice because she'd learned a few healing skills from her mother and from Frau Zieff, who served as both midwife and makeshift doctor to the German community. For her trouble, Mattie demanded two new dresses when she returned in the fall and Vati had agreed. On the first day of the three-day wagon trip, she hated it, but by the second, she realized that the open Texas plains could be beautiful. There was a certain grandeur about such wide spaces beneath a huge sky. Escorted by her brother-in-law, Liam, and his top hand, Boone Wilson, Mattie began to enjoy the trip. She marveled at the birds and some of the wildlife. And by the second day, she'd adjusted her thinking about cowboys – at least some of them.

Her brother-in-law might own a ranch now, but he'd begun as a humble cowpoke. He treated her with polite familiarity as befitted a family member and it was apparent that he was capable. It was the other cowboy, the one named Boone, who changed her mind. Although taciturn, he behaved like a gentleman and a guardian as well. Mattie noticed that Boone was always watching, ever alert. If there was a rattlesnake coiled up along the rutted road, he saw it first and dispatched it. When a party of strangers met them along the way, Boone was aware and ready. From the talk around the nightly campfire, Mattie gathered the two men had served together in the late war and that Boone had experienced his own share of troubles since, being shot and expected to die, then accused of a murder he didn't commit. From their talk, he'd escaped the noose at the last possible moment. At night, both men slept on a bedroll under the stars, and on the one night, it rained, beneath the wagon.

He impressed her mightily, and she might have developed a flirtation, except he was married and pined for his wife, Rachel. Mattie could see that his love for Rachel and his devotion to his family topped everything else, and she admired that. Unlike the cowboys she'd seen in San Antonio, he was anything but rough or rowdy, and he gained her respect.

After arriving at the Double B, Matilda kept busy helping her sister, who was great with child. She cooked, tended her small niece, Grace, worked in the small garden, mended clothes, and did whatever needed doing to make Maggie's load lighter. Ranch life turned out not to be the exile she thought it would be, and she began to enjoy the rural pace. Both dawn and sunset were often glorious, bright with color, and viewed without any obstruction. Since arriving she hadn't been to town, the closest of which was Laredo and at least twenty miles distant. She hadn't gone shopping for as much as a bit of lace or a sarsaparilla. Nor had she worn anything but simple calico dresses, nothing with ruffles or a bustle. Funny thing is, she liked the freedom.

When she first saw Moses Wilson in the garden, she mistook him for Boone. He did favor his brother, but after a few moments, she had noticed the difference. Moses wasn't as sober-faced as his brother, and she thought he might be a bit younger. His manner had more merriment in it, and by the time they sat down to supper, she had decided she liked Moses just fine.

He could spin a good story, she noticed, and he liked to laugh – even if it was at himself.

"So, Maggie, how long has Boone's brother Moses worked on the ranch?" she asked her sister the next morning as they sat on the front porch, stitching gowns for the new baby. Inside the house, it was hot, and the porch at least offered an occasional breeze. Mattie schooled her voice to be casual. "He looks a good bit like Boone, and I thought it was him at first."

"They are similar in looks," Maggie replied. "He's been here since Boone became top hand, about three years or so. Boone's been with Liam a good five years before that. They served together in the war, and they're as close as brothers. Ezekiel, the youngest Wilson, came first from Kentucky in 1870, I believe. Moses came later when Boone was in jail, but I suppose he liked Texas enough to stay."

"Wasn't Boone almost hanged?" she asked. "I remember them talking about it on the way here."

"He was," Maggie said. "Liam wouldn't give up, although it was Moses who finally got the real murderer caught so Boone could go free. And that after Boone was shot in the chest and near died, would have if it wasn't for Rachel."

Mattie tried not to sigh. She knew the bare bones of Boone's story – it was Moses she'd like to hear about. "How did Moses do that?"

"You'll have to ask Liam for all the details, but I know he can be a charmer, talk the birds out of the trees, Liam told me."

"Boone served in the war with Liam," Mattie said, recalling talk she'd heard between the two men on the trail. "Did Moses?"

"He was too young. He wasn't, but about eighteen when

they first came to the ranch, all three of the brothers, and that's about three years ago, so he's just twenty-one or so now," Maggie replied. "Just a little older than you."

"No wonder Boone is more serious-minded." Older, a war veteran, and a seasoned cowboy, Mattie thought, and a family man. "Moses seems to be of a merrier nature."

"True, but he can be just as sober and steady. Liam said Moses was a driven man trying to keep his brother from being hanged and wouldn't quit until he did."

"The brothers are close, then."

"*Jawohl!* All three are very close. You haven't met the youngest one yet, have you? Ezekiel? He came here to find Boone when he wasn't but fifteen years old, came all the way alone from Kentucky."

Recalling the trip from San Antonio to the ranch gave Mattie an appreciation. It had taken six days in the wagon. "He must be brave and tough."

"Oh, he is," Maggie said. "All the Wilsons are. Did you see those peaches Liam had the cowboys pick? There's a good stand of peach trees down by the water."

With her head turned by Moses Wilson, Mattie hadn't noticed. "No, I hadn't."

"I meant to make a peach cake or pie, but I haven't yet. If you'd like to take some over to Rachel, I'm sure she'd be happy. She came early to borrow a couple of eggs because she's cooking up a fine homecoming meal for Moses and Ezekiel, but I forgot to mention the peaches."

Mattie had met Rachel and liked her. "That's Boone's wife, isn't it?"

Maggie nodded. "It is. If I wasn't as big as the broad side of a barn, I'd bake something myself."

"I could bake a peach cobbler and bring it over to her," Mattie said. Rachel was Moses' sister-in-law, so maybe she'd catch a glimpse of the cowboy. She recalled that Rachel had recently suffered a miscarriage. Not only had she lost the child she carried, but she'd also bled hard until Boone despaired of losing her. Since Maggie was with child, Liam refused to let her tend Rachel, so Mattie had helped. It'd been so bad that Liam considered riding out to bring a midwife or even a doctor from Laredo. Boone's concern had been powerful, and so had Rachel's grief.

"That would be *sehr gut,*" Maggie said.

Mattie rolled up her sleeves, sifted flour and cut lard into it, peeled peaches, and pounded sugar until she'd made a fine peach cobbler. The fact that Moses would partake of it inspired her to do her best baking. Unless she was mistaken, it would taste fine, and it looked pretty, too. She'd taken the time to make a lattice top crust, cutting strips of the pie dough she made and then layering them over the peaches until it looked like braids. Mattie sprinkled a little extra sugar on the crust and put a bit of milk on it first so it would brown nicely.

When it had cooled enough to carry, she put it into a basket, took off her apron, and straightened her blue calico dress, the one she liked to think brought out the color of her eyes. Then she strolled toward the cabin where Boone Wilson's family lived, taking a detour past the corrals where some of the men were working with the horses. She could hear their shouts and whoops as they broke some new horses Liam had just acquired.

At the largest corral, she sidled in close and stood beneath the lone shade tree to watch. Moses sat on a paint stallion, one that kicked and bucked in an apparent effort to dislodge him from its back. To Mattie, horses were something you attached to a buggy or wagon. Her family had owned one, an older roan mare named Rose whose primary function was to pull the buggy as needed. She'd seldom ridden a horse and, in fact, had been more than a little frightened when she'd been on one. The animal seemed so far from the ground, and she feared being tossed off. At the edge of the corral, she watched as Boone led another horse, a young mare, on a rope, talking to it in what had to be sweet, gentle tones. Beside him, a young cowboy stood and watched. She wondered if he might be the youngest brother, Ezekiel. Liam had been there earlier but had gone home to see his wife. At this stage of her pregnancy, he was concerned and tried not to leave her alone for too long.

As Mattie watched, the paint horse went from bucking to rearing on both hind legs. The animal whinnied as it thrashed. Moses clung to the saddle horn with both hands. She held her breath as his hat flew from his head and landed outside the corral near where she stood. Mattie fetched it, shifting the basket containing the cobbler to her left arm and held the hat in her right.

The gathered cowboys sitting on the rail fence that surrounded the corral or stood just outside it began hollering words of encouragement to Moses.

"Ride her!" one called.

"Keep yer heid," the cowboy named Mac shouted. She recognized the burr of his Scots accent.

"Hang on," Ezekiel cried.

Moses gave it a valiant effort, but the horse had gone wild. Hooves flew in all directions as the animal contorted in every direction and danced about the corral. It almost seemed as if the horse were intent on stomping something on the ground. At the same time, Boone shouted, Mattie heard the sharp buzz of a rattlesnake. She took two steps back, gazing about to see where the snake might be.

"Snake!" Boone yelled. "Moses, hang on if you can while I get the rattler."

She thought Moses gave his brother a nod, but then he lost his seat and flew over the bucking horse's head to hit the ground hard. Mattie stifled a scream as Boone pulled his pistol from his belt. He walked across the corral on steady legs, aimed, and fired once. The horse bolted, running around the corral as Mattie spotted the snake. Until then, she'd only heard it.

The large rattlesnake still writhed and wiggled, so Boone shot it again. This time, it lay still. He thrust the pistol back into the holster and rushed to his brother's side. Moses had crawled to the edge of the fence to avoid the horse's hooves. He grasped Boone's offered hand and came to his feet, leaning against the fence for support.

"Are you hurt?" Boone asked, his voice harsh with concern. "Did you get bit?"

When Moses didn't immediately answer, Mattie walked toward the corral, worried.

"Naw," he gasped. "Not bad, anyway. Turned my ankle, I reckon, but the rattlesnake didn't get me."

"Are you sure?"

Moses nodded. "I am, Boone."

"Thank God," the older cowboy said. "You'd likely be dead if you'd got bitten. It's a big one. You're bleeding, though."

Mattie saw the gash on Moses' forehead and winced at the blood trailing from it. She dithered about whether to set down the basket, then turned to Liam.

"There was a snake in the corral, and Moses got thrown," she told him. "Boone killed the snake. Take the basket."

She thrust it at her brother-in-law and dashed over to the fence. Unless she crawled under the bottom rung or climbed over, she couldn't get to Moses, but she called his name, and he turned.

"You're hurt," she said and handed him the handkerchief she carried in her pocket. "Here, see if you can stop the blood."

His smile lit up his dirty face as he took it from her hand. "It ain't bleeding too bad," he told her. "I'm more worried about my ankle."

Boone touched the brim of his hat to acknowledge her

presence. "Thank you, Miss Mattie," he said, then to his brother. "Can you stand on it or walk on it?"

Moses glared at his brother. "I'm standing now."

"No, you're leaning on the fence. Give it a try."

Mattie reached between the boards of the corral and touched his shoulder. She remained in place when Moses stepped forward and grimaced. He halted and shook his head.

"It hurts like the dickens when I try, and I swear I thought my leg was gonna give way."

"Let's hope it ain't broke," Boone said. He grasped Moses' arm to steady him. "Let's get you to the bunkhouse and let Cookie take a look."

"I can tend it," Mattie said. "I know more than a little about cures and such."

She hadn't meant to speak up, but the idea of a cook trying to treat Moses' injuries upset her. He might do something that would harm more than help.

"Alright, let's get him to the bunkhouse, then," Boone said. "Rachel can doctor him if need be. She did a fine job with me back when I was shot and near dead."

Liam stepped forward, still holding the basket. "Mattie can't go take care of him at the bunkhouse, and neither can Rachel. Besides, your wife has the children to tend. You'll have to bring him to my house or to yours, Boone."

If they brought him to Liam's, Mattie would have full access, but she'd been to Boone and Rachel's cabin many times, too.

"Take me to your place, Boone," Moses said. "I don't want to be any trouble or be underfoot at Liam's, not with Maggie so near her time."

As the men debated how they would transport Moses, Mattie grabbed the basket back.

"I'll go gather some things to help," she said.

As she hurried back to the house, Mattie made a mental list of the items she would need. Comfrey always helped, she thought, and she knew well that her sister had plenty of ground comfrey root. She'd need some willow bark tea to ease the pain, and if she could get some fresh peach leaves, she could use them in a poultice. Garlic, onions, and cider vinegar were other things on her list as she rushed into the kitchen to gather them. Maybe Maggie had an old sheet that could be torn into strips to use as a bandage, and if not, perhaps Rachel would.

"Didn't they want the cobbler?" Maggie said as Mattie burst into the house.

"They will, I'm sure, but Moses got hurt, so I'm going to Boone's cabin to treat him," she said. She sketched out what had happened, gathered the necessary things, and headed for the cabin at a fast clip.

Moses was already there, seated with his injured leg propped up on another chair. He held a wet compress to his forehead, which had stopped bleeding. Boone stood beside Rachel, one arm around her. She'd passed the younger brother and several other ranch hands on the dog trot porch as she entered. Once inside, however, Mattie became almost tongue-tied, uncertain what to say.

"I brought you a peach cobbler," she told Rachel. "It may be a bit worse for wear since I've carried it over half the ranch by now."

"Thank you," Rachel said. "I'm much obliged. I'm frying chicken for a special homecoming meal for the boys, so now I won't need to fret over dessert. I didn't expect Moses to get himself hurt, either. He's had a bit of willow bark tea, and there's more steeping."

"I'll see what I can do to help him," Mattie said. She put his hat down on the table and stood beside him. "Tell me what hurts."

Moses tilted his head as he looked at her. "I've got a powerful headache," he said. "A few scrapes and such, but my ankle's paining me the most. Boone doesn't think it's broke, though."

Mattie pushed up his trouser leg to get a better look. Already, the ankle was swelling and red. "It's going to bruise," she said. "By tomorrow, it'll look awful and hurt even more."

She touched it, her fingers as light and gentle as she could make them, but a moan escaped his lips. Still, she had to see if it could be broken, so she felt the ankle and decided it wasn't.

"You twisted it," she said. "Sprained it hard. You'll be off it for a bit."

"I'll be up on my feet walking in a couple days," Moses said with bravado he didn't feel.

"You won't unless you want to end up crippled," Mattie replied. Even hurt, he had some sass, and she liked it. There were plenty of men who would be taking on much more than Moses with such an injury.

"I can't get crippled," he said. "I couldn't court you if I was."

Moses smiled at her, the expression sweet and tender despite the pain lines in his face and although she should have chastised him, even discouraged him for being so bold, Mattie smiled back.

"There'll be time enough for that later," she told him. "For now, let's take care of your hurts."

The little girl, Mima, came from the corner where she'd been hiding. She touched Moses' arm then hugged it. "Mo Mo got hurted," she said. "He's my Mo Mo."

Mattie smiled. "Then we need to make him feel better, don't we?"

And she thought but didn't say that, just maybe he might one day be her Moses too.

CHAPTER THREE

His ankle hurt, and so did the spot where he'd bashed his forehead open. Moses sat on a chair in the corner of Boone's main room with his injured ankle propped on another. It could be worse. He remembered all too well the time that a horse called Devil's Mischief had injured Boone badly enough he'd been in bed for days, but unlike Boone, he was awake and fully conscious. One hand clutched the lace-trimmed handkerchief Mattie had handed him at the corral, although it was now stained with blood that had dried to a rust brown. His brothers hovered, Boone, glaring from across the room, with a worry line dividing his forehead. Ezekiel wore a frown as he twisted his hat in his hands.

"Don't fret," Moses said, although he could use more than a little sympathy and some tender care. "I ain't dead or anything."

"You could have been," his oldest brother growled. "Least it doesn't seem to be broken. I can see you're hurting, though."

That was an understatement. Moses couldn't decide what hurt the most – his injured head or his ankle. He figured he might have sprained the wrist he'd landed on, too.

Rachel approached with a steaming cup. "The willow bark tea's ready, and it'll help," she told Moses as she handed it to him. "Drink it slow, though, so it won't make you sick."

His uneasy belly gave a lurch at that, but he nodded and sipped it. She'd sweetened the bitter brew with some honey, so it wasn't too terrible. "Thanks," he told her. "I ain't feelin' good at all."

"Mattie should be here soon," Rachel said. "She'll be a help."

He almost managed to grin. Moses had thought he'd heard her say she would come but when she hadn't, he figured he'd heard wrong. When she sashayed into the room a short time later, he could swear he caught a whiff of sweet lavender.

The first thing she did was look at his ankle, and she winced. When she brushed her fingers across it, he moaned, then wished he hadn't.

"You'll be off it for a spell," she told him.

"I'll be up and walking on it in a day or two," he replied. He wouldn't and knew it.

"If you do, you might be crippled."

She was so pretty, he thought, and he nearly answered without thinking about what to say first.

Mattie raised her head and met his gaze. Moses wondered if he'd been too bold and offended her, but then she smiled. Behind her, Boone frowned.

"Mind your manners, Moses."

"He's probably delirious," Mattie said in a light tone. "Out of his head with the pain, I imagine."

"I didn't think he was that bad," Boone said. He came closer and peered at Moses, brow furrowed as if he might be on his deathbed after all.

"He's not, Boone," Mattie told his brother. "He's cheeky, though."

"Brash," his brother agreed, relief easing his expression. "If he's gonna be laid up, I reckon we need to fetch in a bed so he'll have a place to lay. Ezekiel find Deke and Mac to help, then bring up a cot from the bunkhouse. Mattie, what else will you need?"

"Some fresh-picked peach tree leaves for a poultice," she

said. Moses liked the sweet sound of her voice. "A pillow or two and a blanket."

"Ezekiel can pick the leaves. I'll fetch his gear," Boone said. He kissed Rachel and departed.

First, Mattie scrubbed his face, using extra care around the wound and hands. Then she cleaned the gash, put something on it, then covered it with a paste.

"Try not to move while the comfrey dries," she told him. "It'll hurt, but I'm going to take care of that ankle now."

Moses expected her treatment would smart, but by the time she finished, his ankle throbbed, and he thought sure he might be sick from the harsh pain. Mattie had cleaned the injured ankle, then applied arnica, a poultice with both peach leaves and garlic, then comfrey paste over it all. Then she'd wrapped it tight with strips of linen torn from an old sheet. He longed to lay down. A powerful fatigue made him long to sleep, and he closed his eyes, although his perch on the chair was far from comfortable.

"Moses," Mattie said. "Drink a little more of the willow bark tea if you can. I mixed it with some coneflower, too. It may take a bit longer, but it will help, *ja*?"

He nodded. "I hope to shout."

His hands were a bit shaky, so she steadied the cup as he drank. By the time he'd gotten the infusion down, the camp bed had arrived.

"We can set it up there," Boone said. "Or across the dog trot in the cabin no one uses."

"Leave me right here," Moses said without hesitation. He liked company and wasn't much of a loner. If he was over yonder, he'd spend too much time alone. Besides, here, Mattie could visit – over there, she'd need a chaperone.

He got what he wanted, but it was an ordeal. Rachel and Mattie put their heads together to decide he needed to be wearing clean clothes, so his brothers wrestled him into a change of clothing. They managed the task, but they lacked the gentle hands of the women. It took Boone, Ezekiel, Deacon Lee, and Mac to transfer him to the cot, and although it was delightful to be able to stretch out, Moses realized he was also very sore. His body ached, in addition to his other injuries.

It was hot and close inside the cabin, especially once Rachel started frying chicken. Moses inhaled the delicious aroma and hoped he'd manage to eat some. His belly hadn't settled much, and the pain from his various hurts robbed much of his appetite. He craved a long drink of cool water but said nothing. He might have dozed because he realized Mattie was no longer present, and that made him sit up straighter.

"Where'd Mattie go?" he asked.

"I don't rightly know, but she said she would be back," Boone said. "Did you see this peach cobbler she brought? Looks fine."

"That's one of my favorites," Moses replied. He wasn't sure how he missed the fact she'd come with a gift, but he guessed that maybe being thrown from the horse might have taken all his attention. "I hope she does come back. I don't feel so bad when she's here."

Boone exchanged a glance with Rachel, and both smiled, remembering. They'd met after he had been shot in the chest and expected to die. Rachel had refused to accept that, nursed him, and they married.

"It won't be long till you perk up then," Zeke said. "She's coming yonder."

Moses wallowed his way into a half-sitting position and tried to see through the single front window. The effort increased his headache, though, and he sighed. Rachel shook her head and helped replace the pillows behind him.

Mattie came through the open door like a ray of sunshine, her hair shining in the late afternoon sun. She carried a glass jar and set it on the table before she turned to Moses. Her fingers brushed his cheek, taking care to avoid the injured area above.

"You look so miserable and hot," she said. "I made some lemonade. Do you want some while it's still cold?"

"That's just what I was wanting," he said, although he'd never thought about it until she said the word. "How's it cold, though?"

"There's a spring behind Maggie's house, and the water is very cold," Mattie said. "I used it."

She poured some into one of the tin cups they all used and brought it to his lips. Moses thought he could have easily managed, but he had to admit he liked her attentive care. He sipped and sighed with pleasure. She'd managed the perfect blend of sweet and tart. The cool beverage slid down his throat.

"That's fine," he said. "Thank you kindly."

"Where did you get lemons?" Rachel asked from near the hearth, where she turned pieces of chicken over in a cast iron skillet.

"Maggie bottled the juice," Mattie told her. "I suppose Liam brought her some lemons some time ago. I thought it would taste good to Moses, so I made some. Do you want some more?"

Moses did, but he had been raised not to be greedy. "Let the little ones have some first," he said. "I don't reckon they've ever had lemonade before. Rachel might appreciate a sip, too, cooking over that hot fire."

"There's plenty," Mattie told him. She half-filled another cup, and he drank it. Then she dipped a clean rag into another jar, this one with spring water, and wiped his face. It felt wonderful against his hot skin. "You might keep a bit to wash away the taste of the willow bark. You'll need more of it, I'm sure."

"You're more than welcome to take supper with us," Boone told her.

"I will, thanks," the young woman said. "I helped Maggie

finish up their meal, and Liam said it'd be fine if I stay here a bit. He said Rachel likely needs another pair of hands, more than my sister does right now."

Moses managed a small smile, and he thought Boone looked relieved. Rachel probably hadn't recovered from losing a child, he thought, and shouldn't wear herself out trying to tend him. He just wished he didn't hurt as much as he did so he could enjoy Mattie's company more.

Not only did Mattie stay to share the meal, but she also assisted Moses with his. Although he fumbled at first, the fried chicken was crisp and tender, a true treat after months on the trail, and he began to perk up enough to handle the mashed 'taters with milk gravy, the sweet green peas picked from the small garden Rachel had out back, and the biscuits. He sopped his with more gravy and savored the taste. He didn't eat more than about half what he normally would, saving room for a generous slice of the peach cobbler Mattie brought.

"That's the best cobbler I ever put in my mouth," he told her when he'd finished. "You've a good hand for light crust, and those peaches are sweet."

"I'm pleased you liked it," Mattie said. She took the dish from his hands.

"Ma ever gets here, don't let her hear you say that," Ezekiel said, with a smirk. "Ma's always figured she's the best pie and cobbler maker anywhere."

"Ma's runs a close second," Moses replied. The delicious food, topped off with the fine cobbler, made him forget about his injuries a little. "If she ever makes it to Texas, I reckon we'd be so glad to see her. We'd watch our mouths well."

Rachel paused as she stacked dishes from the table. "Do you think she'll really come someday?"

Boone grinned. "She will if she takes the notion. She's got more of her boys here than in Kentucky now. I reckon she'd like to see her namesake here and young Rob, too. I wish she would, Rachel. I've not seen her in so long."

"And you meant to go back once you healed," Rachel told him. "If I hadn't been in a delicate condition, we'd likely have gone to Kentucky."

Moses watched his brother shrug, knowing it was true. He was glad, though, that they hadn't. He liked Texas and ranch life. There was nothing back in Kentucky he missed except his mother and siblings.

"I'm glad we're here, right where we're at," Moses said with a sideways glance at Mattie. If they'd gone home, he wouldn't have met her, and that would have been a sorrow.

She smiled at him as if she understood what he didn't say. "Would you like a little more?"

He shook his head. "Best not. I'm plumb full now."

"It can keep till tomorrow," Mattie said. She put a serving in a dish and covered it with a cloth. Then she set it on the mantle over the fireplace. "Rachel, I'll do those dishes and all if you'd like to sit outside and get some evening air."

Rachel protested, but once persuaded, Boone took her outside with the children. Moses noted the look of gratitude his brother sent Mattie's way and almost smiled. Now that he'd eaten, fatigue had come down over him like a heavy rain shower. Moses watched her clean up, admiring the graceful way she moved and the way she was efficient, then fell asleep.

He woke to the sound of heavy boots outside on the breezeway between the cabins and the sound of men talking. For a moment, Moses was startled, then recognized Liam's voice. He roused and realized that Mattie had pulled Rachel's rocking chair beside the bed to sit beside him. She touched his face. "I didn't want to wake you."

"Is it mornin'?"

She shook her head. "It's barely dark out, though Rachel

and the children have already gone to bed. I imagine Liam's come to take me back to the main house."

Boone entered with Liam on his heels. Ezekiel followed the pair.

"I come to see how this rascal's faring," Liam said. "That and give you boys your wages from the drive. How are you, Moses? Bedfast, I see."

"I'll do," Moses replied. He did his best to look less ill. It wasn't likely, but if Liam should cut his job for someone who could pull their weight, he'd understand. "Least it's no worse than a sprained ankle and a busted head. It'll be a day or two or more before I can walk on it, though, or do my job."

Liam waved his hand to dismiss what he said. "Don't fret. I'll find something you can do once you're up till you can walk and ride again. There's never an end to the work around here, Moses, and you're a good hand. You got banged up trying to break that horse of mine, so I'll pay you half wages till you heal and keep you on."

Relief made Moses almost giddy. "I'm much obliged, Liam, and I thank you."

"Pshaw, it's nothing much," the boss told him. "Let me get you and Ezekiel paid."

Liam paid well and at the going rate. His brother Boone earned a fair $40 a month plus a house to live in and some of his food. Moses and Zeke, when they were working on the ranch and not out trailing cattle, made about $50 a month plus their bunk, meals, ammunition, a horse to ride, and most of the supplies they needed.

He reached into his saddlebag he'd carried inside and counted out a stack of coins for each of them. They'd be gone on the drive for three and a half long months. The usual pay was a dollar a day, but Liam tended to be generous. At the usual rate, wages would come to just over $110 but Liam counted out $150 to each of them. He paid in a combination of gold and silver dollars, creating a sizeable stack. On the months they weren't trailing cattle, Liam paid the others $30 plus their board.

"That's more than fair, Liam," Moses said. "Thank you."

"*De nada,*" the other man said. "You earned it. I rode that trail too many times not to remember. Don't rush your recovery, but when you can, I'll have some jobs for you, nothing too hard. There's tack to be mended and more. Now, before it's altogether dark, I'll take Mattie home with me."

"I meant to stay the night," Mattie said, still seated in the rocker. That was the first Moses had heard of it, but he wished she could.

"You can come back come morning," Liam said. "Your sister needs your help with little Grace. Let's go, then."

"I'll meet you outside," she said.

Boone offered a lantern to light their way back to the main house, then walked outside with Liam. Zeke scooped up his wages and put them in his saddle bag, so Moses figured he must have been expecting the boss to pay.

"I'd best head back to the bunkhouse myself," Ezekiel said. "Moses, I'll stop by tomorrow, then come Saturday evening, I'm headin' to Laredo."

Mattie remained seated until Ezekiel went outside, then she stood and approached the bed.

"Good night, Moses," she said in her sweetest tone. "I'll come back tomorrow, at least for a bit, to see how you're faring."

"I'd like that," he said. He hated to see her go. Her presence made him notice his various hurts less.

"Then I'll be here, early as I can," she said. Then she leaned as close as she could and kissed the uninjured side of his forehead. Her lips were as light and swift as a floating butterfly, but he would swear he felt the small caress down to his feet.

"Good night, Mattie," Moses said and wanted to say so

much more but he didn't have the words. She picked up her now empty basket.

Moses watched her walk through the door and sighed when she vanished out of sight. If it wouldn't hurt, he would have twisted around to catch a glimpse of her, but it would, and it was dark. Boone returned and took up the rocker.

"You're gonna look uglier than a sow's back end," he said as he rolled a smoke. "And come tomorrow, I reckon you'll be bruised worse than if you'd been if you'd tangled with wild coyotes, but I'm glad you're still above snakes."

"I am, too," Moses said. He could well have died in that corral. Men had, and he'd seen some of them pass. He could easily have broken an arm, leg, or his fool neck. That rattler could have nailed him, and he doubted, from the size of the thing, he'd have survived. "Gonna have to keep an eye out for snakes, though. Ma always said where there's one, there's another."

"Or more," Boone agreed, blowing out smoke. He held out the cigarette to offer it to Moses, but he shook his head. "Ain't the first one I've killed round here. Rachel's some scared one will get under the house, and the little ones won't see it before it sees them."

Moses shuddered at the idea. "I'll help keep an eye out."

"I appreciate that," Boone said. "Moses, I have a notion Rachel might be in the family way again."

"That's good news, brother."

Boone nodded, but he wore a sober expression. "It is, I reckon, but since I near lost her a few months ago, it worries me. I love my children, and I want more, a big family like we had back home, but I couldn't bear to lose Rachel. Once you're back on your feet, will you help me?"

"You know I will, anyway that I can."

"All I want is for you to help watch over her, make sure she's not doing anything she ought not, lifting heavy things and such. Carrying the water for her from the well, too. I don't want her straining over the big kettle on laundry day, and if I should be tied up out on the ranch, if you or Ezekiel could help her, I'd be obliged."

Moses nodded. He'd do near about anything in his power to help his brother and Rachel, even if it took away from his ranch hand duties. Even if Liam saw fit to dock his wages a bit, if he was giving Rachel a hand, he wouldn't mind much. He would have once and griped plenty, but he realized if he were around the cabin, he was more likely to see Mattie than he was out on the ranch or down at the corrals.

And he liked that, maybe more than he should, but there it was.

"I'll be more than glad to help, Boone."

Boone grasped his hand and shook it. Moses figured if he hadn't been all bunged up and in bed, it would have been a bear hug instead.

CHAPTER FOUR

Mattie's dreams of a fine home on one of San Antonio's nicest streets had changed. She no longer thought she wanted the size and responsibility of a three-story house with multiple rooms or the fine parquet floors or hardwood she'd have to polish to a fare-thee-well. The appeal of a neat yard with short, cropped grass and lovely, well-tended flowers had faded. So had her notion of a prosperous husband who might be German. Now, she dreamed of becoming a cowboy's wife and life on a ranch. She couldn't live with a husband who wore pin-striped trousers with a cut-away morning coat with a white dress shirt, a patterned vest, a silk tie, and a top hat. Mattie's taste now ran to cotton shirts, simple vests, and wool pants in brown or gray and boots. She found chaps to be an interesting part of a man's wardrobe and liked the look of a tall, crowned, wide-brimmed hat. Mattie preferred heeled cowboy boots to pince-nez spectacles or, worse, a monocle.

She fancied Moses Wilson, and the Texas she had first disdained had an appeal she couldn't deny. Something about the wide, sweeping acres of grass where the cattle roamed fired her imagination, and she adored the flowers that dotted the land. She'd caught the last of the bluebells when she arrived, but now, she found the black-eyed Susan's, daisies, and Indian paintbrush prettier than the cultivated zinnias, roses, and marigolds back in San Antonio. Ranch life had its' own pace and rhythm, and as she adjusted, Mattie realized she liked it. There was a freedom to it that she had lacked in town.

First, her brother-in-law and then Boone had changed her ideas about cowboys in general, but it was Moses who made the biggest difference. Boone had demonstrated responsibility, dependability, and a gentleman's approach to her safety. Liam had done the same, but Moses impressed her with his wit, his charm, and his caring. The Wilsons were a strong family, and she admired that. Being part of it wouldn't be the worst thing that could ever happen.

Liam had gained at least part of his land by homesteading in Texas, and she thought perhaps Boone or Moses might do the same one day. Mattie had a notion maybe the three brothers could go together on a spread, but she hadn't mentioned that to anybody.

When she arrived home after dark, her sister had all but scolded her for staying out so long, but Mattie had argued that Moses needed her.

"He has Rachel," Maggie replied. "I need you, too. Don't forget that's why you're here."

For a moment, Mattie had a few guilty qualms, but then she rallied. "I know, sister," she said. "But Rachel is still recovering from losing a child, and she works hard to care for her family. If I help with Moses, it's less trouble for her."

Her sister scrutinized her and then smiled. "You're smitten," she said, and then added an old proverb in German. "*Wider die Liebe ist kein Krat gewachsen.*"

Mattie preferred to use English, but she understood what Maggie told her, that there is no cure for love. She replied in the same tongue with another adage, "*Der Liebe is kein Ding unmoblike.*"

Then, because she considered herself an American woman, she repeated the sentiment in English, "Nothing's impossible in love."

"Mama and Papa expect you back in San Antonio this autumn after the baby comes."

"And they want me to marry a German man as well," Mattie countered. "Just as they did with you."

"That was before I met Liam."

"And before I met Moses."

Maggie's eyebrows flew upward. "Are you already thinking about love or even marriage?"

She might as well be hanged for a sheep as for a lamb, Mattie thought and smiled without answering. "Good night, Maggie. I'm going to bed because, in the morning, I plan to go back and see how Moses is faring."

Then, because she was a responsible person, she added, "After I make breakfast and get Grace dressed, and anything else you need me to do."

Then she climbed the stairs to the small room where she slept. Through the night, she thought about Moses more than she slept.

Before Liam left, he extracted her promise she'd be home long before dark and in time to assist Maggie with supper.

The sun had climbed high into the sky by the time she'd fixed breakfast, baked some molasses cookies, dressed her niece, and braided Grace's hair, and weeded the garden. While there, Mattie also picked some peas, more carrots, and some herbs. She put a pot of fresh green beans seasoned with some bacon and onion to cook for supper, to go with the always available beefsteak. While it simmered, she made some peppermint tea from fresh picked leaves for Moses and, after pouring it into a stone bottle, set out for the Wilson cabin, leaving the rest of the meal to her sister.

Halfway there, Mattie saw Boone riding. He slowed and tipped his hat to her with a grin.

"He's been waiting for you since sunup," he told her.

"And he's meaner than a bear caught in a briar patch today 'cause he's hurting. Second day's the worst. I reckon he'll perk right up when you get there, though."

"I hope so."

Boone chuckled. "Only time he wasn't bellyaching was when he finished up the peach cobbler you brought. Maybe it sweetened up his temper a bit."

Mattie smiled. "Maybe so, and perhaps these molasses cookies will."

"If they don't, then nothing would," Boone remarked. "I picked some fresh peach leaves this morning. They're at the house if you should need them."

He tipped his hat again, then kicked the sides of his mount. She watched him go, then trekked onward to the cabin. Rachel sat on the bench in the dogtrot run between the cabins, mending one of Boone's shirts while little Rob played near her feet. She glanced up when Mattie mounted the steps and smiled.

"I told Moses you'd come," she said. "He's been fractious all morning. I know he's sore, so I brewed him a fresh batch of willow bark tea and sweetened it with honey, but he hasn't had it yet. He was sick, puking in the night. Mima's tending him now."

Before she had time to wonder how a child so small could care for a grown man, Mattie heard her singing in her high, clear, young voice. She'd heard Liam sing the same tune and on the trip from San Antonio, both Boone and Liam had sung it as well. It was an Irish song, and she remembered the words so with a wink and smile from Rachel, Mattie began to sing along. Her alto voice blended with the little girl's soprano as she entered.

Moses lay on the bed with his left arm over his eyes. He appeared to be enduring more than enjoying until the moment he realized his niece no longer sang alone. As they ended the duet with the last refrain, he scooted higher on the pillows and removed his arm.

"Good morning," Mattie said. The bruises had fully come out now and darkened his face. The worst one centered around the gash on his forehead, but one cheek was also tinted a nasty purple with yellow. His right eye was also black, and the flesh around it swollen. His features were harsh and tight from his pain. "How are you faring?"

"I hurt," he replied in a voice as faded as old wallpaper. "Belly's been riled up too."

Mima crawled onto the foot of the bed, inches from his bad ankle. Mattie winced, but Moses didn't complain. "That was a nice song, baby girl," he said with an effort. "I liked it real well."

Mima smiled. "I can sing more, Mo-Mo."

"Maybe in a bit," he said. "Thank you, honey."

She skipped outside to find her mother, and Mattie sat in the rocking chair, dragging it close to the cot. Moses stretched out his hand and grasped hers.

"I was beginning to think you weren't coming."

Mattie brushed back some unruly locks of hair from his forehead. "I had to help my sister first. I brought some peppermint tea. I thought it would be refreshing, but it should ease your stomach too. If you keep it down, Rachel said she brewed more willow bark, and that ought to help your pain."

"Don't know why I'm feelin' sick," he muttered, putting his right hand over his belly.

"I imagine it's from the pain," she said, with what she hoped was a soothing tone. "What hurts the most?"

"Ankle."

Without asking, Mattie uncovered it and flinched. The ankle and the foot below were both swollen and had to be sore. Both were also bruised a deep purple. She tried not to touch it any more than necessary as she reapplied the remedies she'd used yesterday. The peach leaves Boone had picked were on the table, and she used them in a new poultice, then covered it with a new layer of comfrey paste.

"I wish I had ice," she murmured.

"It's July."

Mattie laughed. "I know, but there's an icehouse over in San Antonio where they store it, and you can often get a bit of ice, even in the summer. It would help your poor ankle."

"If I was a horse, they'd have shot me by now."

Her protest faded when she realized he was kidding. "Your brother would never allow it, and I wouldn't either. Your bed's a mess. Would you like to sit up for a little bit in this chair?"

His good eye widened with surprise. "I'd like it right, well, but I don't know if I can, Mattie."

"It'll be easier to drink some tea if you're sitting," she said. "I'll help you. I promise to be gentle."

Moses managed to swing his legs over the side of the bed and sit on his own power. Mattie put an arm around him so that he could stand on one foot, then hobble into the rocker she'd vacated. That required turning around first, which proved to be an effort. He groaned several times as she assisted him. By the time he sat in the chair, and she'd dragged over another to prop his ankle, he'd turned pale, and heavy perspiration coated his face. His breathing was ragged, and he looked almost green. Fearful he might either vomit or faint, Mattie grabbed a brown crockery bowl from the table, but he waved it away.

"I'm alright," he said. "Moving set my ankle on fire, but it'll pass. It's good to be sitting up."

Once he'd settled, she poured him some of the peppermint tea, and he sipped it slow. More than once, he closed his eyes and frowned, but after a good bit, Moses smiled at her, the first genuine smile she'd seen today.

"That helped," he told her.

"I'm glad," Mattie said. While he rested, she straightened the covers on the bed, smoothing them out, and plumped the pillows so when he did return, it would be more comfortable. Then she coaxed him into downing some of the willow bark tea.

Rachel came in with her children in tow, arms filled with fresh green beans she'd picked from her small garden patch, along with a few other vegetables. Mima ran to her uncle, and Rob toddled in the same direction, both chattering at him with delight.

"So, you got him out of bed," Rachel said with a grin. "That's good. Maybe it will improve his temper."

Mattie stilled her tongue so she didn't say something sharp in return. To her, it was apparent Moses didn't feel well at all, and if he'd been cross, it was no wonder. Instead, she forced a smile. "I believe it will, especially once I give him a cookie or two."

"That should do the trick," Rachel replied. "I've got beans cooking with a bit of salt pork, and I'll make cornbread to go with them. I've got these green beans to string for leather britches beans, and I thought I might fry a few 'taters if it doesn't get too hot. I reckon Moses is hungry along with everything else."

"I am," he said. "What kind of cookies?"

"Molasses," Mattie said. "Do you want one?"

"Two," he answered, and she laughed.

After he'd eaten the cookies, she washed his face, using care around his injuries, and combed his hair. He could use a shave, but that could wait until the bruises faded. Mattie sat on the edge of the cot and talked to him while he remained in the rocking chair. The teas must have eased some of his discomfort because he brightened up.

"I didn't know a German girl knew any old Irish songs," he told her.

Mattie lifted her chin high. "I'm an American girl," she replied. "Liam sings that old song to Grace sometimes."

"Our ma always sang it, too. Boone sings to the little 'uns

sometimes. We all sing out on the range. It calms the stock."

She'd never heard that, but she was a town girl. "Are you fooling me?"

Moses gazed at her, his dark brown eyes steady as they met hers. "No, ma'am. It's the truth. Rachel, don't cowboys sing to the cows?"

She turned around. "They do. Boone sang to me back before we were married, and he sings to the babies. Rocks them to sleep, too."

That moved Mattie almost to tears. "Your husband is a good man, Rachel."

"He is, but Moses and Zeke sometimes sing too," the other woman told her.

Moses spoke up. "When I'm back on my feet, I'll sing to you if you want, Mattie, though I fear I've not the voice for it that Boone does."

Although it was already hot in the cabin, warmth crawled up her cheeks at the idea. "I'd like that," she told him.

He'd become drowsy, and she suggested he return to bed. Moses protested and argued that he'd rather go outside. Although he made a stubborn case for it, Mattie prevailed, and she tucked him back into bed. Once she had him settled, he fell asleep within moments. She took a moment to sit in the rocker, then offered Rachel her help.

"I'd be glad to fry the potatoes or make the cornbread," she told the other woman. "It's not supper time yet, and I left my sister with it ready to serve when it's time."

Rachel sat down at the table and wiped her sweaty face with her apron. It dawned on Mattie that she'd been taking the woman's comfortable chair and made a move to rise. Rachel saw it and waved a hand to dismiss it.

"You can sit there. You've more than earned it," she said. "I appreciate your help with Moses. I'm frazzled enough now with the housework and our babies. It took me longer than I thought it would after what happened with the last one. Boone appreciates it too, more than he'll say, probably. He dotes on his brothers almost as much as the children. I'm just glad that though Moses hurt himself with the horse, he's not bad, not like Boone was when we first met."

"I understand he'd been shot," Mattie said.

"He thought he was dying when I met him," Rachel said. Remembering softened her expression. "And he was very ill, that's for sure. The bullet was still lodged in his chest, he burned with fever, and he was weaker than a newborn kitten. His friends gave him up for dead, but he lived, thank God. I got that bullet out and nursed him till he healed. We got married, then we had a bad time when I thought he'd hang, but Moses came all the way from Kentucky and got Boone free. Moses may hurt, but there's no danger he'll die, and that's a blessing."

Rachel must be made of stronger stuff than she, Mattie thought. She couldn't imagine how she'd feel if Moses were as sick as Boone must have been, and she doubted she could dig a bullet out of a wound. "It is."

Mattie peeled and sliced the potatoes to fry and mixed the cornbread batter. Busy with the work of her hands, she never noticed that the little girl had crawled up and fell asleep beside her uncle in the narrow bed. Rachel had put the boy down for a nap on the trundle in the bedroom and went to sit outside to catch a breeze.

She eavesdropped when Boone came in, Ezekiel right behind him, trailed by their friends, Deacon Lee and Mac.

"How's Moses?" Boone asked. From the sound of it, he'd sat down on the bench beside his wife and lit a smoke.

"Sleeping, but he spent a good part of the day sitting up in the rocker," Rachel said. "He'll do, Boone."

"Give me a little sugar," he said. Mattie, listening, sighed and dreamed of how it might feel if Moses kissed her. "Then I'll go wash up a bit before supper."

Ezekiel burst into the cabin but stopped short when he saw Moses asleep. His eyes lit up when he noticed the cookies and plucked one to eat. His arrival woke Mima, who stirred, and Moses woke, too.

Zeke plucked the girl from the bed before she rolled off and whirled her about until she giggled. Rob began to cry in the other room, and Rachel returned to retrieve her son. The quiet cabin now echoed with the noise of a family, and Mattie savored it. She sat down on the edge of the cot with care. "Are you feeling any better?"

Moses nodded. "I still hurt but not as much, and I'm awful hungry."

"It would probably help if you can drink a bit more willow bark now," Mattie said, unable to resist touching his uninjured cheek. "There's beans, fried potatoes, and cornbread for supper. I helped Rachel."

"She did the 'taters and baked the cornpone," Rachel said, with her son in her arms. "Soon as Boone's washed, we'll eat."

The Wilsons asked her to stay for supper, but Mattie didn't, remembering her promise to Liam. She remained long enough to see Moses eat, then brushed his cheek with her fingers again.

"You are leavin' so soon?" he asked, sounding disappointed.

"Maggie needs my help too," she told him. "But I'll come back tomorrow if you'd like."

"I would," Moses told her. "And maybe then you can sing to me."

A smile stretched her lips, and she nodded. "Maybe I can, Moses Wilson."

She wanted to run back to the main house or fly, but she walked, her skirts swaying as she walked, her heart blooming like the wildflowers on the edges of the dooryard, her mind brimming full.

She would come back tomorrow, she thought and remembered a line from Shakespeare she'd learned in school, 'tomorrow and tomorrow and tomorrow.' Mattie wanted to be there for all those days and more.

CHAPTER FIVE

Moses didn't stay in bed nearly as long as he probably should have, but he couldn't bear lying there as if he were really sick. He had to be up and doing, or he'd lose his mind. After the first time Mattie assisted him to the rocker, he'd sat in a chair each day. Twice, with Boone's stronger arms to support him, Moses had ventured out to sit on the bench in the dog trot between the two cabins. The fresh air, although hot and humid, had done him good. So did Mattie's daily visits.

On Saturday, three days after Liam paid their wages, Ezekiel took off early for Laredo. If Moses hadn't been all stove up, he might have gone too, although he had no interest in drink or women or even cards. After what had almost happened to Boone there, Moses wasn't overfond of the town, but it was the closest one if he wanted to buy anything. Besides, he would have gone to look after the kid, though Zeke had long since proven himself more than capable and to be as much a man as he or Boone.

He did hand over a few dollars to his younger brother to purchase a small gift for Mattie as a token of his appreciation and to begin his courtship. Moses wasn't sure what to have Zeke buy. He considered a hand mirror, but it seemed both fragile and expensive to bring back on horseback. He'd rather not end up with a broken mirror and seven years bad luck, so he discarded that idea. Hair ribbons seemed more like something for a child, and he did ask his brother to bring back some for little Mima and maybe a toy horse for Rob. He added penny candy for both young ones to the list but still pondered what to get Mattie.

He decided on maybe a paper or two of pins or needles, simple and inexpensive. Then, because he liked to read when he had the time and because he knew Mattie had gone to school, Moses asked Ezekiel to see if he couldn't find a copy of Alfred Tennyson's poems published by Harper. He'd read a few and liked them, so he figured Mattie might enjoy the poetry. If he recollected right, the lines from the poem 'Beggar Maid,' "so sweet a face, such angel grace," could have been written about Mattie.

Ezekiel returned with everything Moses had asked for and more. He brought a wooden walking stick, fashioned from a stout tree limb but sanded smooth and carved in a few places.

"Figured you wouldn't stay off that ankle for long," Zeke told him when he presented it with a flourish. "Reckoned maybe this would help you not cripple yourself too awful bad once you start limping around."

"Thank you," Moses said, accepting the staff from where he sat in Rachel's rocking chair. He liked the sturdy feel of it in his hands and, even more, his brother's thoughtfulness. "That'll help get me out and around."

"*De nada*," Zeke replied. He'd picked up the odd bit of Spanish, and he'd brought home a passel of the tamales he'd been craving, too. "Just don't hurt yourself more, or Boone'll have my hide, or Miss Mattie might even slap my face."

"I don't intend to, but it'll be grand to get out and about. I might even hitch my way up to see Mattie at the house once I get the hang of this."

Rachel tucked the spools of thread Ezekiel brought her from Laredo and peered out the window. "You won't need to this morning. She's on her way here, coming across the dooryard now. And Boone's likely looking out for you, Ezekiel, since you waited till this morning to come home."

The youngest Wilson flushed. "I figured it was safer not to ride back at night," he said. "I slept at the livery stable."

"I have no doubt," Moses said as he and Rachel laughed. He meant it, too. Their ma had raised them to be upright men, and they seldom strayed from her teaching. "I'd best go, though, and get some work done. You're gonna have the tamales for supper, though, right?"

"I am," Rachel told him. "And I'll make those *frijoles* the way you and Boone favor since I did learn how from Graciela."

Zeke grinned, then headed out to where he'd tied up his horse, a young paint he'd been riding since their return to the Double B. He leaped into the saddle and galloped off, letting off steam with a wild rebel yell, though he'd been just a boy during the war.

Moses used the walking stick to stand and tried a tentative step, then another. Using it, he could put most of his weight on his good leg, favoring the sprained ankle on the other. Maneuvering was a bit trickier, but he found he could manage.

"I'll mosey out to meet Mattie," he said.

He made his way across the floor and out onto the dog trot space with slow progress. Once there, Moses stepped toward the front and watched Mattie as she approached. She wore a simple dress with buttons down the front trimmed with a touch of lace at her wrists and the bottom of the skirt. The pale green calico fabric bloomed with small yellow flowers, and it suited her. It was fancier than what most women, including Rachel, wore for every day, but he liked it. That basket she toted most days was on her arm, and he wondered what she brought.

When she was about ten feet from the cabin, he hailed her.

"Good morning, Mattie."

She halted and stared, then her face lit with a smile.

"Moses, you're on your feet!"

"I am with the help of this fine stick," he replied. "Zeke brought it from Laredo."

Mattie mounted the few steps, and although Moses wanted to offer her a hand, he didn't. If he lost his balance and fell on his face, it would end his show of bravado.

"You look fine," she told him. "Your bruises have faded a fair bit, and your forehead's got a good scab. How's your ankle?"

"Paining me less," he told her. "I'm favoring it, so it won't get any worse."

"*Sehr gut, sehr gut,*" she said in her milk tongue. That surprised him. She seldom had spoken any German, not in his presence. Then she stepped closer, put down her basket, and cupped his face between her hands. Mattie kissed his lips in a light brush that sent sweet fire through his veins. Moses hadn't expected that, and he teetered for a moment, afraid he'd fall.

"I had to," she told him, her cheeks bright pink. "You've worried me so and to see you standing upright made me so glad I had to kiss you. I hope you won't think I'm shameless or too bold."

He'd show her shameless if he'd had his full strength and wasn't leaning on a stick. "Never, honey," Moses told her. "Before long, I'm going to be giving you genuine kisses."

She tilted her face up to his, and although unsteady on his feet, he lowered his mouth to hers. He had just touched lips when he heard a horse at fast gallop approaching so he stepped back, wary.

Boone rode into the yard at top speed, so Moses knew something was amiss.

"What is it?" he asked, fearing some mishap with Zeke or a disaster like a wildfire creeping across the land.

"Maggie's time has come," his brother replied as he pulled his horse to a stop. "Mattie's needed, and Liam wants Rachel to come, too."

Mattie's eyes became wild, and her expression worried. "Now? She was fine when I left."

"Her water broke," Boone said. "Liam sent me to fetch you and Rachel."

He paused, then noticed his brother standing. "Well, you're upright and outside. That's grand. Is that the cane Zeke brought you from Laredo?"

Moses nodded. "It is. Boone, if Rachel leaves, who's gonna keep the little ones?"

"You are," the older man replied. "I'll send Ezekiel over to help in a bit, too. Where's Rachel?"

She stepped out, wiping her hands dry on her apron. "I'm here, Boone. What's the matter?"

"Maggie's time is here," he said. "Liam wants Mattie home and for you to come, too. Moses will mind the children. Get what you need, and I'll take you to Liam's on Sprat. Mattie can follow on foot."

Mattie turned to Moses. "I'd like to stay, but I mustn't."

"I know," he replied. "Go to your sister, and I'll see you soon."

She reached into the basket and handed him donuts wrapped in a clean towel. "I brought these for you – there are plenty more at home. Take care, Moses."

He touched his hand to hers. "I will, and I'll be thinking of you."

Mattie began walking back the way she'd come while Boone rolled a smoke. He smoked while waiting for Rachel, who emerged from the cabin with a clean apron and a bundle. Boone maneuvered Sprat up alongside the porch steps and offered his wife a hand. She took it, and he pulled her onto the saddle in front of him.

"Zeke will be along soon," he said. "Mind the young ones,

Moses."

Before Moses could say that he would, Boone wheeled the horse around and headed off toward Liam's. His niece came out and held out her arms to be picked up. Moses obliged, and she clung to him.

"Mama said you'll take care of us while she's gone."

"You know I will," he told her. "Let's go see what your brother's doing."

Robert sat on the floor with the wooden toy horse Ezekiel had brought from Moses' list. The surprisingly realistic animal had been painted brown, much like Moses' own horse, Buttons, and was complete with mane, tail, and saddle. It sat on a board with wheels so it could roll back and forth, so Rob pushed it to and fro, trying to make cowboy talk. He wore a grin, as well as a smock-like dress like all little boys did. Moses couldn't remember wearing one himself, but he could just recall when Zeke had.

"Play, Mo-Mo," the kid demanded. He had Boone's stubborn expression and wasn't likely to take 'no' for an answer, but Moses doubted he could manage to scramble back up if he got on the floor.

"How about a donut instead, kid?"

Moses unwrapped the donuts Maggie brought and tasted one. The sweet taste flooded his mouth, and he savored it. Since he'd eaten a hearty bowl of porridge – what Rachel called oatmeal – with the rest, he ate just one and let each child have a donut, too. That kept them busy for a short while. Then he taught them to play a game he recalled from his own boyhood, one that his mother used to entertain them on rainy or snowy days called 'Simon Says.' He took the role as Simon, reminding the babies they had to do what he said but only if he prefaced it with 'Simon Says.'

"Simon says stick out your tongue," Moses said, starting the game and laughing when both did. He had them hopping on one foot, sitting, standing, crawling, and dancing, but by the time Zeke arrived, he was worn out, but the kids were happy.

"Thought by now you'd taught them to play faro," Zeke said as he came inside. "Might be a good skill to have, for it's served me well enough."

"You won, then, in town."

"I did, a fair bit."

"Cards near cost Boone his life," Moses said. He hadn't been in town when his oldest brother took a bullet to the chest and almost died from it, but he'd arrived in time to see him withering in jail.

Ezekiel turned one of the chairs around backwards and sat down. "I ain't forgot. I was here for that, watched him burn with fever, getting weaker every day until Rachel had the guts to pick up a knife and dig the bullet out. She wouldn't give him up for dead, and so he lived. Don't mean faro's bad luck, though."

Moses shrugged. "Might not be, but I ain't seen him play cards since."

Zeke laughed. "He don't exactly have the opportunity out here on the ranch, although he could over at the bunkhouse, but he's a family man now. So, we're minding the tots?"

He nodded. "Guess it's too soon to hear if Liam's got a new son or daughter."

"Yep, I stopped by there and talked to Boone. Gonna be awhile yet, he said. Heard Mattie brought over some donuts."

"On the table, help yourself."

Zeke turned to grab one. He munched it down. "She's a fair hand with cooking."

The compliment made Moses proud. "Mattie is."

"I reckon she'll be going home before long, now that the baby's almost here."

Moses lost hold of the walking stick, and it clattered to the floor. Somehow, that thought hadn't occurred to him. "Why would she?"

"It's why she came in the first place, to help her sister. Once this kid is born and Maggie's back on her feet, I reckon Mattie will head back to San Antonio."

He had known but had pushed it out of his mind. His plans to court her were in jeopardy if she left. The book of Tennyson's poems lay on the table beside the papers of pins and needles. In the rush, Moses hadn't given them to her yet. He'd meant them to be the first of many tokens of affection, leading up to a traditional courtship, then marriage. He had fancied her from the moment he saw her, but now he loved her. The idea of Mattie leaving put him in a dither, and he sat, his thoughts flying faster than birds over a cornfield.

"Moses?"

"Yeah?"

"You ain't taking a bad turn, are you?" his brother asked. "You went white, and you ain't said a thing for a spell."

"Naw, I'm good," he said, but inside, he feared his heart might break at the thought. He wanted to rush up to the ranch house and give her the gifts, but he knew she'd be busy. She wouldn't have time to see him, so he would wait. "I'm just figuring what to do next with these young 'uns."

"I can teach them to play naughts and crosses," Zeke said. "They're big enough, I reckon. We'll go outside, and I'll draw in the dirt 'cause I doubt Rachel's got much paper to waste. Maybe you could rustle up something to eat. It's past noon now."

"There's those tamales."

"I doubt much these kids can eat that spicy stuff and 'sides, I planned to keep them for Boone. Maybe keep them warm and cook up something else."

"I can do that," Moses said. Earlier, he'd had an appetite, but right now, it'd gone with the realization Mattie would be heading back to San Antonio. A gal that pretty would likely have her pick of suitors, and a humble ranch hand, a cowboy, might not stack up against tradesmen, or storekeepers, or bankers, or lawyers, or even soldiers.

Ezekiel led the babies outside. Moses watched from the door as he drew out the lines, then let them guess if they wanted to put an 'x' or an 'o' in the boxes to make three of a kind. He limped back inside, peeled a few potatoes to fry, and fried some bacon. Ma had taught all her children, including her sons, to cook and tend house if needed. Those skills had served him well.

After the meal, Mima got her doll and mothered it outside on the breezeway under Ezekiel's watch. Moses cleaned up the dishes they used and noticed Rob was heavy-eyed. He still napped, and Moses wouldn't mind one himself. He picked up the boy and rocked him, singing to pass the time. He sang a few of his mother's Irish ditties and then a haunting song he'd learned from Mac out on the trail called 'Glenlogie.' It, like many of the old ballads, was a love story and, as he sang, one of the lines stood out to him in a way it hadn't before, 'I've laid my love on you and you're aye in my mind.' It summed up how he felt about Mattie, so he sang it twice. Then he sang a few of the tunes they used to soothe the herd by night.

"Got the bellyache, or are you singing?" Zeke asked when he came in, carrying a sleepy little girl.

Moses shot him an annoyed look. "I ain't as sweet-tongued as Boone, but I'm singing the kid to sleep."

Boone had a good tenor voice and could carry the tune well. Moses knew he tended to wander around it a bit, but the cattle never cared, and he figured the wee ones wouldn't notice.

"I'm just picking at you," Ezekiel said. "Mima got tired too. I'll put her down on her folks' bed, and if Rob's sleeping, I'll move him there, too. Then, if you want to rest a spell, you can."

"I will, thanks." He could use it and knew it. His ankle throbbed in a way it hadn't for a couple of days, so once the children were settled, Moses stretched out on his cot. He didn't think he'd be able to sleep, thinking about Mattie's departure, but he did and didn't wake until Zeke served a light supper.

"I made them some cornbread and scrambled some eggs," he told Moses. "We can eat the same or sneak a few tamales. There'll still be some left for Boone and Rachel when they come home."

"They ain't back yet?"

Ezekiel shook his head. "Naw. I reckon they'll come when they can, not before."

It was near midnight when they did, Boone riding at a slow walk with Rachel before him in the saddle. Zeke had fallen asleep on the camp bed, but Moses rested after his nap, sat outside to enjoy the relative cool of the night. Ma had always cautioned against being out at night because of the vapors, air that might bring sickness with it. Funny, Moses thought now, she hadn't minded a bit when they rose before dawn, still in darkness, to tend the stock or start the day.

Boone halted the horse and called, "Is that Moses or Ezekiel?"

He'd thought he would be invisible in the dark, but Boone had always had the vision of a cat, even at night.

"It's me, Moses."

"Can you help Rachel down? I'll put the horse up and be back."

"I will. So, the child's here?"

It was too dark to see his face, but Moses heard the grin in Boone's voice. "It's a boy, weighed almost ten pounds. They named him Seamus Heinrich Rafferty, and he's lively. Fussed about being born, howling, and carrying on worse than a wildcat."

Moses lifted Rachel down from the saddle, and she hugged him.

"Thank you," she said. "I'm so tired I could sleep standing

up, I believe."

"Go on to bed, honey," Boone told her. "I'll be there soon enough. Got any grub, Moses?"

"We kept the tamales warm, saved some back for you."

"That'll do."

Inside, Rachel lit a lamp, and the glow roused Ezekiel. He sat up, scrubbed his face with both hands, and yawned. Once he heard the good news about Liam's son, he headed for the bunkhouse. Moses took his place on the narrow cot and turned his face to the wall, so Boone and Rachel could have some measure of privacy.

He could have listened to their soft whispers but didn't. His mind and focus were all on Mattie Baumann and how much he wanted her for his bride.

CHAPTER SIX

Mattie longed to go to Moses once her sister's baby, a big, healthy boy, had been born, but she knew she didn't dare. By the time Seamus had arrived, been washed and swaddled, dark had fallen. Maggie had delivered the afterbirth, and she needed to be cleaned up, which Mattie did with Rachel's help. When the time came for the baby to be pushed out, Liam had taken over and brought his son into the world, but until then, the women tended Maggie.

There had been several times when Mattie was present for a birth, but until now, there had always been a midwife or doctor present. Out here, on this ranch deep in the Texas countryside, there had been no one, just the three of them. Boone had stayed with Liam, smoking and talking as they waited, and Mattie thanked God for his presence. He'd kept her brother-in-law calm and out of the room until the crucial moment. Rachel had been steadfast, always placid and gentle.

If Rachel thought about how she'd suffered a bad miscarriage and came near bleeding to death, she didn't show it. Mattie had been there to provide what skills she could, but in her experience assisting Frau Zieff, most women didn't lose nearly as much blood as Rachel. It had been unusual, and she hoped it wouldn't happen again. Rachel showed signs she might be with child again, and if Mattie had noticed them, she would have guessed it from the way Boone treated her as if she were fragile, breakable as if fashioned from spun glass. More than once, he'd stuck his head through the door to make sure Rachel wasn't lifting anything heavy or overdoing it. Although Boone was as tough a man as she'd ever known, his tenderness for his wife was evident.

Once the Wilsons headed home and Liam settled in with his wife and new son, Mattie checked on Grace, who'd been put to bed hours earlier, then retired. She didn't even bother to change out of her dress into a nightgown. She woke early and started coffee before daybreak, then prepared breakfast.

Liam emerged from the bedroom wearing a jovial smile. "Good morning, Matilda. It's a fine day, isn't it?"

"It is. Sausage and biscuits are almost ready."

"Smells like heaven. I don't think I ever had a bite to eat yesterday, nothing but coffee and a slice of bread with butter," Liam replied. "Maggie appreciated you and Rachel very much. When Grace came, it was just me and Cookie, no other women. I do believe it made a difference."

Mattie tried to imagine enduring Maggie's pain. It had been difficult enough, although her sister had been brave and never screamed, not once. Alone, though, it would be almost unthinkable.

"I expect that it did."

She poured Liam coffee and put a plate down before him. Then she poured a much-needed cup of her own and joined him.

"You'll be glad, then, to return home in a few weeks, a month at most," Liam said.

The hot beverage went down wrong, and she spluttered, choking. "Home?"

"Back to San Antonio," he replied with a chuckle. "I recall how you weren't too happy about coming in the first place, so we'll get you home as soon as Maggie can spare you."

Moses had blinded her, she realized. She had forgotten

that she would be returned home once the child came and her sister could manage alone. Her zeal to get back to San Antonio had vanished somewhere during the hot summer days. Still reluctant when Liam and Boone transported her to the ranch, she'd changed her thinking about many things. Before, Mattie had believed that the ranch must lie in a barren desert, a wasteland where only skinny cattle afflicted with the mange lived, where everything was brown and sparse. She'd figured that the ranch house would be a shack, a mere step up from uninhabitable, and that the cowboys would be gauche, rough men with no redeeming qualities.

Instead, she saw the beauty in the Texas plains, in the well-fed cattle, in the green vegetation, and the wildflowers. Mattie had found the ranch house to be a fine home, spacious and with a small second story. It remained relatively cool in the summer heat, and she expected it would be warm in the winter. And the ranch hands had proven to be good men, possessed of character and manners and intelligence. They were open and honest, far more so than many of the gentlemen she'd met back home. They lived their own code of honor, and although she hadn't spoken the thought aloud, she thought of men like Boone, Moses, and Ezekiel, and the others as 'knights of the prairie.' The knights of old had to be strong and tough, too, she had realized.

Now, she hated to think of going home and even more of leaving Moses Wilson behind.

"I'm in no rush," she told Liam. "I can stay as long as Maggie needs me."

"Pshaw, it won't be that long. She'll be up in a week and have the two children in hand soon after. I'd like you to stay until she's fully on her feet and has a routine, but I plan to get you home as soon as I can."

At home, she would return to a life where she tended her younger siblings, two girls, Minna (Wilhelmina) and Marlene

(Lena), ages twelve and ten, and a brother, Manfred (Freddy), who was fifteen. She would help around the house, go shopping, and perhaps accompany Frau Zieff on a few midwife calls. Mattie no longer wanted to teach school or marry a prosperous man.

"I'm in no hurry," she told him. If she said more, she might as well blurt out that she was rather smitten with Moses Wilson.

"You'll not want to be here when the fall rains come," Liam told her, polishing off his breakfast. "I gave Boone the day off since he was here so late with Rachel, so I'm heading down to check on the hands. I'll be back in plenty of time for dinner."

At the main house, unlike at Rachel's, the main meal of the day was served at midday because Liam always came home for it. Rachel served hers in the evening after Boone returned from a long day in the saddle. Although she'd been up very late as well, apparently, Liam expected her to make dinner. With a sigh, Mattie went about finding something to cook and cooking it. She settled on the green beans she'd picked the day before, seasoned with bacon and served with ham slices that she cut from a ham in the smokehouse, one they whittled at as needed. She could boil or fry some potatoes to go with it, she thought, and it would be enough.

The first free moment she had, Mattie went to see her sister and the baby. Maggie sat up in bed with Grace curled up beside her. Young Seamus nursed at Maggie's breast.

"Something smells good," Maggie said. "I'm hungry."

"I'll bring you something to eat soon," Mattie answered. "Looks like your son was hungry, too."

"That he is and greedy."

"He looks like Liam."

Her sister's smile was sweet. "I think so, too."

After they'd all eaten dinner, Maggie in the bedroom on a tray, Liam said he would spend the rest of the day at home. Mattie put the kitchen in order and made sure Grace would stay with her parents. Using the excuse that she would be in the garden, she set out for the cabin, her feet hurrying so fast she almost stumbled more than once. Her need to see Moses was almost as powerful as her need to breathe. The heat of the day baked the earth, and she perspired as she rushed. More than halfway there, Mattie paused to draw a deep breath and saw Moses.

He made his way toward her, leaning on the walking stick, a bundle in his hand, head down, as he concentrated on each step. Delight shot through her, and she called out to him.

"Moses!"

When he glanced up, a grin spread across his face as she dashed to meet him. He held open the arm that didn't hold the stick, and Mattie ran to him. Moses held her close, bold now that he knew she would be going away soon, and for the first time, he kissed her proper, full on the lips. His mouth reminded her of warm honey with the same rich sweetness.

"I was coming over," she told him, stepping back, blushing.

"I was headed to see you," Moses replied. "I got a couple little gifts for you, to show my uh, regard and to thank you for tending me. I would likely still be abed if you hadn't."

"I don't know if you should be up and walking on that ankle, but I'm pleased to see you. Come on, since you came this far, let's go sit in the garden. It's cooler there, and there's a small bench."

Moses lifted his gaze skyward, and for the first time, Mattie noticed that clouds were moving in, swift and dark. "I reckon it's gonna rain soon. We might get wet."

"I don't care if we do."

He grinned. "Well, I do, honey. For one thing, I'd rather not be soaked to the skin without a slicker, and I don't want this gift wet, either. Mud'll make it slower going back to the cabin, too."

"Let's go sit on the porch at the ranch house."

"Will Liam mind?"

"Why would he?"

The first fat drops of rain splattered between the neat rows in the garden, so they headed for the porch. Mattie paced herself with Moses' slow progress, so they still got wet. Laughing, they fell onto the bench there, and she dashed inside for towels. Liam poked his head out of the bedroom.

"Is it raining?" he asked. "Who's here? One of the hands?"

"It's Moses," she said.

"He came on foot? He must be improving."

"Ezekiel brought him a walking stick from Laredo," she replied. "I believe he was trying it out."

Liam popped onto the porch and greeted Moses. "So, you're up and about?"

"I'm trying to be," Moses told him. "It's my first effort, and I hope not to fall on my face. Once I can do that, I can get back to work."

"Take your time. There's no hurry," Liam said with a wave of his hand. "You're a good hand, and I value that. I'll still pay half wages until you can get back to work."

"I do appreciate that, Liam."

Mattie listened, pleased, then reached for the towels and handed Moses one. "Dry off before you take cold," she told him. "Liam, Maggie asked for you."

"Stay as long as you like on the porch," Liam said as he opened the door. "I don't expect it to rain long, though."

As soon as his footsteps retreated, Moses toweled his hair so that it was half-dry. He approached Mattie and put the wrapped bundle in her lap.

"For you," he said with a flourish of his hand. Then he sang softly, *"I'd buy for you a paper of pins, for that's the way my love begins."*

Her cheeks turned hot, and she knew she must be blushing.

Mattie kept her head down, intent on opening the package. He left out the lines "if you will marry me," but she didn't sing back the traditional lines either, so she didn't sing the ones about rejection. The rhythm of her heart increased.

"Thank you," she said. "I can always use some good needles and pins. Maybe I'll make you a shirt."

"I'd like that fine. But that's not all."

Mattie undid the cloth and pulled out the poetry volume. It was a handsome book, the cover a light green edged in gold with gilt letters. "Oh! It's a book of Tennyson's poems," she cried. "Moses, this is a wonderful present. I like poetry, and Lord Alfred Tennyson's a favorite."

"I reckon we might read a few poems together sometime."

"We could." She liked the book, he could tell by the bright sparkle in her eyes and the happy lilt of her voice. "Do you like to read? Do you like poetry?"

"I do," he replied, surprising her. "I read when I can, and I toted a couple of books along on the drive last spring. I like Tennyson, too."

Moses leaned back and recited the opening lines of 'The Lady of Shallot' from memory.

"On either side the river lies long fields of barley and of rye, that clothe the wold and meet the sky; And thro' the field the road runs by to many-tower'd Camelot."

Mattie blended her voice with his, and together they recited the poem.

"I learned that to recite at school," Moses told her when they finished.

"He uses such lovely language," Mattie said. Then she stared straight into his eyes and asked, "Did you mean that you sang from the song, that's the way your love begins?"

Moses rose, his motions stiff, and with effort, he knelt before her chair.

"With all my heart," he told her and with his fingers crossed his chest where his heart would be. "I mean to court you, Mattie, and I will."

Her heart skipped a beat, and she smiled. She touched his face with her fingers, a soft caress, and he smiled back. Then she remembered and began to cry. His expression faded, and his mouth turned down in a frown. He used the walking stick to stand.

"What's wrong, Mattie? I thought you wanted to be courted," he said. His voice had the edge of brittle glass. "If you don't, then I offer my apology to you, and I'll take my leave."

She came to her feet in a rush that made her head spin. "Don't go, Moses, don't. I do want you to court me."

He didn't smile. "Then why the tears?"

"Because Liam plans to take me home to San Antonio in a few weeks," she told him, the words tumbling from her mouth like scattered marbles. "Moses, I don't want to go but…"

"You'll have to," he said. "I know. Zeke reminded me a bit ago. I'm not happy about it neither."

"I wouldn't go, but my Mama and Papa expect me back," she told him, still crying. "I want to be here, with you, on this ranch. I don't want to go back to town."

She doubted he would understand and would turn away from her. He'd find himself a gal in Laredo or on some other ranch to court. Her life would be lived out as a spinster in San Antonio for Mattie couldn't imagine being with anyone but Moses now.

"It won't be forever," Moses said. "We can figure it out. Ma used to tell us if there's a will, there's a way, and I believe it."

He offered her hope, like a lifeline thrown to someone drowning, and she took it.

"I want to, too. But how?"

"I don't rightly know, but we'll find a way. Mattie, I love you."

His words touched her, moved her to the depths of her soul, and resonated.

"Moses, I love you too," she told him.

Already standing, he took a step closer and wrapped his arms around her. He kissed her full on the mouth, his lips sweet and tender. "I'll court you," he told her. "I want to make you my wife. Would you marry me, honey?"

"*Jawohl*," she replied. "Yes, yes, yes, Moses. But we'll have to wait a bit."

He nuzzled her nose with his. "I know that woman, but now we're promised, and I'm a man of my word."

Her love for this sweet man filled her heart until she thought it would burst, and so much joy that she thought she could probably fly. Mattie had to be realistic, though. "It might be a year before we can," she told him. "My mama and papa are strict about such things."

"I'd marry you tomorrow, but I can wait. You're worth it, darlin'."

This time, brash as it was, Mattie was the one to kiss Moses.

And his brother Boone rode up in time to witness it.

"Well, don't that beat all?" Boone drawled with a grin. "I come out to see if this yahoo fell on his face in the mud, and instead, he's getting some sugar. Got my drawers in a knot for nothing."

Moses laughed, and after a moment, Mattie did too, although she knew by the rush of heat to her cheeks she blushed. "Don't say anything to Liam, Boone."

His eyes narrowed with interest, and he nodded. "I won't. Ain't my place to cause anyone grief. If you want a ride back, jump up behind me, Moses."

Mattie's eyes met his. She longed for him to stay, but she had supper to serve, and little Grace would be searching for her auntie. "It'll save you walking back on that ankle," she said. "I'll come see you tomorrow and make sure you didn't injure it more."

His grin delighted her. "I'd like that, Mattie."

He handed the walking stick to his brother and, in one swift, graceful motion, mounted behind Boone. Moses raised a hand in farewell. Mattie stood on the porch and watched them go, waiting until they were out of sight before she sighed and went back inside to do her duty.

Although she served supper, she never tasted it. Mattie went through the motions of washing dishes, helping Grace get ready to turn in, taking a turn rocking the new baby, and talking with her sister, but though she was there in body, her mind flew free, dreaming of all things bridal.

Like any young woman, she'd dreamed of love and romance. Back in San Antonio, Mattie had imagined a fancy wedding with a satin dress trimmed in Chantilly lace, a ceremony with multiple attendants, a veil to cover her features, and a groom wearing a long morning coat in a dove gray with a top hat to match. Her ideas were simpler now but centered on Moses Wilson with his slow grin and soft brown eyes that lit up at the sight of her.

Maggie noticed her distraction but didn't ask. Maybe she was still too tired after giving birth. As Mattie held little Seamus, she imagined cradling an infant of her own, one with Moses' features. Until now, she'd not thought much about becoming a mother. She'd spent too much time tending her younger siblings to crave babies of her own. Now, Mattie thought she'd like very well to raise children with the man who held her heart.

Liam seemed to observe her preoccupation as well. "Are you feeling well, Mattie?" he asked. "You've not said more than a few words."

"I'm well," she told him. "Just a little weary."

"Was Moses Wilson deviling you? He's a good man, but he's not as sober as his brother Boone."

She smiled and didn't try to hide it. "He's no trouble to me, Liam."

Her brother-in-law nodded. "Glad to hear it. Don't get any starry-eyed notions about him, though. Your parents expect you back in San Antonio, and they've high hopes of you making a good marriage. I doubt they've ever recovered from the shock of Maggie marrying me and coming to live on the ranch."

The phrase 'a good marriage' distressed Mattie. She understood what her parents meant by it, and it wasn't a dream she shared. They wanted her to marry well to gain both social standing and financial security. Her idea of what a good marriage might be now included deep and abiding mutual love, more valuable than wealth or station. Mattie would marry Moses or not at all, she thought. She wouldn't settle for second best.

"Good night, Liam," she told him without responding to what he said. "Sleep well, Maggie. If you need any help with your little man here, just give me a shout."

Upstairs, in the tiny room, she unbraided her hair and stood at the window staring toward the double dog trot cabin where Moses lived and touched her fingers to her mouth. She could still feel his kiss and felt confident there would be many more to come.

CHAPTER SEVEN

Moses probably should have waited, but he was back in the saddle and riding the range by mid-August. His ankle had healed, although he still had an occasional moment when it pained him or proved weak. Boone's days were longer than his, often from before dawn until near dark or after, so Moses started each day by heading over to draw water for Rachel. He would spend a few sweet minutes with his niece and nephew. Most days, Rachel would fix him breakfast before he began his duties. On wash day, he lingered longer to fill the heavy kettles for her and often to help. Liam knew and didn't protest.

For now, Mattie remained on the ranch, which was dandy, but each day that passed brought them closer to the inevitable parting. In the evenings, he often spent time with Mattie, enough that it was no secret to anyone that they were courting. Moses wasn't sure if Liam approved because the man said little.

Rachel walked up to the main ranch house each morning to give little Grace Rafferty a few lessons in reading, writing, and arithmetic. Once a school marm, always a school marm, Moses thought. Rachel had also been teaching Mima a few words, so he planned to get her a slate board and pencil so she could practice for her birthday come September. That would require a trip to Laredo, but once Mattie left, he would have time heavy on his hands.

The heat they'd experienced in July continued into August

and became hotter. The wind blew hard most days, delivering clouds of dust that almost made Rachel cuss since it was difficult to keep the dust out. On laundry day, the blown dust could and often did dirty the fresh washed clothes, so Moses rigged up a clothesline to the side of the cabin, which served as a windbreak.

Liam hired two new hands, a young, slender fellow from north Texas named Jim and a stocky Civil War veteran who'd served with Boone and Liam. The former Confederate's name was Beau and he originally hailed from southern Virginia. Liam meant to hire a third, although the bunkhouse was already crowded.

On a rare day when rain spit from the sky, Moses rode back in early, washed off, and sought Mattie. He found her in the garden and managed to steal a kiss. She wore a scowl, though, so he asked, "What's amiss?"

"Liam said this morning I'm leaving at the end of the month, and that's less than three weeks," she told him. "My father wrote and asked why I haven't returned, so Liam is set on it."

His cheerful mood fizzled, but he did his best to rally. "It won't be forever, and I'm hopin' I'll be one of the hands who will escort you back. It won't be Liam, not with a new baby nor Boone, not when Rachel's in a family way."

"He's already asked that Beau and Jim to do it," Mattie replied with a frown. "I asked why it couldn't be you and Zeke, but Liam says you're needed here."

"Well, that sours my milk," he told her. "I've been counting on being there. I'd rather go, not just so I can have those few more days with you but to make sure you travel safe."

"I'd prefer your company myself. Oh, Moses, I'm going to miss you so."

That required another kiss, a longer one this time. "Just remember it ain't gonna be forever," he told her. "And I plan to come to see you whilst you're in town."

"It's a long way for that."

"I will, though."

"I doubt Liam will allow you to be gone for days. To go there and back will take almost two weeks!"

"That's by wagon. I can travel quicker on horseback, and if he doesn't like it, I'll kick up a row."

"Moses, you're a caution," she said.

Her tiny smile encouraged him, and he said, "I strive for it, my heart."

He lingered a little longer, then headed to Boone's. He'd rather take the evening meal there than at the bunkhouse. The time spent with family had become more precious to him, and he'd rather not listen to the new hands talk of their upcoming trip to escort Mattie home. Ezekiel joined them, too, and after they ate, he sat out on the porch with his brothers. Boone fired a smoke and said, "Liam come to talk to me today."

"I reckon he told you he's asked Jim and Beau to take Mattie home."

"He did, but that wasn't all," Boone said. "I know well that you'd rather be going on that trip, but this might perk you up a tad."

"I doubt it, but go ahead and tell me."

"Since the bunkhouse is crowded, Liam said you and Ezekiel can move into the other side of the cabin," Boone told him. "Might be someday I'll want to use it as well as my family grows, but for now, I like the notion of having the two of you close."

So did Moses. "It's a fine idea."

"I'm ready – can we move in tonight?" Zeke asked with a huge grin.

"Whenever you want," Boone said. "You don't need much house plunder. Liam offered to send a table and chairs over. If one of you will make the trip to Laredo, he'll loan the wagon and I'll spot you each a bedstead, a couple pots and pans, a dish or two. Till you can go, you can bunk with your bedrolls or even out here while the weather's fine."

"I'd rather have escorted Mattie," Moses said. "But there's something to be said for bunking close, too, at least while we're all here. Still thinking on getting a ranch of our own one day?"

While Moses had been down with his ankle, Boone had mentioned that maybe they should investigate the possibility of homesteading their own place. With the three of them, the potential was there to get a large bit of land to build a ranch.

"I am, and I'm not," his brother replied. "Take a lot of doing to start from scratch. That leads to the other thing – Liam asked if we might want to buy into the Double B, put up some stakes, and be partners with him. He has big dreams for this place, and I told him I'd study on it awhile. Besides, I wanted to see what the pair of you think. It'd be all of us if we do it."

Zeke whistled sharp and long. "We'd be in tall cotton."

"We would," Boone said. "But it's something we cain't walk away from, so there's no changing our minds later. It'll put us in Texas for good."

"Where else would we be?" Zeke asked. Moses kept silent as he mulled over the possibilities.

Boone shrugged. "There's always Kentucky. I recollect we first planned to head home once I got out of the hoosegow, but because Rachel was with child, we couldn't make the trip. Or there's more places than this if we ever should get itchy feet."

"I didn't know you still thought about going back home," Moses said. Sometimes, he did – or had until he met Mattie. Kentucky had some positives, but he missed his folks, especially Ma, more than he cared for the land.

"I don't much," Boone said and echoed Moses' thought. "I'd surely like to see Ma again, though, along with the rest of our brood."

"I'm good to stay or go," Zeke said. "Thought I favor Texas a good bit."

Boone drew the last drag of his smoke. "Well, we don't have to decide any time soon. Liam's in no hurry. I'm tuckered out, so I'm calling it a night. Sleep tight."

"G'night, Boone," they said in unison.

Moses looked at Ezekiel. "Let's go get our gear and bedrolls tonight. I've had about enough of the close quarters over there."

"That and talk that we get favored because we're Boone's brothers."

"I hadn't heard that said."

"It's come up a few times. Come on, let's do it before I get sleepy."

Hauling up their bedrolls, packs, and gear took time, and so did hauling it all over on horseback. Then, they had to put their mounts up for the night.

"Boone needs to build us a stable," Ezekiel said on their way back on foot.

"It's a thought," Moses said. Maybe in the winter season, they could.

Although the floor was hard, once he stretched out, Moses soon slept. He liked the privacy of not sharing space with a dozen other men who were often fitful in their sleep and known to pass gas so that the whole place stunk like an outhouse. Instead of rising to catcalls and men's morning nonsense, Moses woke to find Mima kneeling beside his bedroll.

"Mo Mo, there's coffee made, and Mama says come eat."

Rachel's biscuits were lighter and tastier than anything Cookie had ever made, and the bacon was fried to a nice crisp, not half-burned or half-raw. He enjoyed drinking coffee with his brothers and Mima's chatter. Rob didn't talk as much as his sister, but he could now hold his own. So far, his favorite seemed to be "Da," which delighted Boone. Although they rose with dawn and left early, breakfast was far more pleasant with family than in the raucous atmosphere of the bunkhouse. If it wasn't for Mattie's upcoming departure, Moses would have been as content as he'd ever been.

On the Saturday before Mattie's return to San Antonio, Liam agreed that both Moses and Zeke could have the day off and make the trip to Laredo for furniture. He also said that Mattie could ride along. Although it would make for a long day's trip, Moses anticipated it with pleasure. In polite society, probably up in San Antonio, there would be a chaperone, but with only two women on the ranch, it wasn't possible. Maggie was a new mother, and Rachel was in the family way. Liam conceded that Mattie would be safe with two of the Wilson brothers, and so, on the next to last Saturday in August, they set out just after first light.

Since they would be hauling back supplies from a list Liam provided along with money and Rachel's long list as well as furniture, they used the covered wagon, the same one used to make the move from Laredo a few years earlier.

Mattie, pretty in a wide-brimmed straw hat decorated with silk flowers and ribbons that tied beneath her chin, perched on the seat beside Moses. She wore a dark green damask dress worn with a white lace fichu pinned in place with a cameo brooch. He figured it had to be the best dress she'd brought to the ranch and found it quite fetching.

Ezekiel could have squeezed onto the seat and flanked Mattie like bookends but had chosen to ride his favorite horse, Licorice, alongside the wagon.

"How long will it take to get there?" Mattie asked as she gazed about, admiring the scenery.

"Five hours, maybe," Moses said. "Reckon, we'll get there by ten o'clock in the morning or so. It'll give us time to get all the supplies. Both Liam and Rachel gave me long lists. Then we got to pick out a couple of beds and a few other things. I thought you might want to do a little shopping, too."

She turned toward him with a bright smile. "I would, Moses."

"And I figured we might get a bite to eat in a restaurant before we head back to the ranch."

He'd seldom dined in any establishment, but Moses figured it would be a treat for his lady, and her response pleased him. Mattie gave a little cry of delight and leaned against him on the seat, close enough he could smell her lavender fragrance.

Zeke rode close and said, "I'll be hungry enough to eat a horse by then. We won't get back to the ranch until late, though."

"As long as we home by dark, it's all good," Moses said. "I've every confidence we'll manage it."

Laredo, when they arrived, seemed uglier than he remembered. Maybe it was because he'd seen San Antonio since he'd been here, but the streets seemed muddier, the buildings more faded and in poor repair. The saloon, The Out of Luck, where Boone had been shot, still stood but appeared seedier.

If Mattie found the place a poor second to her hometown, she didn't mention it. Instead, she sat straight on the edge of the wagon seat, her eyes darting to and fro to take it all in. Moses wondered if any town seemed thrilling after a summer spent on the ranch.

Once he found a place for the wagon, he lifted her down from the seat and set her on the sidewalk with care. His ankle twinged a little, but he ignored it. At the mercantile they'd patronized before, Moses swept her inside. He pulled the lists he carried from a pocket, and as she perused the selection of ladies' finery, everything from lace to ready-made dress goods and jewelry, he stepped up to the counter.

"Moses, I'm gonna step over and say hidy-do to Mary

over at the saloon," Zeke said. "Then I'll head over to the livery for a spell."

"Give her my regards," Moses said. Mary, the saloonkeeper and the madam for a small bevy of painted ladies, had given Boone shelter after he'd been shot. She probably wouldn't have if he hadn't been expected to die, he figured. Still, she'd had a small input that aided his quest to prove his brother's innocence. "If Graciela's about, see if you can buy some tamales that we can take back with us. Boone favors 'em, and Rachel's got *frijoles* down well, but she's never caught the knack of the tamales."

Ezekiel nodded and touched the brim of his hat to Mattie, then departed.

The storekeeper, Klaus Zimmerman, remembered that Moses was Boone's brother and that Boone had been a good customer. Mattie spoke to him in German, and when she did, he lit up like a church on Christmas Eve. Their conversation seemed to please them both, which made Moses glad.

At the counter, Moses began the order, that included many items that the ranch couldn't provide, including sugar, gunpowder, salt, coffee, flour, cornmeal, tobacco and cigarette papers, and various spices. Some items duplicated on Liam's and Boone's list. Boone wanted some dress goods for Rachel and some flannel, plus a trinket or two. Rachel requested some raisins and dried apples if any were to be had.

Once those necessary items had been procured and loaded into the wagon, he picked out two of the simplest beds in the place. There was no need for mattresses, just some cloth to make straw ticks for both. He added some blankets. He also, with Mattie's able assistance, chose two frying pans, a couple of pots, some tinware including cups, plates, and silverware, and a few other household items.

She had chosen a few sewing notions, a bit of lace, some scented soap, and some candy sticks, which she said were for the little ones. Since it wasn't long until Boone's birthday, Moses had it in mind to get him some small gift. Boone had several good knives, but he found a fine Bowie knife and bought it for his brother. Although Jim Bowie died at the Alamo, the style of knives that carried his name continued to be made, and he thought Boone would like it.

Ezekiel turned up just after the wagon was loaded, bearing tamales and town gossip. Little of it had any interest to Moses or Mattie since she wasn't familiar. By then, it was past noon, so they headed for the closest café. Although he had a suspicion that Mattie had dined in far finer establishments with a larger variety, Moses liked the place. It was small but clean. The tables were topped with red and white checked cloths, and the curtains at the windows matched.

Each table held salt and pepper shakers as well as a sugar bowl. The trio settled down at a table near the front windows and looked at the bill of fare. The choices were few, beef steak, beef stew, fried river carp, or bacon with cabbage. After a steady diet that consisted of primarily beef, augmented by the occasional chicken or the game Ezekiel hunted, Moses chose the carp. Some called it a trash fish, true, but he'd eaten it in the past and found it tasty. Mattie also chose carp, noting it was a popular fish among Germans. Their dinners came with a side of fried potatoes and some hominy. Zeke asked for beef stew, and when it was served, Moses almost wished he'd chosen it. The stew was thick with carrots, chunks of potatoes, green peas, and onion as well as beef. The fish, however, was fried to a golden crisp and proved to be delicious, a welcome change from beef.

The meal sat well in his belly, and although Moses would have liked to linger, maybe enjoy a smoke, they returned to the wagon for the long trip back to the ranch. After lifting Mattie onto the seat once more, he did roll and light a cigarette, which surprised her.

"I didn't know you had the habit," she said.

"Do you mind?" If she did, he would give it up.

"I don't," Mattie said. "It came as a surprise, though. I don't believe I've ever seen you smoke."

Moses laughed. "I don't as much as Boone, that's for sure. I never did until I came to Laredo. I seldom get a smoke, but after a fine meal, it can be a pleasure."

She held out her hand. "May I try?"

Her request shocked him. "Mattie, love, nice women don't smoke."

He had only seen a few who did, Mary over at the Out of Luck among them. She smoked thin cigars, and a few of her ladies did as well.

Mattie sighed. "It's just as well if I don't. Papa would have me in the woodshed, I imagine, and I doubt Liam would feel much different."

The trek back to the Double B seemed to take longer, but that was because they didn't have the same anticipation they had when they headed into town. Heat beat down from the full sun onto the wagon, intense enough to see the shimmer in the air. More than once, Moses could have sworn he saw puddles ahead, but they were mirages, nothing but an optical illusion. They stopped more than once so Mattie could relieve herself, and all could drink some water.

Each time, he lifted her down from the wagon. By the time they were in the last stretch, his ankle twinged with pain. Moses realized he'd taxed it too much with the journey, loading the wagon and assisting Mattie. Once home, they would have to lug their purchases from the wagon, but there should be plenty of hands to help with that. He'd rest it once he settled for the evening, he thought, maybe rub it with a little witch hazel or arnica.

Dusk had begun to gather before they reached the ranch.

Ezekiel had ridden ahead but returned. "If you turn around, you'll see a mighty fine sunset," he told them. "You ought to look. It's purty."

The western sky was bright with vivid orange and a few silhouetted clouds that appeared almost black. It was glorious and Moses was glad he took time to view it. By the time he rolled the wagon to a stop near the main house, it was all but dark. Both Liam and Boone were waiting. Zeke rode to get the hands to help unload, and when Moses climbed down, he stepped wrong, and his ankle hurt more. He winced and hoped no one noticed in the dark, but Boone did.

"Looks like your trip didn't do the ankle much good," he commented.

"It's a mite tender, that's all," Moses replied. "I'll be right as rain come morning."

His brother snorted. "Best rest it a bit tomorrow so you don't get laid up again," Boone said. "Hurt?"

"Like the devil," he admitted.

As the supplies were unloaded and most taken to the storehouse Liam had built, Moses limped alongside Mattie and delivered her to the front porch. Glad of the darkness, out of the circle of lanterns that illuminated the work, he kissed her sweet and slow.

"I enjoyed your company today," he told her. "I hope you found the trip to be good."

"I did, but I wish your ankle wasn't troubling you."

"I'll do," he said. "Good night, Mattie."

"Sleep well, Moses."

He began a slow, tedious walk home, and despite his aching ankle, he was happy.

For now, he ignored the fact Mattie would soon be gone and savored the day.

CHAPTER EIGHT

Mattie scarcely had time to draw a deep breath before Liam loaded her trunk and other items onto the same wagon they'd taken to Laredo and sent her back to San Antonio. She would have preferred that Moses accompany her, but Liam said no. Nor would he allow Boone to make the trip, citing Boone's responsibilities as top hand as they went into the fall. It would be a busy season, Liam told her, and his top hand was needed. He had asked the newest hands, Jim and Beau, to escort her, but after she begged, he agreed to allow Ezekiel Wilson to go too.

If it couldn't be Moses, then her mind rested easier to know one of his brothers would be present as they traveled. The plan was to leave early, to make as many miles as possible, although it would take days to reach San Antonio. Liam wanted them to start before the weather turned or the fall rains began.

She rose before dawn on departure day and as they'd planned, she slipped outside as soon as she had dressed to meet Moses, who waited on the porch. Without a word, he opened his arms when he saw her, and she launched into them. He held her tight in a fond embrace, and she clung to him as if she could take his love with her. After a few long moments, he stepped back a little and kissed her, not the tender kisses he'd given before but a powerful kiss that claimed her and fired her senses.

"I love you, Mattie," he told her. "And I'll be proud to make you my wife."

"Oh, Moses, I love you so," she whispered, her voice choked with unshed tears. "I don't want to leave. I'll miss you terribly."

His answer was to kiss her again, this time with gentle lips that caressed.

"I'll come soon as I can to visit and to court you proper," he promised. "We'll be wed as soon as we can."

Mattie had to touch him, to store up the feel of him for the coming separation. Her fingers combed through his hair. She cupped his face between her hands, then touched his shoulders and clasped his hand in hers. They stood, hand in hand, until Liam and Maggie emerged with the children to say farewell. Ezekiel arrived, his bedroll and gear in place on his favorite paint horse, the newer hands riding behind him.

Boone rode up too and dismounted to stand beside Moses.

Jim would drive the wagon, at least on the first leg of the trip, so his mount was tied behind, and he climbed onto the seat. Moses lifted Mattie up, mindful of his ankle, and put her in place, keeping a decent distance between her and the driver.

"I love you," he said and didn't care who heard. "Be well, dear heart."

As she sometimes did when most emotional, she reverted to German, but he knew what she said. "*Ich liebe dich.*"

Moses stood and watched as the wagon set out, never moving until it passed out of sight. Mattie noticed as she turned back to see him for as long as possible. The image of him, one hand upraised to say goodbye, would remain with her.

She cried for an hour, tears trickling down her cheeks no matter how many times she blotted her eyes with a handkerchief. Jim ignored her for the most part, and she thought she made him uncomfortable by crying. Beau and Zeke rode, taking turns ahead and bringing up the rear. Ezekiel sought out Mattie to see how she fared as often as he could, for Moses' sake, which she appreciated, but she had few words and little appetite.

The silent, stocky Beau had taken over meal preparation, cooking over an open fire each night when they camped. She couldn't find much appetite for the beans, bacon, and biscuits that were the foundation of his menus. Once, Ezekiel shot some prairie chickens, which he roasted. Mattie enjoyed the change of pace and told him so.

His slow grin reminded her more of Boone than Moses, but as she came to know him, Mattie realized he was as solid as his brothers. She figured him to be at least her age and was surprised to learn he was just 19 years old. He treated her with the same courtesy that Boone had when she first came to the ranch, although sometimes, he was a little more familiar, enough, she felt almost like a sister.

One clear night, when the stars shone like diamonds in the night sky, she walked out a little from camp to admire them. Lost in thoughts about Moses, wondering what he might be doing and if he missed her as much as she longed for him, Ezekiel startled her when he stood at her side.

"You ought not wander so far from the rest of us," he said in his quiet drawl. "I reckon you're missing Moses, but it ain't safe."

"I am," she replied. "I won't come to any harm, though."

"You might. Just cause it's dark don't mean there may not be a few snakes about. There's wild pigs in these parts, too. And not many but a few Comanche's still roam, and so do some desperados. Moses would have my hide and nail it to the wall if anything happened to you on my watch."

Mattie shivered as he listed the potential dangers, none of which she had realized were possible. His words didn't scare her, though, as much as the part about Moses pleased her.

"He might," she said, with the first smile she'd had since leaving the ranch.

"I've no doubt. I know he means to marry you, thinks on you highly."

She nodded. "I've promised to be his wife. I suppose that makes us family because we will be."

"Right. So come on back to camp with me before anything happens to you," Ezekiel said. "It won't be but about two more days now, and you'll be home."

"It's not where I want to be," Mattie told him. "That old saying, home is where the heart is, is true. I want to be where Moses is."

Ezekiel sighed. "If I know my stubborn brother, you will be as soon as he can make it so."

After that, Mattie's mood wasn't as somber. Having Ezekiel close helped a little.

They entered San Antonio, and her first brief excitement faded fast. The family home on Elm Street hadn't changed in her absence, but now it seemed different. Ezekiel helped her down from the wagon while the other hands unloaded her trunk and valise. Before she could walk up to the front door, her parents rushed out of the house, chattering in a flood of German. For the first time in her life, it sounded foreign to her. Her sisters, Minna and Lena, and brother Freddy, followed them. They all but knocked her over with their exuberant greeting and hugs.

Mattie stood still to be kissed and welcomed but said nothing. Her father and Freddy carried her trunk and valise into the house, presumably up to the same bedroom. Her mother turned to Ezekiel, who stood just behind Mattie, and said, "So is this the cowpoke, the one you fancy?"

Her tone was harsh and her accent heavier than Mattie recalled. Anger bubbled up from deep within. "This is Ezekiel Wilson, *Mutter*," she replied. "He has two brothers, Boone, who is Liam's top hand, and Moses."

"And they are all cowboys?" Ilse Baumann said. She made

'cowboys' sound like something loathsome, belittling the word.

"Like Liam," Mattie answered through gritted teeth. Behind her, Zeke stiffened.

"*Ach, nein,* Liam owns the land," her mother stated. "He has the *geld,* the money not like these."

Ezekiel stepped forward and, without regard to polite manners, said to Mattie, "I reckon we'll go now. We have a long trip back home, and it seems we're not needed here."

She had never heard any of the Wilsons use such a cold tone. "Zeke, don't…"

"Ain't your fault, and I know it," he interrupted. "Write Moses if you can. He'll take this hard, more than you probably know."

"Tell him…"

Before she could finish the sentence, her mother and sisters drew her into the house. Mattie paused on the threshold and turned back toward the wagon.

"Ezekiel, take care," she called. "I'll write Moses, I promise."

He raised one hand in acknowledgement, then swung back into the saddle. Before the heavy front door closed, he, the other hands, and the wagon were gone. Mattie drew a long, deep breath and entered her childhood home.

A narrow, steep staircase led upward from the small entryway. To the left, the dining room held a large table, chairs, and buffet with a kitchen behind it. On the right, a doorway opened into a large parlor thick with furniture and a piano. A door to the rear opened onto a small room where the family sometimes gathered and where the prized Singer Sewing Machine was kept.

"Come, let's sit in the parlor," her mother said, ushering them into the room. As she spoke, Mattie's father and brother descended from upstairs, where she guessed they had put her trunk in the bedroom.

Surprised that her father was at home, not work, and that the children were allowed to miss school, she commented on it and earned a sardonic look from her mother.

"It's Sunday," Ilse said. "Our dinner will be ready soon. I wondered why you would travel on the Sabbath, but I expected nothing more from those cowboys, no better than vagabonds. If you'd come earlier, we would have been at church."

Twenty-one years old and a woman grown, her mother's attitude made her feel younger than her sisters. Mattie didn't want to spoil her homecoming, however, and she knew, despite the bitter words, her parents loved her. "I wish you could see Maggie's new baby," she said in an effort to change the subject. "He was ten pounds when he was born, and he's handsome."

"Ach, *ja,* maybe one day," her mother said with a sigh. "He has a fine middle name, and I wish it had been his first name, not the Irisher one."

"Ilse!" Her father said. "*Schweigen Sie!* I want to see the young man, no matter what his name, and it's wonderful to have Mathilde home again."

The dinner table held so many German dishes Mattie thought it a wonder that it hadn't collapsed. She ate more than her fill of *Schnitzel* and more, noodles and sauerkraut and potato pancakes and fried cabbage. There was bread, of course, since her father was co-owner of a popular bakery where bread was their specialty, with several varieties. For dessert, there was strudel and black forest cake. Mattie ate too much, and the rich, heavy German food didn't sit well on her stomach. Claiming a stomachache, she retreated to her room, but she didn't find the peace she sought.

She sat on her Jenny Lind bed across from Maggie's. The roses still bloomed on the wallpaper, large and bright pink, but they had lost their appeal. With one hand on her stomach, which did hurt, Mattie rose and stood at the window. As far as she could see, houses filled the landscape, both large and small. The light breeze that made the dotted Swiss curtains dance brought the fragrance of honeysuckle and roses in bloom, but she longed for the stronger wind in the open country. She spent the remainder of the day in her room and denied that she was sick, but she was homesick for the ranch and missing Moses so much it hurt.

When her mother insisted that they venture out to Commerce Street, then onto Navarro and St. Mary's Street to shop on Monday, Mattie went. Mutti wanted to find the dress goods that Mattie had begged for if she went to the ranch. Then, it had seemed important, but now she had no interest. She did choose some cloth, however, because otherwise, too many questions would have been raised.

Once, she'd adored the bustle and the busy city. She had liked the stores with their wide variety of wares, the notions store, the shops that sold only trimmings for hats and dresses, and the shoe shops. The old Mattie had coveted it all and more. She had judged prospective suitors by what they wore, from the tailored suits to the handmade hats. She had thought she wanted a large house, one that would dwarf her parents' humble abode, and had dreamed about having domestic help.

Now, the gentleman, German or American, that she saw on the streets or in a business seemed somehow like shadows compared to robust men who worked hard, men who would lay down their life for their woman. Their pale faces made her think they had poor health. Most had hands that lacked character or scars, as white as a lady's who never lifted a hand to work.

San Antonio made her feel caged, and so did the home where she'd been raised. The parlor, her mother's pride and joy, brought out a wild desire to clear away at least half of the heavy furniture and to remove the china knickknacks. Mattie would replace them with flowers, fresh or dried, something simple yet lovely.

If she could ride, and it wasn't so far, Mattie thought she would saddle a horse and set out for the ranch. But, since she lacked the horsewoman skills and knew she'd never make the long trek alone, she dismissed the dream and sat down to write a letter to Moses.

> *Dearest Moses,*
>
> *I am at the house where I grew up, but it isn't home anymore. Home is where you are. Home is the ranch where the sky is big and wide, deep and blue. I am lost here in this town with too many buildings and people. I miss you so much that it hurts, and I want to cry. Nothing is the way I remember it, for I've changed and for the better. Write to me, Moses.*
>
> *I wait for the day when we'll be together again. I pray it is soon, my love.*
>
> *Your Mattie*

She didn't write him about the afternoon teas her mother made her attend or the musical evenings or the dances. Mattie kept back the fact that her family didn't take it seriously that she meant to wed Moses and tried to find her a suitable husband. To her folks, an ideal husband would be German, he would be blonde and big with bright blue eyes, and he would be a gentleman with an education. He should be a banker, or an attorney, or a doctor, something professional so that he could keep her in a fine style to which her mother thought she could easily become accustomed.

When she put on the carnation pink taffeta ballgown that bared her shoulders and her neck, Mattie wanted to cover it with a wrap. The furbelows and flounces seemed too fussy to her, and she disliked the bustle even more. She suspected that Moses wouldn't find it attractive but that he'd be appalled. She hated dancing with young men who fumbled at conversation, and worse, she loathed the ones who maneuvered her into remote corners where they tried to steal a kiss.

As the weeks passed, a local banker, Gunther Hammerschmidt, became her most frequent escort. He was a guest at her parents' dinner table at least two nights a week. He brought Mattie flowers and trinkets, a pair of kid gloves, a silk ribbon, cameo earrings, and a prayer book. She tossed his offerings into a drawer and ignored them. When she wasn't socializing, she made two shirts, one linen, one calico, for Moses, although she kept that quiet. And she waited.

Near the end of September, a letter came for her from Moses.

> *Sweet Mattie,*
>
> *I miss you more than I know how to say. I don't eat much or sleep much. Boone says I'm downright distracted, and I reckon he's right. A big rattler almost nailed me a week ago because I never saw it until it was almost too late. Your nephew Seamus is growing very fast. Little Mima sends her regards to you and Rob asks where's Miss Mattie at least once a week.*
>
> *We've been cutting hay for the winter, moving the stock to different pastures, riding fence lines, and weaning calves. I'm busy from dawn till dark, but there's not a minute I don't think about you and wish you were here.*
>
> *Liam says once the fall work eases, I can come to San Antonio, so look for me around late October.*
>
> *I love you, honey, and look forward to the time when we're wed when we're man and wife.*
>
> *Until then, till I see you, all my love, Moses Robert Wilson.*

Mattie read it until she knew it by heart, then read it again. She carried it with her, tucked into her bosom, and his sweet words brought tears each time she read it.

On the evenings, her presence wasn't requested at some gala, she stayed at home. Sometimes, she played games with her siblings, and often she read. She'd read the poems in the Tennyson book Moses got her many times. Mattie bought some simple fabrics, pretty calicos, and sturdy wool to make some dresses for when she returned to the ranch. She never doubted that she would, but she had no idea when it might be.

Gunther became bold in his courtship. He began talking about the house he planned to build and the children he hoped to have. Once, he took her on a buggy ride to see the lot where he would build his house, but she said little. The stress made her head ache, and she pleaded to go home.

She retreated to her room to lie down with a very real headache, but he remained downstairs, dining with her family. Mattie crept halfway down the back stairs to eavesdrop, and what she heard curdled her blood.

"I plan to ask her to marry me by Christmas," the pompous banker said. "I have no doubt she'll agree to be my wife. Construction on the house should begin in the spring, and I thought perhaps the wedding could be in the fall of next year."

"You have our blessing," her father said. "Mathilde seems unsettled and needs your guiding hand. I think I made a mistake sending her to that ranch to help Magdalena."

"I agree," Gunther said, although in Mattie's eyes, it was none of his concern. "A year should be time enough to make plans, for her to prepare for a wedding, and our courtship to advance."

"*Jawohl*," her mother said. "Once you are engaged, we'll host a gala party, probably rent a hall."

Mattie bit hard on her lip to avoid crying out. She couldn't bear to hear more. Angry tears poured down her cheeks, and once she returned to her room, she stifled her sobs into a pillow.

No matter what happened, she wouldn't become engaged to Gunther. She was promised to Moses Wilson and no one else. If she didn't wed him, she wouldn't marry at all.

Oh, Moses, she thought, *Come soon, my darling, come soon.*

CHAPTER NINE

Without Mattie, Moses sank into a funk. He was back in the saddle full-time now and worked long days. Normally as good-natured as a man could be, Moses was on the edge of anger too often. He barked at some of the other hands, and if he hadn't been Boone's brother, they would have fought him. Weary at the end of a workday, he'd come home to the dog trot cabin he shared with Zeke. Rachel, although with child now, always had a hot meal prepared, and he was welcome at the table. Sometimes he ate with the family, sometimes he didn't. If he missed out, Moses didn't eat. He might beg a bite of corn pone or bacon from Cookie at the bunkhouse, but he lived on black coffee, and he'd started smoking more than he ever had.

Rachel made some of his favorite dishes to tempt his appetite, and when she did, he made the effort to eat. Nothing tasted good, though, and too often, anything he ate soured in his gut. Headaches plagued him, fueled by fatigue because he failed to rest easy or sleep much. Zeke trod lightly around Moses these days, unwilling to start or finish a fight.

Two weeks after Mattie's departure, Boone hurt his back while breaking a horse. It wasn't the same mare that tossed Moses back in the summer, but one even wilder. Although Boone held his seat and rode it into submission, the wild gyrations of the animal strained his back. It wasn't a serious injury, but painful. Moses could see that in the way Boone held himself and how he walked with a stiffer gait than normal. Boone refused bed rest, although each night, Rachel rubbed the sore muscles and applied Lone Star Liniment.

Despite being taciturn and saying little, Moses worried about his brother's back. To help out, he took over rocking the babies each night and singing to them. Boone usually did it, but Moses figured his brother could use Rachel's care more, and it was a task he could do. Young Jemima and Robert were the only people he always treated with kindness. He never griped at them or had any sharp words. Since Rob was the youngest, he rocked the boy first then let Rachel put him to bed. Then Moses would rock Mima and sing to her. Her devotion eased a small fraction of his sadness, his ever-present loneliness for Mattie.

The first song he sang was one of Mima's favorites, 'Skip To My Lou,' a cheerful and cute song. She sang with him but, after it, became sleepy and curled tighter against his chest. He didn't think too hard about what to sing next, just began the song that came into his head, then a Stephen Foster tune that included the words "Weep no more, my lady, oh weep no more today, we will sing one song for the old Kentucky home, for the old Kentucky home far away." That one made him homesick a little, so he switched to one of the songs Ma had sung them, a love song that ended tragically, 'Ballinderry,' ending with the lines "now it's as sad as sad could be, for the ship that sailed with Felidmid Eamon is sunk forever beneath the sea."

Then Moses sang a song from the war, Boone's war, that always made him sad, but since he already was, it didn't matter. "Weeping, sad and lonely," he sang the refrain. "Hopes and fears how vain, when this cruel war is over, praying that we'll meet again."

It suited his dark spirits, but Boone objected.

"Tarnation, Moses," he cried. "Leave off the sad songs, would you? That baby girl's gonna have bad dreams if you keep on like that."

"I cain't help it," Moses said. "I been a bit forlorn since Mattie left."

"I know that, but man, she ain't dead, and she'll be back."

Moses sighed. "I hope so, Boone, but there ain't no guarantee."

"I can guess how you feel. I'd be lost without Rachel, and I can't imagine how I'd have felt if we were parted for a spell, but you gotta have heart, Moses. Sing something happy, would you?"

"I don't hardly know what to sing."

"Sing 'The Royal Forester,' and I'll sing with you."

Their voices blended in the old ballad, a song about mistaken identity and love. Afterward, Boone reached to take his sleeping daughter but winced when his back twinged when he tried to lift her, so Moses carried her to bed. He tucked her into the trundle beside her brother, and Rachel, already in bed, stirred. "Boone?"

Before Moses could answer, his brother did.

"I'm right here, honey."

"Are you coming to bed?"

"I will directly."

"Is your back paining you much?"

"It's alright, not bad," Boone replied. "I'm gonna sit out for a smoke with Moses, then I'll be in."

Listening to their banter was one more thing that made Moses' heart ache for Mattie. He turned and headed outside, taking a seat on the steps. Boone joined him there.

"You never used to smoke much," Boone said after he'd rolled and fired a cigarette.

"Didn't used to have the habit," Moses replied, drawing on his own. "Picked it up at that saloon trying to prove you were innocent. I didn't smoke much till Mattie left, but now it seems like a small comfort."

"You needn't take on so," his brother said. "You're grieving like she's dead, but she's just over to San Antonio."

"Might as well be on the moon for the good it does me."

Boone laughed. "Quit yer bellyachin'. Being lovesick's got you distracted, and that's dangerous. Ezekiel said you near stepped on a rattler the other day 'cause you didn't notice it. Ol' Jim told me that you rode off without your saddle on tight and got tossed, too."

Moses took a long drag from his smoke. Both were true.

"You ain't gonna do that gal any good if you get yourself hurt or killed," Boone told him. "You'll get down sick or something, all the frettin' you been doing. And for love of the Lord Jesus, mind your temper and tongue. Zeke's got his drawers in a knot 'cause you want to disagree with every word that comes out of his mouth and spar with him. Half the other hands are either mad at you or afraid you're gonna fight them. Besides that, you're off your feed, and it's making you skinny as a slat cat. I figure you ain't sleepin' much neither."

He hadn't been very aware, but when Boone pointed it all out in his quiet drawl, Moses saw his behavior had been pitiful. "I ain't."

"What do you think Mathilde would have to say about the way you're acting?"

Moses would rather not imagine what his pretty lady would think. "She'd scold me, most likely."

"I imagine so."

He took the last drag from his smoke, then said, "Boone, thing is, I love Mattie. We're promised, and I mean to make her my wife."

"I have every confidence that you will," his brother said. "It might not be easy – look at me and Rachel. First, she had to keep me from dying, then we wed, then the next morning, I got hauled off to the hoosegow. I thought I might well hang, but thank God I didn't. Might have if it weren't for you and Liam. I can't recall what the Bible might say, but ol' Shakespeare wrote something about how the course of true love is never smooth. That's no lie, Moses, but it'll work out for you."

"I hope you're right about that."

"I am, being the older and wiser brother," Boone said with a flash of humor.

Moses had been just seven years old when their daddy died. Boone had filled those shoes for twice that long. If anyone else said the things his brother did, Moses would be fighting mad but because it was Boone, he listened.

"I'll try to do better," he said.

"You will. Just pull your head out of the sand," Boone said. He took one last hit and pitched his smoke. "I'm heading for bed. Don't tell Rachel, but my back is giving me some misery. Don't let the bed bugs bite."

That line from their childhood, back when Jemima Wilson would have burned the house overhead before she allowed a single bug in their beds, brought a smile. "Good night, Boone."

Moses lingered in the September night. Although not as sweltering as August, it didn't feel like autumn yet. The pleasant evening settled about him, and he did his best to enjoy it. His mind drifted to thoughts of Mattie, and he never noticed Ezekiel had joined him until he spoke.

"It's gettin' late," Zeke said. "You're woolgathering out here. Did Boone talk at you?"

"You could call it that. He nearabout stripped off my hide with his tongue."

Ezekiel laughed. "Aw, he cain't help it. Besides, he worries, and you know it."

"I do," Moses said as he thought about rolling a fresh smoke. "He ought not, though. I'm a man grown now, and so are you."

"True," his brother said. "He's right, though, about you being distracted. I thought that rattler had you, Moses."

"I told him the same as I'll tell you – I'll pay more attention," Moses said. "And I don't mean to be disagreeable. I just have a load on my mind."

"Named Mattie," Zeke said. "It's alright. I just ain't used to you fussing and fighting with me. That's more Jacob or Garrett's way than yours."

First, Boone tore him a new one, now Ezekiel wanted to complain. Moses had had enough, but to keep the peace, his tone remained mild. "I think I'll turn in. We got an early start come morning since we're cutting and hauling hay."

Despite time spent with his brothers, Moses slept poorly and rose grouchy. A long, hot day, almost as bad as July or August, didn't improve his mood. He did join Boone's bunch for dinner and forced himself to eat a good portion of the frijoles Rachel had learned to make like Graciela back in Laredo. If Boone got through with anything, it'd been the part about what would Mattie think of his recent manner. That and telling him how skinny he'd become. He didn't want her to think he was a weakling or sick.

After supper, he sat on the steps and watched Mima play with her dolly. She'd moved out about six or eight feet from the cabin, using a bush as her playhouse. Moses half-listened to her patter, but he wasn't paying full attention, wondering what Mattie might be doing over in San Antonio.

Boone had been over to the bunkhouse to check on the hands and walked up. He came to an abrupt halt not far from his daughter and, in an odd tone of voice, asked, "Who are you talking to, Mima?"

"My friend," the child said. "Mr. Snake. Isn't he pretty? Look at him, Daddy."

Something about the way she said it alerted Moses that something was out of the ordinary. Without ever taking his eyes from Mima, Boone motioned him to stay in place.

"Jemima Ann," Boone said. His voice was slow and deliberate. "Stand right where you are. Don't you move, not one bit. Don't even breathe."

Moses saw why, now. A large timber rattlesnake, mottled with black bands over gray, had coiled not far from Mima. Its tail shook in warning, and it could strike at any time. The girl stilled, and as Moses watched, Boone pulled the Griswold revolver he always wore each time he left home and shot it. His aim was true, and on the first shot, the serpent writhed and thrashed. Concerned for his niece's safety, Moses dashed to scoop her into his arms as Boone fired twice more, his gaze never wavering and without flinching. By the time he stopped, the snake no longer had a head, just a bloody mass at the end of its long body. Moses judged it to be a good four or five feet long and thick as his forearm.

Boone holstered his pistol and walked toward Moses. Mima clung to her uncle, but when her father approached, she flung herself into his open arms.

"You killed my friend!" she said. "That snake was my friend."

"If that rattler had bit you, you'd be dead," Boone said. "It was a rattlesnake and dangerous, Mima. It was no friend."

Rachel and Ezekiel burst from the cabin to stare.

"Boone, what in the world?" Rachel asked, then saw the snake, still wriggling in its death throes. She paled, and her hand went to her throat. "Where did that come from?"

"It was at your daughter's feet," Boone replied. "So, I dispatched it to hell where it belonged."

"You could have shot her!" Rachel's voice went high and sharp.

"Boone's a better shot than that," Ezekiel said, standing beside her.

"No, I couldn't have. She minded me when I told her not to move," Boone said. "She's a brave little thing and obedient. Scared the fire out of me, Rachel."

Rachel began to cry. Boone handed the little girl to Moses, then crossed the porch and took his wife into his arms. "Hush," he said. "Hush, she wasn't hurt."

"She might have died," Rachel wept. "Oh, Boone."

Moses watched as his brother swept Rachel into his arms and carried her into the house.

"Were you scared too, Mo Mo?" Mima asked.

His heart hadn't stopped racing yet. "I was," he replied. "But your daddy took care of it. He had a steady hand and a good eye. Thank the good Lord he was here."

Little Rob, who had followed his mother outside, remained but began to cry. Zeke picked him up and began to sing one of the tunes they used on the drives, one with the refrain, 'get along little dogies,' which quieted the boy.

Moses still held Mima, but his hands trembled. The impact of what might have happened hit him hard. If not for the fact that Boone always paid attention, that he'd seen what his daughter was focused on and had dispatched the venomous creature without hesitation, the child he held close could be dying or dead. Judging from the size of the snake and her small size, she wouldn't have had a chance if bitten.

And if she had been, it would have been his fault. He'd been meant to be watching her with his full attention, not half an eye, while he daydreamed about Mattie. Moses had heard her singsong talk but assumed she crooned to her doll. Until Boone's arrival, he failed to see the snake that had slithered into view or even heard the unmistakable sound of its rattles. Folks said that rattlers could strike half its length, and judging by the size of the snake, it could easily have struck Mima. With his mind on Mattie, Moses wouldn't have noticed until too late. Maybe Mima would have screamed, but it could have been so quick she could have been playing one moment, stretched out dead the next.

In his arms, she was alive, even wiggling as she asked to get down. Moses put her down. Guilt soured his stomach and he bolted into the yard, as far away from the coiled reptile as he could get, then puked up his dinner. He retched until he had nothing more to bring up, then stood, gasping to catch his breath. The shadows lengthened into dusk and still he stood there. Ezekiel carried off the dying snake using a shovel.

"Moses?"

He turned, expecting Zeke, but found Boone instead. His brother wore a serious expression, but there was no anger in his eyes. Moses had expected Boone to be mad, even to punch him, and at the least to give him a tongue lashing. If anyone else, another hand or even Ezekiel had done what Moses had, endangered a child through inattention, he would have used his fists.

"Boone, I'm sorry," he said, facing his brother. "If that snake had got her, it would have been my fault. I couldn't have lived with that on my conscience or stayed."

Moses would have had to leave and become a hermit or wander in the desert like Jesus had for forty days or more. His heart couldn't have stood burying his tiny niece or watching his family grieve.

"Aw, Moses. You ought to have been minding her closer, and that's the truth, but I ain't mad at you. Nothing happened to Mima. Even if you'd been aware, you didn't have a pistol, and if you'd tried to snatch her out of harm's way, it could have nailed both of you. That would've been two to bury and praise Jesus, no one's dead, and there's no grave to dig."

Boone's quiet words absolved some of his terrible guilt.

"Ain't you gonna at least black my eyes or break my nose?" Moses asked, attempting to joke, although he wouldn't blame his brother if he did either.

A slow grin spread across Boone's face and lightened his grim expression. "Naw, I ain't, though, Rachel might have."

"I reckon she'd like to leave my body for crow bait."

"That or carve out your liver. She was frightened, and rightly so, but Rachel's all right now. All that matters to her is that Jemima's unhurt."

"Boone, I'd rather die myself than let anything happen to that baby girl."

His brother laid a hand on his shoulder. "I know that very well. Come on back to the house. Let's have a smoke before we hit the hay."

They sat, smoking, in a companionable silence for a bit. Moses' jangled nerves began to ease, and he apologized one more time, adding, "I've learnt my lesson, Moses. I won't be distracted anymore. I'll pay mind to all that's around me. I sure don't want anything bad to happen if I don't."

"Then good's come out of it," Boone said. He sounded as philosophical as their mother sometimes did. "We sure don't need anything bad to come to pass. Besides, though I might not often say it, I'm right fond of you, Moses Robert Wilson."

Comforted by his brother's love, Moses released his guilt. "Same, brother, same."

"I know it. Don't fret too much about your Mattie. It'll all come out in the wash."

That old, familiar phrase had often come from their mother's lips to reassure them everything would come right in the end. Said now, after an averted tragedy, it was a balm to Moses' spirits.

Inside the cabin he shared with Ezekiel, he sat up for a time, deep in thought. Zeke snored from the bedroom, and in time, when Moses retired to his own bed, he fell asleep.

When he woke in the morning, his mood was fine and fair until he remembered two things. He'd almost watched Mima die, and Mattie was in San Antonio. But his outlook had shifted, and instead of reverting to despair, he thought of what could be, what would be in time.

He vowed he'd head for San Antonio near the end of October. Moses made it a goal, not a dream, and set out to do a good day's work in a way that would make Boone proud.

CHAPTER TEN

Mattie marked the day when two months had passed since she left the ranch and her heart behind. Then, it had been high summer, days of heat and dust and toil. Now, as October waned, fall colors touched the hardwoods in the city, and there was a slight crispness to the air. Autumn had long been her favorite season, but this year, it lacked the same appeal. While she still admired the vivid orange, yellow, and scarlets that replaced summer green on the leaves and enjoyed the taste of a good apple strudel or pumpkin bread, it wasn't the same.

Each morning, she kept her hands busy, often sewing or doing her part in cooking for their family. Many afternoons, her mother insisted she make social calls, so Mattie went along to various homes for tea and conversation, which usually bordered on gossip. She had little time to accompany Frau Zieff, which was the one thing she wanted to do.

Although she preferred quiet evenings at home, reading, playing the piano, or spent with the family, Mattie was swept into the ongoing swirl of events. It seemed there were always lectures or plays or concerts to attend, musicales and evening parties. Balls, thankfully, were major events, so they were held no more than a few times each year. Gunther Hammerschmidt was present at most and her escort for many of the events.

As often as she could, Mattie begged not to participate. She remained always aware of the conversation she overheard and Gunther's intentions. Her parents welcomed and encouraged him, but she did not. If he wasn't present at any of the frequent event galas, he appeared as a guest at the family table or arrived on a Sunday afternoon to offer a buggy ride or other outing.

There had been no more letters from Moses although she wrote two more. She worried that he was no longer smitten with her or that he'd found a new love in Laredo, although her heart said he would never do that. Her appetite waned, and already slim, she grew slimmer. Between that and the fact she wasn't as vivacious as in the past, her parents forced her to drink an iron tonic once each day. It was black and tasted vile.

When an elaborate masquerade ball invitation arrived for the 30th of October at the Menger House, her mother brought in a dressmaker for a fancy ball gown. Those who attended were to wear masks but not costumes. Although her passion for fashion had changed, Mattie still found it to be a beautiful garment when delivered. It was modest for an evening dress, made from watermelon hued silk taffeta and decorated with a darker rose silk macrame trim. Buttons formed a line from throat to bodice and a small bustle. The colors would flatter her blonde hair and blue eyes, but she wished Moses could see her in it, not Gunther, who would be her escort.

Still, no more letters had arrived from Moses, and the few from her sister didn't mention any of the Wilsons. On the day of the masquerade, the house was in an uproar in preparation for the gala event. Her younger siblings were sent to stay at an aunt's house so that the focus could be on the masquerade. In the morning, Mattie was descending the stairs when someone knocked at the door. Since it was Saturday, she thought it might be Gunther or a delivery of flowers to wear that evening, and she almost bolted, allowing her mother to answer the door. With a sigh, however, she opened the door, and her heart halted.

Moses Wilson, resplendent in a white shirt with black

pinstripes, black woolen trousers, a black vest, and a gentleman's jacket, stood there, his hat in his hands over his chest. His eyes glowed with joy, and a slow grin spread across his lips.

"Moses!" she cried, "Oh, Moses!"

Without thought for propriety, Mattie threw her arms around him and almost crushed his hat. He moved it to the side in time to avoid it being smashed. She drew him into the hallway, where he placed his hat on a table near the door, then he took her into his arms and kissed her.

It wasn't a light kiss or a short one. His lips claimed hers with longing and need, sweet and yet powerful. Mattie's head spun, and her skin tingled. She forgot that anyone might walk into the hall and find them there until he released her.

"I've been lonesome for you, Mattie," he said.

"I've missed you, too. Come into the parlor."

She had always thought the room to be spacious, although crowded with the three-seat sofa and the matching parlor chairs, the upright piano, and the carved walnut turtle top table with the ornate oil lamp in the center. Dried flowers and china figurines decorated the mantlepiece on the fireplace, and the tables had velvet cloths. Several tintype photos were placed about the room, including one of Maggie and Liam on their wedding day. An oil painting of the Danube River in Germany claimed space on one wall. It was a busy, fussy room, and with Moses seated on the sofa, it seemed smaller. Mattie settled her skirt and sat on the other end of the sofa.

Her mouth still prickled from his kiss, and she wanted to hold his hand or touch him. He was as handsome as ever to her eyes, but in the unfamiliar setting, he looked as out of place as a grand piano in a quiet forest. His masculine presence made the dainty frills and furbelows in the room appear silly. He belonged on the open plains, on horseback, not perched on the edge of a settee.

"You look well," she told him. "When did you get to San Antonio?"

"Late yesterday," he said. "I rode hard to get here in just four days. I was dusty and dirty, plum tuckered out. I figured I needed a bath, a shave, and a haircut before I came to see you. Bought some new duds too, all but the jacket, and I borrowed it from Phineas."

She didn't know the name. "Who's that?"

He smiled, and she almost forgot the question. "He served with Boone and Liam in the war," he told her. "Phineas D. Dawson. He has a mercantile store on one of the plazas here. I'm bunking at his house while I'm here."

"Dawson's Emporium," Mattie said. She knew the place and had shopped there.

Moses nodded. "Oh, Mattie, I have so much I want to tell you…"

A screech interrupted him. Ilse Baumann sailed into the room like a full-rigged ship, eyes blazing and her jaw set hard. "*Was ist das? Wer ist dieser Mann?*"

Mattie replied in English. "Mutti, this is Moses Wilson from the Double B Ranch. Moses, this is my mother, Frau Ilse Baumann."

Moses stood and bowed. "I'm right pleased to meet you, ma'am."

"You are a *cowboy*," Ilse said. "A hired hand, right? Why are you here? Did you bring news from my son-in-law?"

Her tone was sharp and meant to be insulting. From the way Moses' face shifted from a happy to a bland expression, he understood that well. His smile vanished, and his lips pressed into a thin line.

"I've brought no news from my *partner*," he replied after a moment's pause. "My brothers and I are buying into the ranch. We'll be owners as much as Liam is, and we're fixing to change the name. I'm here to court your daughter, Miz Baumann."

Mattie gasped. She'd hoped and prayed that the Wilson brothers might one day get a ranch, but she'd never imagined they would become partners with Liam. Excited and delighted, she said, "That's wonderful news, Moses."

"I reckon so," he told her, and she realized that under his calm expression, he was angry. "Least for those who value money over a man's worth."

She rose and stood beside him, then placed one hand on his arm. "I don't, Moses."

He turned toward her, and his hard expression softened a fraction. "I know you don't, Mattie, but it seems some do."

Ilse huffed, then said, "*Jawohl*, I do, and I won't stand for you to court my daughter. I don't even know if it's true that you're partners with Liam Rafferty, but you need to go back to the cows."

"I'll say who courts me and who doesn't," she told her mother, cheeky and bold. "And Moses will."

If her mother said much more, she'd probably blurt out that she'd already agreed to marry him, although that would cause a major storm.

"I will not have it," Ilse began as Hans Baumann walked into the parlor.

Every muscle in Mattie's body tensed as she waited to see what her father might say. If he agreed with her mother, she would pack a bag and leave with Moses today.

"It is not yours to say," Hans said to his wife. "I'm her father, and it is my decision."

He spoke in the precise tones he'd adopted, never happy to speak in broken English or with much accent.

Moses stepped forward with his right hand extended to shake. "Moses Wilson," he said. "From the Double B Ranch and partners with your son-in-law, Liam Rafferty."

Hans shook hands with him. "And you want to court my daughter, I hear."

"I do, sir."

"You are not the only one," Mattie's father said. "A banker, Gunther Hammerschmidt, has been paying suit to Mathilde. And there are many others who would like to court her."

Mattie blushed as Moses sent a shocked look in her direction. Since she'd rather he'd not think that she'd been fickle, she said in a low tone for him to hear, "I've not welcomed his attention, Moses, nor that of anyone else."

"I'd hope not," he said.

Her father looked at his daughter, then at Moses.

"So, daughter, tell me who you would want to court you."

"Moses Wilson," she said without hesitation.

"*Ach du Lieber Gott,*" Hans said after his wife gave a wordless squawk. "Then I will say this – let both men court you, and then you can choose. I will stand by your decision. That seems what an American papa might do, and you have long said you're an American girl."

"I am, *Vati.*"

"Then so it will be," Hans said. "Please join us for dinner at noon, Mr. Wilson. You are welcome at our table."

"Thank you kindly," Moses replied. "I'd like to take Mattie on a buggy ride. We'll be back in plenty of time to eat."

"It is for her to say."

"I'll go get my wrap," Mattie said. "Moses, I'll be right down."

She descended the stairs fifteen minutes later after changing into one of the new dresses she'd made since returning to San Antonio. The bright green and white of the gingham garment suited her. She'd added a shawl and donned a hat trimmed with flowers.

Moses waited in the hallway, and when she reached him,

he offered her his arm, and she took it. A buggy waited on the street with the one horse tied to the hitching rail. He helped her into it, then joined her and took the reins.

As the buggy moved forward, he turned to her. "So, you've been courtin' a banker?"

"No," she said. "He's been trying to court me."

"Good, because I still mean to marry you unless that's not what you want."

"It is, Moses. I love you."

His face lightened, and he smiled for the first time since her mother had come into the parlor.

"Well, those are sweet words for these ears, dearest. I love you, Mattie."

He stole a quick kiss without losing control of the reins or horse.

"Where are we going?"

"I figured down by this San Antonio River," he said. "I saw a quiet place or two with willows where we can talk."

Mattie scooted over as close as she could get to him. "So, you and your brothers are partners in the ranch?"

"Not yet, but we will be. Liam's asked, and Boone figures we'll do it. Details ain't been worked out yet, though. I plan to build us a cabin, maybe even a house of our own, Mattie. It won't be as big nor as fancy as where you live, though."

She'd never thought their home to be elegant, just larger than most.

"I don't care about that," she told him.

"I'd thought maybe I'd persuade you to get hitched and come back to the ranch with me," Moses said after a moment. "But thanks to your daddy, guess we'll have to wait."

"Why?" she repeated.

"That's what he said. Let both me and that banker court you," Moses said. "I don't reckon to wait that long. We'll leave to drive cattle in April, most likely, and I'm not waiting till I come back from the trail. We'll figure something out and get married before then."

"I'd marry you today, Moses."

"I know it, but I'll be as honorable as I can for your family's sake. Besides, right now, we'd have to kick Zeke out and send him back to the bunkhouse if we wanted to live in that dog trot cabin across from Boone's."

When they reached the river, he parked the buggy and secured the horse. Then he lifted her down, and they walked along the bank beneath the willows, yellow now for autumn. They linked hands, and Mattie's happiness soared like a bird into the sky.

"Tell me what to expect at dinner," he said.

"It'll be in the dining room, and we eat our main meal at noon. More fashionable people eat dinner in the evening, but we're still old-fashioned. It will be my parents, the two of us, and maybe a relative or two. My sisters and brothers are at my Aunt Gertrude's."

"Will it be fancy?"

"Substantial," she said. "There should be soup, then meat and vegetables and bread, then something sweet and probably some cheese."

"What are you doing this evening? I'd thought to maybe take you to a restaurant or find some entertainment."

She had almost forgotten the masquerade but remembered.

"Moses, there's a masquerade tonight at The Menger House, it's a hotel on the plaza. I must go – my parents had a dress made. Most aren't dressing in costumes, but it's fancy dress, and guests must wear masks until midnight. Mine covers my eyes only – that's how most of them will be."

"I'd be proud to escort you, Mattie, though I'm not familiar with such things."

Her stomach clenched tight. "I'd like it if you could, Moses, but Gunther will attend me. I'm sorry…"

"So am I," he said. "I'll be there, though. Wild horses couldn't keep me away."

"You have to have an invitation."

"Phineas and his wife are going," he replied. "I understand now what they were talking about. I didn't before. I'll go as their guest, and you can dance with me."

It was bold, she thought, but she liked it. "I will, then, Moses. I'll dance as many dances with you as I can. Gunther won't like it, though."

"He can go to the devil for all I care."

Mattie laughed. She felt the same. "Kiss me again, Moses."

He obliged her, then they settled down to sit on a large rock near the river. She wanted to know all the news from the ranch, so he told her how baby Seamus was growing, how tender Boone was with Rachel, who was expecting a child in early spring, and how he'd missed her.

When he told her about how close Mima had come to being bitten by a rattlesnake, she shivered.

"Oh, Moses!"

"Would have been my fault if she had been."

"No, it wouldn't. Are there many snakes, though? I don't like them, and they scare me."

"A few, no more. How many did you see when you spent the summer on the ranch?"

"Just the one in the corral, the day you were hurt."

"And that's about how many you'll see in a year. Let's get you back before they fuss or send a search party."

The noon meal began with a rich potato soup followed by a roast chicken with spätzle noodles, creamed peas, green beans cooked with bacon and onion, rye bread as well as a black bread, Bavarian cream served in glass dishes, and a plum cake.

Her family peppered Moses with questions throughout the meal, and he answered them all with a patience Mattie wouldn't have had. By the end of the dinner, the family knew he came from Kentucky, how many siblings he had, how long he'd gone to school (which hadn't been long), that he liked to read, and how he'd come to be in Texas.

When it came time to leave, Moses didn't protest or kiss her. The masquerade hadn't been mentioned at all, but as he bowed, he whispered, "I'll see you tonight, I promise."

Her smile had been her answer.

The afternoon was spent in a long nap so she could stay up late at the gala event, then two hours were spent in primping and preparing. Instead of her usual braids pinned around her head, Mattie's hair was curled into long ringlets caught up in back. Although she wore no cosmetics – nice women didn't – her mother had powdered her face so it wouldn't be shiny. Once the gown was on and in place over several petticoats, she slid her feet into shoes, added an evening wrap of lace, and picked up her best reticule.

Gunther arrived, resplendent in evening dress, and ushered them all into his large carriage for the trek to The Menger House. The two-story structure was bright with lights, and a steady stream of carriages brought guests to the door. They climbed the sweeping stair to the ballroom upstairs, a large room made festive with floral and fall decorations. Tomorrow would be Halloween, not a date that most observed other than to bob for apples, drink cider, or tell scary tales, but tonight, it was one of the biggest parties of the season.

Mattie, like all the ladies present, was given a dance card with a tiny pencil attached. The notion was to fill the card with the names of those gentlemen who would dance with her. Each one was named a waltz or a two-step. Gunter reached for it and would have written his name on most of the lines, but she snatched it back. He frowned, and she tried to explain.

"I have to share dances with several," she said. "Otherwise, it would look improper. We're not engaged to be married, so you can't take all the dances."

Although her eyes scanned the crowd frequently, Mattie had yet to spot Moses. She stood along the wall as the first waltz was about to begin, and he tapped her shoulder.

"May I have this dance?"

She whirled to find Moses, masked and wearing a fine suit. His eyes, though, were the same and his voice. "Yes, you may," she said and bowed to him so they could begin.

Unsure if he would know how to dance, Moses pulled her into the correct position and twirled her onto the floor. He kept time and didn't tromp on her feet, moving with grace.

"I reckon you thought I didn't dance," he said.

"I wasn't sure."

"Ma taught us a bit back home," Moses said. "She always wanted us to be ready for whatever might come in life, but Phin's wife took pity on me and gave me a few quick lessons."

In his arms, as the musicians tucked into one corner played the Blue Danube Waltz, they danced. She savored the experience, for she had never dreamed that Moses might ever be her partner for any dance or at a ball. If she hadn't already given him her heart, she would have that night.

She danced a few rounds with Gunther, but the rest were in Moses' strong arms. Near the end, when guests prepared to unmask, they headed outside and he kissed her long and sweet.

"I'll see you tomorrow," he told her.

"How?"

He laughed. "Your daddy invited me to Sunday dinner."

Then he vanished into the dark, and she rode home, quiet, but her thoughts and heart were full of Moses Wilson.

CHAPTER ELEVEN

Double B Ranch

When he headed out for San Antonio, Moses never figured on attending any kind of dance, let alone a masquerade ball, but that was exactly what he did. The long-ago days when Ma had taught him – and each of the others – to dance the waltz and two-step in the kitchen now proved handy. Phin's wife had given him a few quick lessons as well, once she learned he would accompany them to the ball. His new clothes weren't fine enough for such an evening, so Phineas loaned him the use of a suit, one that would return to his closet the next day.

Mattie had been resplendent in a fine gown, and with her hair down in curls, he thought she'd never been lovelier. He preferred her, though in calicos and cotton with her customary braids. Gussied up, she reminded him of a porcelain doll, fragile and too easy to break.

He'd come to town to spend a few days and stayed almost a week. More than once, he dined at the Baumann table, and he'd managed not to break any fine china or commit any social blunders. The food, although tasty, had been too high-brow for his taste, but he didn't complain. He could hold his own in the conversation when it centered on books, and he answered the many prying questions without fail, for Mattie's sake. If it were up to him, he would have told them all to leave off, and he would have gone.

The worst meal had been Sunday, when Mattie's other beau, the wealthy and blond Gunther, was also a guest. The man had appeared to be at ease, but Moses was tense throughout the meal and the afternoon that followed. Mattie had confided she had no regard for the man, and that made Moses glad, for he saw no value in him. He was as empty as a suit of clothing without a body but seemed to think quite highly on himself. It was obvious he thought himself to be Moses' better, and though that rankled, he swallowed his anger and said nothing.

He took Mattie for buggy rides, brought her to shop at the Dawson Mercantile, paid for a meal in a restaurant, and came to formal high tea at her home twice. Sometimes, they managed no more than an afternoon in the stuffy parlor where he would sit stiff and near silent but still glad to be near Mattie. Sometimes, they read poetry, some of her favorites and his.

Moses arrived on a Friday and headed back on a Thursday. By then, it was November, and the weather had taken a cooler turn. The fall rains would start soon, and if he could, he'd prefer to ride ahead of them. He took his leave of her Thursday morning, early, down near the river. They had spooned for a bit, then he talked of serious things.

"I can't and won't wait until May to marry you," Moses told her, blunt and honest. "I don't know when I can be back, but I will. It makes me no never mind whether we wed here with a judge or in a church with a preacher, whether it's in San Antonio or on the ranch or in Laredo, but we will get married. I love you, woman, and it's gonna be hard to part."

"I'll be ready whenever you come," Mattie had told him. "I'm not partial to any special place as long as we say our vows."

In his arms, as the river made its' own music, she put her head against his shoulder.

"I love you, Moses, more than anything," she said, then

quoted from Elizabeth Barrett Browning's poetry. "'I love thee to the level of every day's most quiet need, by sun or candlelight."

He liked the words fine but remembered the poet had but a short time with her beloved husband and had been dead now for more than ten years. "I love you all the time, Mattie, for always."

The trip back to the ranch was long and tedious. Rain began to fall on the second day, and he rode wet more often than not. He had never been one for solitude, preferring company to being alone, so he became lonely. Once back, however, welcomed by his family, Moses found a calm he had lacked before. He would marry Mattie before May. That was certain. Figuring out the where and how would come.

Mima and Rob had missed him but he had brought home trinkets for them from San Antonio. He bought the little girl a Susie Simple paper doll with four paper outfits that could be put onto the doll and a small cast iron toy revolver for the boy. At less than three, he was too young for it, but he could grow into it, Moses thought.

He shifted back into ranch mode, his daily chores, riding out after lost or strayed cattle, working with the horses, mucking out the stables, and anything else he was asked to do. A letter came from Kentucky a week or so before Thanksgiving, written in early October.

To my sons and their family, greetings from Kentucky

We are all well. The tobacco crop did well this year, and we are provisioned for the winter at hand. I hope this finds each of you well, Boone and Rachel, Moses and Ezekiel, as well as the little ones. I someday hope to see those grandchildren, especially that girl who bears my name. Maybe one day I will come to Texas. Jacob's wife is with child once again as the family continues to grow.

We plan to kill a hog for Thanksgiving.

There is not much else of any importance to write. Life goes on as it always has, but know that I miss each of you very much.

Your loving mother, Jemima Wilson

Boone read it out to them all over supper one evening, then it was passed from hand to hand until the paper frayed more than a little. When he had time, Boone sat down with pen and paper to write an answer, his duty as the eldest son.

Dear Ma and all,

We are well here in Texas, and I long to see you someday. My children are growing. Little Jemima, who we call Mima most of the time, turned 4 years old in September, and our son Robert will be three come January. Rachel is in the family way and, so we should have another child come spring.

Moses is courting a young lady, and I do believe he means to marry her someday. Ezekiel is a man now – you would hardly recognize him. They are both well.

Life here on the ranch is good. We are probably going to buy into it and become partners. Tell Jacob and Garrett there would always be room for another hand or two.

Enjoy that roast hog come Thanksgiving. We eat more beef here than anything else, so that sounds tasty. Ezekiel does some hunting to give us something different on the table.

I wish you all well, that you stay prosperous and safe. I think of you often, Ma, and do pray that someday you will come here or we can make the journey back there.

I doubt another letter would arrive in time, so Merry Christmas to all.

Your loving son, Boone Benjamin Wilson.

"I'm glad to be in Texas," Moses said after his brother shared the letter he would mail back home. "I do miss Ma, though, and wish we could see her."

"I feel the same. I'd make the trip home for that if I thought we could, but with the little ones and Rachel in the family way, I don't see any way it could be."

Moses didn't either. Once, he'd considered making the journey, but he'd done it once, to arrive in Texas to save Boone, and it had been an arduous trip. Now that Mattie was in his life, he didn't want to leave her for so long. Trailing cattle would be more separation than he wanted from her. If Zeke ever imagined returning as the prodigal, he had never mentioned it and Moses suspected he was rooted well in Texas.

On Thanksgiving, Liam gave all the hands the day off. He did, to Moses' surprise, roast a whole hog, but he also had Cookie prepare steaks and other beef cuts for all. Since the weather had remained mild, for now, dinner was outside.

Although no formal papers were drawn up as yet, the Wilsons anticipated partnering with Liam on the ranch. Boone sometimes spoke of building a larger house for Rachel, necessary as his family grew. If that happened, Moses could have one cabin and Ezekiel the other. It would serve, Moses thought, as a place to set up housekeeping, but he thought he'd like to build one day too. Toward that end and for his upcoming marriage, whenever it might take place, he saved almost every cent that he earned. Ezekiel ventured into Laredo and sometimes played faro. Now that he was a family man, Boone almost never did either.

As December loomed, Moses missed Mattie and wished he could be with her on Christmas Day. He began to tentatively plan to make the trip back to San Antonio in March, after Boone's child was born. He would return married, he thought, or with a bride. For that, he could bide his time and wait.

******

San Antonio

As soon as Moses departed, Gunther stepped up his courtship of Mattie. Ever mindful of what she'd overheard, Mattie did her best to remain elusive. She did nothing to encourage his pursuit, although she had to be polite. If Gunther suspected he came in a distant second to Moses, he didn't let it show. Mattie thought her father knew where her heart lay, but her mother continued to push the German banker. Ilse wanted her daughter to marry well, into a life of wealth and privilege. Maybe once, Mattie reasoned, her mother had dreamed of such an existence. If so, then she shouldn't have come to America, to the frontier with her baker husband.

On the last Thursday in November, the day proclaimed by President Grant, her family hosted a huge Thanksgiving dinner. All her aunts, uncles, and cousins were invited. The closest family friends were included, and so was Gunther. To be more fashionable, dinner was served later on that day, at five o'clock in the evening.

The meal began with oyster soup and a beef consommé, followed by saddle of mutton, duck, ham, and a roast turkey. Side dishes included mashed and riced potatoes, creamed onions, peas, carrots in a rich, sweet sauce and bread dressing. There were multiple types of pie for dessert, along with a few cakes. Her father outdid himself with various breads, all served with butter. After the rich meal, there were salted almonds, raisins, fruit, and cheese.

Aware that it was one month until Christmas Day, the deadline Gunther had given her parents when he would ask her to wed, Mattie had little appetite. She tasted bits of this or that, but her plate, unlike the others, was never heaping, nor did she suffer indigestion afterward. Usually honest to a fault, however, she claimed pains in her belly as an excuse to retire from the revelry to her bedroom. She stood at the window that faced west for a very long time, wishing she could send her thoughts of love to Moses. Mattie wondered how he spent the day and if he missed her.

Her lie worked so well that she continued to complain of stomach troubles to avoid the festive circle of events until her parents called her bluff and brought in a doctor. Mattie overheard her mother confide she feared her daughter might be in a family way, that perhaps she'd done what she shouldn't with Moses Wilson. That suggestion brought anger and a real stomachache, especially when Mutti suggested that if she were with child, she should be married to Gunther with haste. Then he'd never know of her reckless sin, and the child could be raised as his.

It stung that her mother could entertain such a thought or think so ill of either her or Moses. They'd done no more than kiss. If she had found herself carrying a child, Mattie thought she would have found a way to the ranch and Moses, not marry in haste.

Although Dr. Hermann pushed and prodded on her belly, questioned her, looked into her eyes, and studied her tongue, he could find no evidence of any illness. Instead, after talking with her and based on her short answers, he told her parents she suffered from the megrims, a young woman's unhappy condition. Unashamed, Mattie eavesdropped to hear the doctor's verdict.

"I imagine it's from not having a husband or home of her own yet," he said. "How old is she now, twenty?"

"She'll be twenty-one on her next birthday," Vati said.

"Ah, well, that's it. A woman her age isn't a girl any longer, and she yearns to be a woman in every way. Matilde is far from the first I've seen to suffer and be moody. She won't be happy until she can play the bride and manage her own household."

That won't happen, not with Gunther, Mattie thought.

If Moses couldn't yet come to her, she would find a way to get to the ranch. As the rest of the family decorated the house for Christmas with holly leaves, as they prepared to cut a tree to decorate on Christmas Eve and planned gifts to give, Mattie sulked, and she made sure everyone knew it. She picked at her food, refused the black tonic, and sometimes walked around with one hand on her stomach, although it didn't hurt. Her sighs were long and deep, and she did her best not to smile, which wasn't hard with Gunther turning up daily.

She retired early and rose late. It was all part of a plan to see if she might persuade her parents to send her to Maggie's for the holiday. If they thought the trip might cheer her up, she thought they might.

Her actions angered her parents more than it seemed to concern them, but she didn't yield at all.

It was no more than a game, one meant to get her way at first, but then, one night, she had a dream about Moses. She woke troubled, for he had been wandering in a terrible snowstorm, a dream so vivid she woke cold. For two or three days, her mind revisited it, and she worried. The weather had grown cooler, but it hadn't snowed, so she chalked it up to imagination until a dinner guest spoke of the sudden snowstorm that had struck south, near Laredo. In her vision, he had been covered with snow, and she realized it might be true.

About the same time, she became cognizant of the fact if she acted too weak or ill, they would never let her embark on a five-day or more journey to the ranch. Mattie stopped play acting that her stomach gave her trouble. She ate more at the table and consented to attend a few events, two with Gunther.

"You're looking well these days, Mathilde," he told her one night at a concert. She hated the way he usually used her full name. "I'd begun to fear you might be ill, but I'm certain now you're not."

"Thank you, Gunther," she said, forcing her tone to sound sweet.

"I know you've been moody, and that's to be expected for an unmarried woman," he had responded in his pompous way. "But I have a notion you'll be overcome with joy soon, possibly before Christmas."

"I wish I could see my sister and her children for Christmas," she said. This time, her sigh wasn't faked. She knew too well what he alluded to – a proposal that she would refuse. "I would love to go to the ranch to be with them."

Gunther frowned. "That's a long journey, too hard for a young lady this time of year."

"I've made it before."

He dismissed her and changed the subject to the new house he was going to build on East Guenther Street. He liked the similarity to his name, and from the plan he described, it would be a mansion. Once, she'd dreamed of such, but no more. Mattie figured he told her because he intended to build it for his bride, but that woman would never be her.

As he detailed wallpapers and mahogany paneling for the dining room and the possibility of a ballroom on the top floor, she pretended to listen, but her thoughts flew wild and free.

On the ranch, it would be winter, she thought and tried to imagine the place without green hued grass, tall weeds, a garden providing ample vegetables, or trees without full leaf.

Twenty times, she started a letter to Moses, and twenty times, she tore it up to start again. The right words refused to come. Mattie didn't want words on a page, and she doubted that Moses did either. She wanted to look into his eyes as she shared her heart with him or confided her dreams.

There was so much she wanted to tell him, good and bad. He would be as irate as she'd been to think her mother suspected she might be with child, Mattie knew.

Soon, she thought, soon as she eyed the calendar. Once Christmas and New Year's Day were past, it would be a few short months until spring. Surely, she could wait until then. When she thought she wouldn't be able to hold out, though, Mattie schemed for ways to make the trip to the ranch. Although she did want to see her sister and her family, to hold that precious little new nephew once again, it was Moses she wanted most of all, and Moses that she needed.

As the December days came then went, she became more restless than she'd ever been. Mattie continued to dream about Moses, caught in a terrible snowstorm. As disturbing as that dream had been, it grew worse. She dreamed of him coughing and fighting a runny nose. Then, as time went on, she saw him hot with fever, sick, and asking for her.

She woke distressed and afraid. Mattie told herself it was nothing but a bad dream, a nightmare induced because she missed him so much and worried.

The thought wouldn't go away, though, that Moses needed her, and by the Saturday before Christmas, all she could think about was Moses. She made up her mind – she was going, no matter what it might take. Although she wasn't much of a rider and could barely sit a horse, Mattie considered riding to the ranch.

Unless her fears eased, she knew what she had to do – just not how she would manage to do it.

CHAPTER TWELVE

By the middle of December, Moses was edgy and unusually fretful. Rachel and Boone marked their fifth wedding anniversary on the 10th, and following the tradition of what gifts were proper for each year married, Boone presented his wife with a small cedar box he'd made in his spare time. Rachel had no gift in return, but she made chicken and dumplings for dinner, and Boone joked she gave him children for presents.

The visit he'd made to San Antonio at the end of October had lifted his spirits for a while, but as the weeks passed, he found he missed Mattie more than ever. They'd talked about a spring wedding, but it seemed far away. Fickle Texas weather made for dreary days. Half the hands were gone for winter since Liam dismissed them until March. Those who remained, including the Wilsons, had more duties.

Moses caught a cold, a nasty one, which didn't help his mood at all. At first, he didn't complain, just endured his daily work despite his symptoms. He had trouble sleeping, though, with a congested head and his vittles didn't taste right. He hadn't even been smoking since it irritated his already suffering nose and throat. One night, he couldn't finish his supper, a rich beef stew Rachel had made, and excused himself early.

"I'm going to bed," he told them. "This cold is tapping me out."

Mima would have jumped up for a kiss, but her daddy

caught her. "Tell Moses good night from here," he said. "I don't want you getting a snot nose."

Moses nodded. Boone valued his children above all else. Little ones could sicken quickly, and too many died. "Your daddy's right, baby girl," he said. "I wouldn't wish this nasty cold on anyone, especially you."

Across the dog trot, he poked up the fire and then burrowed into bed. It took a long time for his aching body to become warm, and his sleep was fitful. He woke to cough or to blow his nose, or sneeze. Once he'd dropped off with total exhaustion, he woke to Ezekiel shaking him.

"Get up, Moses, get up," Zeke cried. He sounded delighted and excited, which soured Moses' mood.

"Go away. I wanna sleep," he muttered and tried to roll over.

"Get up – it's like springtime outside, and the sun's shining. Let's go to Laredo today."

Moses didn't want to roll out of bed, let alone ride to town. "For what?"

"Fun," Ezekiel said. "Besides, we can get some more Christmas plunder, candy, maybe an orange or two, things for the little ones. I want some tamales, too."

Right now, he didn't feel up to saddling his mount or riding for hours. "No," Moses said with a groan. "I feel awful, Zeke."

"Aw, quit your caterwauling, and don't be a namby pamby," his brother said. "You'd feel better up and doing, I reckon."

"I don't, and I ain't going. Leave me be."

With that, he pulled up the covers and turned away. His head ached, his throat hurt, his body twinged, and his nose was plugged. The only place he wanted to be was here in bed.

"All right, I'm going. You're gonna miss the fun."

Moses tried but couldn't get back to sleep or find a comfortable position. He gave up the effort by noon and rolled out of bed, then dressed quickly. He craved coffee, seeking the heat and the energy it might bring. The fire in the hearth had gone down to embers, and rather than poke it up, he headed over to Boone's. Rachel would likely have the coffee pot on, he figured, and he could use a bit of sympathy.

He opened the door and shivered. If it had been spring-like and warm earlier, it wasn't now. A sharp wind whistled between the cabins, frigid and harsh enough that he shivered. Heavy clouds, heavy with precipitation, hung low in the sky, and snow fell, thick and fast. Several inches already covered the ground. Ezekiel had surely changed his mind, he thought, and entered Boone's home.

His brother glanced from the table where he sharpened knives with a whetstone. Rachel sat in the rocker while her two babies played at her feet. Something bubbled over the fire, but Moses couldn't smell it, although he wished he could. He glanced around and asked, "Where's Zeke?"

Boone's hands paused in his task. "Ain't he over across the way with you?"

"Naw, he tried to wake me up earlier, said it was like spring outside, and he was heading to town."

"I ain't seen him," Boone replied as he came to his feet. "I surely hope he didn't go – not in weather like this. They don't get many snowstorms like this in this part of Texas, but I've seen them before. It may snow several feet before it quits, and it's cold enough to freeze a man's family jewels."

When several hours passed and Zeke didn't return, Boone wrapped up in all his cold weather gear and went to inquire at the bunkhouse. When he came back, a worry line furrowed his forehead. He stamped his feet free of snow and stood before the fire, warming his hands.

"His horse is gone, and so is he," he said without preamble. "The boys all say he set out for town a while ago, but I doubt he could get far in this snow."

"Surely, he took shelter when the storm struck," Rachel said.

Moses spoke up. "There ain't much between here and Laredo," he said. "It's mostly open country. I don't even think he dressed for cold weather. He told me it was like springtime."

Boone snorted. "It was early, but I wish he'd told me. I'd have warned him that usually means a norther is headed this way. Now he's out there, and he's liable to freeze to death."

A finger of dread uncurled within Moses' belly. Back home in Kentucky, he'd heard tales about hunters who lay down and froze to death at the foot of a tree. He'd been told about people who got frostbite, then lost fingers or toes or limbs. Some took such cold that they became sick and died.

"Surely he won't, Boone," Rachel said with concern.

"He might." Boone's lips were pressed into a straight, grim line. "I reckon there's a good foot or more out there now. He could be froze now. Ain't much we can do about it but pray."

"We'd best go see if we can find him," Moses said. Despite his ills, he couldn't sit still by the fire while his youngest brother possibly died.

Boone shook his head. "I cain't leave Rachel and the little ones here alone, not in the shape she's in, Moses, and you're poorly."

"I'm not ailing so bad I won't go try to find Ezekiel," Moses said. "Ma would take it hard if he died from being out in the cold."

"We all would," Boone said. "He ought not to have took off half-cocked, not knowing what the weather might do, though. It was foolish."

Moses made his decision. It really didn't require any

thought. "I'm going out after him. He ain't even twenty years old yet."

Rachel gasped, and Boone whirled about to glare at him. "I know you're worried," he said. "I am, too, but you're not likely to find him. It's snowing so hard out there I could barely see a foot ahead of me, and that's here at the ranch, where I'm familiar. Out in the open, you won't have nothing to tell where you're at, and the snow'll drift high. Stay home, Moses, and we'll hope he makes it in."

If it was him out there, Moses figured Zeke would come after him, and so would Boone.

"I'm going, Boone," he said.

They argued for a few minutes, then Boone groaned. "You're stubborn as, as a mule…"

"Stubborn as you," Moses replied.

"I can see you're doing this crazy thing. Take my duster, these gloves, and wear one of my wool caps, a scarf too. Better put on as many clothes as you can still ride wearing, too. Wear the duster over your own coat, Moses."

"And take some blankets along," Rachel added. "You or Zeke may need them."

Although it was just mid-afternoon when he set out, dressed in so much clothing, he felt like a stuffed sausage. It was almost dark. Gypsy, his horse, protested the moment he led him out of the barn with a sharp whinny, but Moses led him onward. He tied a lit lantern to the saddle horn and mounted. All his gear, including his rifle and the extra blankets, were in place as he rode off in the general direction of Laredo.

It was most likely a fool's errand, and he knew it, but he had to make the effort. Snowflakes flew at him, thick and fast, and the wind buffeted him hard in the saddle. Even with the lantern's feeble illumination, Moses could see little. It made it especially difficult because any sign or trail Zeke might have left had vanished beneath the snow. He called his brother's name, but the wind carried the sound away. Even if he were within calling distance, it wasn't likely he would hear.

A series of sneezes shook his body, and beneath his bandana, his nose ran. He doubted he would ever get warm again and decided it likely he could die out here with Ezekiel. That would make Mattie angry, he figured, but sad too. The idea of Mattie mourning gave him the resolve to go on when otherwise he might have faltered. He'd lost track of time and had no idea exactly where he might be at in the brush country.

He'd been riding for at least a couple of hours, maybe more, when his horse stumbled, and when he pulled Gypsy back, Moses realized they were on the edge of one of the small arroyos. He halted the horse and, on a hunch, he mustered all his strength and shouted, "Ezekiel!"

Moses repeated it several times, raising his volume to be heard over the howling wind. When no answer came, he turned to mount his horse when he heard a faint cry. He paused and listened. The sound repeated, and he tied Gypsy to a scrub bush, then walked to the edge of the arroyo. He yelled again, and this time, he heard his name carried on the wind.

He leapt into the arroyo, almost wrecking his bad ankle, and shouted one more time, "Ezekiel!"

His brother's head popped out from a crude shelter, eyes round with surprise. "Moses?"

"It's me," he said. "And I'm near frozen to death. Are you hurt?"

"Just cold," Zeke said. "When it started snowing so hard and turned colder than a witch's heart, I looked for shelter. Ain't much out here, but I got down in the arroyo and cut some scrub to make a sort of shelter. Horse took off, though. I figured I'd be a dead man by morning."

"We feared you might freeze," Moses said, coughing

hard. Relief made him dizzy, though. "Boone wanted to wait, but I started out to find you."

"You did, and I'm much obliged," Zeke said. "Though now I fear you might be a goner, too."

"I'll get us back home," Moses said, although that was a good part bravado. "Gypsy can carry us both. The trick will be finding the way back. Might be easier if we wait for daylight."

"Unless we're frozen stiff. Give the horse his head – he might can find the way back."

Options were few. They could shelter in the arroyo and hope for the best, but Moses doubted they'd last the night. Or they could mount and pray the horse could find his way back to the ranch. Swathed in the extra blankets, they rode double, shivering and doing their best to stay as warm as they could. Their combined body heat helped a little.

Moses was so tired he would have likely fell from the saddle into the snow without Ezekiel's guiding hand and supporting bulk. Their journey became a long blur of white and frigid wind, an endurance test he feared both might fail. About the time he had decided they might as well give it up, he caught a glimpse of a structure ahead. He nudged Zeke and peered hard into the dark. When he realized it was the main barn, he summoned the energy to whoop.

Weary as they were, they still unsaddled the horse and cared for him, then made the dangerous trek across the ranch to the cabins. More than once, they fell but managed to rise. When they drew closer, Moses saw a lamp burning in the window at Boone's and made for the light.

Together, clutching one another, they managed the steps and fumbled to open the door to Boone's cabin. They fell inside, tangled in a heap as Boone, roused from sleeping, stood with one hand on his Griswold pistol.

"What in the Sam Hill?" Boone cried.

"It's us," Moses said, then coughed hard. "We're back, both of us. I found Zeke and brought him home. His horse got away, though."

"I'll be blessed," Boone said. His voice was thick with emotion. "Are either of you hurt?"

"Naw," Moses said. "I still feel rotten, though."

He fussed over them almost as bad as Ma would have, insisting they get out of any wet garments and that they huddle close to the fire. Rachel and the children were asleep, so he spoke in hushed tones but made fresh coffee and gave them some stew she'd made earlier. He inspected their skin for any indication of frostbite and made Moses drink some whiskey laced with honey. None of them ever drank except for medicinal purposes. Moses didn't like the rank taste of the liquor but downed it, hoping it might break up his cold.

By daybreak, a fire blazed in their own hearth, and the cabin Moses shared with Zeke was toasty. Moses had put on his spare garments because they were dry and curled up in bed. He wasn't as cold as he'd been out in the weather, but he wasn't warm, either.

Boone gave both his brothers a tongue lashing, his words harsh, although his relief both were back, alive and in one piece, was evident. "Fools, the pair of you," he said when he'd finished his piece. "They say God watches over fools and little children. I'm pleased I don't have to bury either one of you. That's true. I doubt anyone could have dug a grave till spring. I don't know that I would have had the words to write Ma or tell Moses' pretty gal if you hadn't made it."

Once the snow stopped, Liam told them it'd measured two feet high, as tall as five feet in drifts. In the contrary way of Texas weather, it melted the following day, leaving behind mud and puddles. Moses did his best to get some rest and fight the cold that still dogged him hard, but with little success. He still couldn't taste anything beyond hot or cold. His nose turned red from running and chapped his skin from the same. His cough turned deep, and he refused any more of the whiskey treatment. Rachel fed him honey mixed with lemon juice left from Mattie's lemonade making. It soothed for a short time but not long.

On Saturday, Moses realized it was a week until Christmas. He felt too bad to be festive about it, although he had a few gifts squirreled away. The main thing he wanted was to shake the cold so he could enjoy the day. No matter how much he tried to sleep by day or night, despite the endless coffee and cups of tea Rachel provided, nothing changed, and he felt almost ill.

He woke on the Sunday before Christmas feeling worse than ever. His bones ached, and so did his muscles until he hurt all over. His cough continued, but he brought nothing up, no mucous that might have given a little relief. Moses had a headache, too, and he lacked any energy to get out of bed. When Boone came to see if he would join them for dinner, Moses sat up on the edge of the bed.

"Boone, I fear I'm taking sick with something more than a cold," he said.

His brother's eyes narrowed. "Do you feel worse?"

"I do," Moses admitted. His chest had begun to ache, and he could hear a strangle crackle when he breathed. He didn't want to borrow trouble, but he had the awful thought that he was very ill. He touched his hand to his forehead but couldn't gauge if he had a temperature or not. "I think I'm starting a fever."

Boone put the back of his hand against Moses' face and frowned. "You're on fire, Moses."

It must be bad because Boone fetched Rachel. With Ezekiel's help, they moved his bed into the front room so he could be closer to the fire. Someone helped him put on his only nightshirt and tucked him into bed with a hot water bottle at his feet. Rachel brought him a cup of cool water, then later some willow bark tea. Even sweetened with honey, Moses had a hard time getting it down. She bathed his face and neck, then put her hand on his chest.

"Boone, he's awfully sick," he heard her say.

"It looks like pneumonia," Boone replied. "It's what our daddy died from, so I hope I'm wrong."

"He's young and hale," she said, but her tone was uncertain. "He'll be all right, but he's going to have a hard time for a few days."

Moses listened and wanted to believe her. Rachel, a schoolteacher before she married Boone, was smart, and if she said something, it must be so. He wasn't sure, though, for he couldn't remember being this sick.

"You'd best go back home," Boone told his wife. "I don't want you coming down with anything, honey."

"Who will take care of Moses, then?" she asked. "Liam won't spare Maggie. I have no doubt Mattie would if she were here, but she's not."

"I'll tend to him," his brother stated in his gruff voice.

Lord, Moses hoped Boone had learned a bit from Ma, then. His headache intensified, and he shut his eyes, weary and sick.

He must be bad, for sure, because Rachel kissed him on his fevered forehead.

"Sleep well, Moses," she said. "I hope you're better soon."

A slight rush of cooler air reached him in her wake, and he wanted to respond, to say something, but he lacked the strength, so he didn't. Instead, he yielded to the darkness that waited and slept haunted with fever dreams.

CHAPTER THIRTEEN

Something was very wrong, and she knew it, felt it to the bottom of her bones and within her soul. Plagued by nightmares where Moses was in peril, Mattie knew she had to go to him. It might sound like an exaggeration, but she believed he needed her. So, she stepped up her campaign to go visit her sister for Christmas.

"*Nein, nein, nein,*" her mother said when she asked about the possibility. "Have you lost your mind, daughter? It's a hard trip in the fair weather, let alone now in December."

"You sent me to the ranch last summer," Mattie countered. "No one seemed concerned that it was a difficult journey then."

"That was different. Your sister needed your help."

"And how do you know she might not need me now?"

The question, a valid one, hung between them in the air, heavy and almost tangible to touch. Ilse couldn't answer that easily. They usually received at least a letter a month from their eldest daughter, but none had come since early October. Although they had all clung to the notion that no news was good news, each of the Baumans had wondered if all was well on the ranch.

"I don't," Ilse said, after some thought. "But even if you were to go, how would we know if she does or doesn't. A letter still takes time to send."

"I would write as soon as I got there, and I'm sure Liam or one of the hands would take it to mail in Laredo."

"No," Ilse said.

"Otherwise, you might not hear anything until spring."

Mattie knew it was a mean thing to say, but she would use anything so she could go to Moses.

Gunther, when consulted by her mother, backed her up and refused to have any part in transporting Mattie to the ranch. He may not have said, but surely knew she fancied the cowboy who'd come calling last October.

She appealed to her father. He had liked Moses once they got acquainted and had, more than once, said he was a man's man. Sometimes, she had suspected he wasn't as fond of Gunther as her mother.

"Your mother says no, *liebling,*" Hans told her. "And your beau, the banker says he'll have no part in it. I would take you myself but I'm not much at horses or wagons or travel. I'm a baker."

"Hire someone," Mattie suggested. "There ought to be some at the livery stable who would do it for money."

Hans shook his head. "They are strangers, and I would not trust them to see you safe, not so far and over such rough country."

"But, *Vati…*"

"You can't bend life to your will, daughter. I see no way. Wait until spring, then the Moses Wilson will come back."

Her premonition that Moses needed her now, that his life might be in danger, washed over her, stronger than yesterday's coffee. If she waited, he might not live to return. Cold chills crept down her spine as she thought, "goose is walking on my grave.".

"I will go," she told her father. "If I find someone you trust, then will you agree?"

"It is not possible, but yes, in that case, I would," her father said. "You inherited your grandmother, my mother's stubborn nature, it seems. She could wear down rocks, they said."

So would she, Mattie vowed, so would she. She refused to give up, and she would go, even if she had to walk every step of the way in her little calfskin shoes.

Mattie racked her brain for any possibilities. She counted what little money she had and doubted it would be enough. Then she prayed. In the meantime, she continued to have bad dreams about Moses and an uneasy spirit.

She refused a new gown for a Christmas dance and rejected Gunther's offer to escort her to it. The others in the family had chosen gifts for one another, mostly small trinkets, but selected with thought. Mattie hadn't bought or made anything. Her mother had been busy baking cookies and making Christmas candies, but Mattie was little help. One day, frosting sugar cookies, she'd sat, butter knife in hand, and instead of spreading icing, she stared into space, desperate to discern what might be amiss with Moses.

"Mathilde," her mother said. "You're no help at all. Sulking and pouting does not become a young lady. Go shopping. Get Gunther to take you if you want."

"No."

"Well, go to stores, pick out some little trifles to give on Christmas," Ilse said. "Have you bought anything at all?"

Mattie shook her head. "No, I haven't."

"Then get out, shoo, go."

With little interest, Mattie put on a coat and a hat. She refused any offer of the buggy and chose to walk. Going on foot helped to clear her mind, and she hoped she might find an answer to her dilemma. As she strolled, she paid little attention to where she was headed but found herself outside Dawson's Mercantile. Moses had stayed with the Dawsons, she recalled, because his brother – and her brother-in-law – had served in the war with Phineas.

She stepped into the store, which was more of a notions

emporium than a general store. As Mattie perused the goods for sale without enthusiasm, Phineas Dawson appeared in the aisle.

"Good day, miss," he said. "May I assist you?"

Mattie parted her lips to thank him and say no, she wasn't seeking buttons or lace or novelties, then realized this could be a slim chance. "Perhaps," she said. "You're a friend to my brother-in-law, Liam Rafferty, and to Boone Wilson."

His face brightened. "Yes, yes, I am. They are my comrades from the late war between the states. Boone's young brother stayed here this fall."

"Moses."

Realization dawned. "You're the young lady Moses fancies," he cried. "You danced with him at the masquerade."

A feeble hope formed in her chest. "I did, Mr. Dawson. We're to be wed, Moses and I, although it's not been announced. He is at the ranch near Laredo, and I'm here, but I must go there as soon as I can."

"Oh, ma'am, it's a long journey," he replied. "I've made it myself."

Mattie pulled herself up as straight and tall as she could. "So have I. I have to get there. Do you know anyone who would take me?"

Dawson drew her toward the rear of the store and pointed to a chair near a pot-bellied stove that gave off warmth.

"Sit down," he said. "And tell me why you want to make that trip, why it is so important."

She hesitated but just for a moment and told him the truth.

"I have this terrible feeling that something is wrong," she told him. "I fear that Moses is sick or hurt, that he might even be dying. I have to go. My mother says I can't. My father says there is no way, but I will not stop trying until I get there."

When he said nothing, her heart went cold. "You must think I'm a lunatic," she said. Mattie rose and prepared to leave, but he shook his head.

"I don't, young lady. My grandmother, God rest her soul, had a way of knowing things without a good way to find out. She had that knack, and it served her well. If you feel it so strongly, I'd wager there's something to it. Besides, Boone Wilson once carried me off a battlefield where I was wounded. He took me to a field hospital, and when the surgeon wanted to cut off my leg, Boone argued with him. He used some grass cure he said his mama back in Kentucky taught him and another that the Confederate surgeons often used. Otherwise, I might have lived, but I durned sure wouldn't have a leg."

She held her breath, afraid to hope.

"I found his young brother a good man, too," he said. "That Moses. If he's in trouble, I'll take you myself."

Her heart pounded, and for a second, she couldn't breathe. Fearing she'd faint, she sat back down. "What about your family? It's Christmas. You'll never get me there and back in time."

Dawson laughed. "My wife's over to Corpus Christi with her family, been there since Thanksgiving and not coming home till after the new year. I stayed to mind the store. When do you want to leave?"

"Is tomorrow too soon? Will you mind closing your store?":

The next day was Saturday, December 18. The same instinct that burned in her brain that she had to go also insisted she had to be there before Christmas. It would work if he was willing.

"I won't mind at all, missy. I'd like to leave as soon as the sun is up to make as many miles as we can. Can you rise that early?"

"I can," Mattie said. "Thank you – I don't know how I'll ever thank you."

"No need for it – but tell me your name."

"Mattie Baumann," she said. "And you can just call me Mattie."

Tears overflowed her eyes as she realized she might just make it to Moses.

"And you call me Phin," he said. "One question, though, are your parents going to mind?"

She shrugged. "Maybe, but it doesn't matter. I'm going."

When she broke the news at home, her mother wept, then raged. Her little sisters cried, thinking she would be in mortal danger. Her brother said nothing, but her father, after a long silence, sighed and lit his pipe. "I can see your mind is made up, and you're a woman grown," he said. "Phineas Dawson is a respected man here in San Antonio. I might like it better if he were *Deutsch*, but you can go with my blessing, daughter."

"She can't go tomorrow," Ilse cried. "She'll miss the Christmas dance."

"I was never planning to go," Mattie said.

"But if you don't go with Gunther, he's going to take Sylvania Epperson," Ilse said. "He told me so."

"Then he can take her. I'd rather he would escort her than me anyway."

"You don't understand, Mathilde. He meant to ask you to become his wife."

Rather than say she knew and admit to eavesdropping, Mattie shook her head. "If I'm to be a wife, I'll be Moses' wife."

She rose long before daybreak and dressed in her warmest traveling gown. Her brother Freddy carried her two trunks downstairs and out to Dawson's waiting covered wagon. Mattie said her farewells and shed a few tears. Leaving a week before Christmas seemed unkind, even cruel, but she had to reach Moses. She still couldn't explain it, but she knew it.

By the time the sun had fully risen, they were on their way, headed for the Double B Ranch. Mattie did not look back at

San Antonio.

The weather held cool, sometimes even cold, but fair. No rain or snow fell as they trekked on the slow journey toward the ranch. Each night, they stopped before dark and set up camp. Mattie cooked basic meals over the campfire, beans and biscuits or fried bacon. There was always strong coffee and like Phineas, she drank it black. She slept in the wagon, and he camped out beneath the stars. He swore the fire and his bedroll kept him warm. Mattie didn't dispute it.

In the morning, they drank coffee made over the fire and cold biscuits or cornpone, then set out. At midday, they stopped to eat but usually didn't take time for a fire or warm food. Phineas proved to be a decent traveling companion. Sometimes, he talked, recounting tales of his war years with Boone and Liam. He said little about the battles but shared stories about the men. Phin spoke of his wife, who he dearly loved, and his three children. If a silence fell, it was never awkward, and in those lulls, Mattie might drift into a doze. If she became truly weary, she might climb into the covered wagon and sleep for a short while.

Her mind was always on Moses and she wished there was a way to let him know she was on the way. The sense of something amiss didn't abate but increased the closer they came to the ranch. On December 23rd, at her urging, they pushed the team harder and covered more miles. Phin told her they should reach the ranch by evening, maybe even before dark.

She refused to stop at noon for a meal but insisted they continue. Evening shadows had begun to yield to night when the wagon rolled to a stop near the main ranch house. Phineas yelled, "Hello, the house."

The traditional greeting was often used to prevent the occupant from shooting first and asking questions later. Phineas set the wagon brake as the front door opened, and Liam burst outside, rifle in hand. He halted at the sight of Mattie. "Mattie!

What are you doing here? Did you come to keep Christmas?"

His tone was far from light, and she cut straight to the heart of the matter. "Where's Moses?"

Liam helped her down from the wagon seat and met her gaze without blinking. "He's very sick, Mattie. Did someone send for you? I know Ezekiel talked about it, but no one thought there would be time."

She would explain later, but now, just one thing mattered. "Where is he?"

"At the dog trot cabin, in the one across from Boone's," he said. "Mattie, wait. Come in, get warm."

"I need to go to Moses." She hadn't traveled all this way to drink coffee or make polite conversation.

Maggie came outside, wrapped in a shawl. Her eyes grew huge when she saw her sister.

"Mattie, you're here."

"I came for Moses."

"He's dying with lung fever," Maggie said. "Boone's with him, Ezekiel too but they don't expect him to live."

A sudden pain in her heart came as sharp as if she'd been stabbed. "He'll live now," she said with a confidence she didn't feel. Before anyone could try to stop her, she picked up her skirts and, burdened with the heavy coat she wore, half blinded by the woolen scarf around her head, and ran. She remembered the way well enough, but in the darkness, she stumbled more than once. Twice, she almost fell, but she kept running. She reached the cabins separated by the dog trot porch and saw that a light burned on the left side. Gasping for breath with a stitch in her side, she slowed, then halted until she could mount the steps and enter. Some of the hands were gathered there, silent but anxious. Rachel opened her door and peered out. She called something to Mattie, but the words were lost in the wind. They made no sense anyway.

Without knocking, she entered. Moses lay, still and very pale, in his bed, which had been moved into the main room. His brothers stood beside the bed, singing 'Nearer My God To Thee.' The poignant song slashed her heart and made her want to weep, but she refused to cry. The song stopped when they saw her, and Boone stepped back.

She took Moses' hand in hers and winced at the terrible fever heat. Mattie leaned down to kiss his forehead, then his mouth. Then, with a cheerful confidence she didn't really feel, she said, "That's no song to be singing. We're not at a funeral, and there's not going to be one. Moses will live."

Moses opened his eyes a little. In a voice she could barely recognize, he whispered her name.

"I'm here," she told him. "I'm here, and I'll stay."

She didn't realize that Liam had entered behind her or that he'd followed her mad dash to the cabin until he spoke to Boone.

"Let her care for him," Liam said. "You need some sleep and some food, or you'll get down sick yourself. Go home, Boone."

"I ought to be here."

Mattie touched his arm. "Go, Boone. I'll be here, and Ezekiel can stay."

Her words convinced him because he left, Liam too. Zeke's eyes were heavy, but before he sought a little shuteye, Mattie wanted a few answers.

"How long's he been sick?" she asked.

The young man scrubbed his face with both hands. "He had a bad cold already before the snow came," he said. "It all runs together now. I was a fool and got lost in the snow, and Moses came to find me. That was about a week ago, I reckon. Come Sunday, Moses woke up taken bad, burning with fever. He's got worse every day, and Boone's been in a state. I feared he'd die, and it'd be my fault, for if I hadn't been out in the weather, he wouldn't have come after me."

Mattie tried to imagine a calendar and count the days. Her dark premotion had begun before the snow fell, she thought, and they'd left San Antonio the day before Moses' cold settled in his lungs. If she hadn't left when she did, they wouldn't have made it in time for anything but a funeral.

"He won't blame you," she told Zeke in a soft voice.

He turned his bleary, tortured gaze on her. "I hope not. Do you really reckon he'll live?"

She wasn't as certain as she would like to be but nodded. "He must," she said. "You're weary. Go sleep awhile, Ezekiel. I'll need your help, yours and Boone's come morning."

Fatigue weighed heavy, but Mattie refused to yield to it. She sat beside the sickbed through the long night, holding Moses' hand and bathing his head with cool water. Sometimes, she talked to him, keeping her voice low and sweet.

Every treatment and cure she'd ever heard for pneumonia came to mind. She weighed each one and considered it. Mattie thought back to two winters again when Frau Zieff she'd gone to nurse a desperately sick woman. She had pneumonia, too, and her breathing was so labored Mattie thought she'd die at any moment. The older woman, though, a veteran with remedies, had said they would try an onion poultice.

"It seldom fails," Frau Zieff had stated.

It had been a pungent mess, and the results were nasty, but the woman lived.

Mattie planned every step of the treatment during the slow hours, and as soon as she thought Rachel might be awake, she crossed the dog trot to ask her help. By dawn, they'd peeled many onions and the first batch frying in the largest skillet available.

It would work, Mattie thought, because it had to succeed.

She would not, could not lose Moses.

From what she'd seen and what Boone told her, they

had given up and expected him to die. They'd kept vigil at his bedside, anticipating the worst, and although she was here, he wasn't out of danger yet. She tried to envision what had been before her arrival and couldn't help but be glad she'd missed the terrible days of waiting and watching, worried.

CHAPTER FOURTEEN

His ma had always told them that hearing was the last of the senses to go before death, and although he hadn't disputed it, Moses Wilson knew now she'd spoke truth. Sicker than he'd ever been in his life, bones baking with a fever that wouldn't abate except when he shivered with harsh chills, chest aching as if he'd been stabbed in a saloon brawl, and a cough that hurt, he believed her and he wished she was there. Hard to rouse and finding it difficult to respond, Moses remained aware of what went on around him and could listen to what was said. It was muted, reminding him of the way he and his brothers used to duck underwater while swimming. What reached him was muffled, not always clear, and hard to fathom.

He did remember they'd moved his bed into the main room of the cabin he'd been sharing with Ezekiel to be closer to the fire and easier to access. Rachel had been there at first, but Boone had sent her away, worried she'd overdo and lose the child she carried. Her hands had been gentle against his burning skin, and her voice gentle. Since she'd gone, Boone tended him, and he was more than a little clumsy. His tone, when he spoke, whether it was to Moses or to Ezekiel, was rough with fatigue and harsh with concern.

As Moses lay now, hot and miserable, he could smell the tang of Boone's tobacco as he smoked. He might be no more than half-awake, but he listened to their conversation.

"He's taken bad," Boone said, sounding as if he sat near the fire.

"I can ride to Laredo to fetch the doctor," his younger brother said. "It ain't the same one as when you were shot. That one drank himself to death. This one is young, fresh from back East somewhere. He might know of a cure or medicine we don't."

"He'd likely do more harm than good," Boone replied. "In the war, the sawbones would purge men sick with lung fever but all I saw it do was weaken them more. Ain't no medicine I know about that will help, just home remedies. I wish Ma was here. She'd know what to do if anything can be done."

Moses longed for their mother, too. If she was here, her stubborn nature and granny cure knowledge might have a chance to heal him. He hadn't seen her in about four years now, and he missed her. The letters from home came often enough to keep them in the know but it wasn't the same.

"Reckon more willow bark tea might help?"

"It hasn't yet, and he chokes on it," Boone said with a sad note in his voice. "He's struggling to breathe now, Zeke. I don't rightly know if there's much that we can do for him."

With sharp clarity, he heard Ezekiel's wordless cry. "Doesn't Rachel know something? She saved you, Boone."

"She did, but sickness is different than a festering wound, and she's with child. I can ask her if she knows any grass cures."

"What about Liam or Cookie?" There was a desperate note in Zeke's voice.

"Ezekiel," Boone said, and something in the way he spoke the name made Moses think there wasn't much hope. "They can't help. I don't know who could, and that's a fact."

Through the fog, Moses thought about Mattie. In his mind, he could see her pretty face, her golden hair braided and put up across her head, her blue eyes, and her smile. She'd tended him after the horse threw him, he recalled, and she knew a little about doctoring. He had been pining for her since the day Liam took her back to San Antonio and had ridden over once to see her. They wrote a couple of letters, but he needed her, not words on a page. With effort, he pushed through the fever and the mental fog to ask for her. Maybe Boone would fetch her, he thought.

"He's gettin' restless again," Ezekiel said.

"Moses," Boone said, his voice now at the bedside. "Here, now, don't fret. We're here, Ezekiel and me."

Moses managed to open his eyes and saw Boone standing beside the bed, face hard and haggard. "Boone," he croaked.

"Save your strength," his brother replied in the tone he usually used with his children in tender moments. "Do you need a drink of water?"

"Mattie," he said. "Fetch Mattie."

"Ah, man, I would if I could," Boone said. "Take too long, Moses."

"Need Mattie," he said, and then, because it was too hard, he closed his eyes.

"I'll go bring her, Moses," Ezekiel said.

"I know you would, but it would take too long," Boone said. "We spent six days bringing her here, Liam and me, in the wagon. Even riding, she'd likely get here too late."

"Too late for what?"

Too late to tell me goodbye, Moses thought.

Boone's tone dropped so low he couldn't hardly hear him. "Ezekiel, short of a miracle, Moses won't last six days. He's barely made it for three. Besides, it's December and cold, so the going would likely be slower. Six days was in the spring."

"He can't die!" For the first time in a very long time, Zeke sounded like a kid, not a man. "Boone, Moses has got to live through this."

"I'm hoping he does," Boone said. "But we gotta be ready if he don't."

From the sounds he heard, Ezekiel muttered and then slammed out of the cabin, banging the door behind him. Boone came as close to swearing as he ever did and put his hand across Moses' forehead.

"You're burning up," he said. "Reckon you can down some of the willow bark tea since you're awake?"

He nodded because it took too much strength he didn't have to speak and managed a few sips, although he thought he'd surely puke afterward. Then Moses shut his eyes and let his mind drift, ill and tired and probably soon to die.

Maybe he fell into delirium, or perhaps he dreamed, but Moses slipped back to another time and place.

He'd been a boy the night his father, Robert Wilson, died of lung fever. Until the last, Ma had kept them away from the sickbed and hadn't let on how ill his pa was. Moses had done what he'd been told and helped the others do chores. Boone, at 15, had been a man, and when their mother asked them to mind their brother, they had included Moses.

Ezekiel had been three, just toddling around after the older children. Boone had asked him to mind Zeke. He had, throughout the long day, as the tension mounted and they all realized that their father was dying. Moses had gone out to milk with the tiny boy following in his footsteps. He'd taken comfort in the familiar barn, resting his forehead against the warm side of the milk cow, then carried the pail of milk back to the house. Somewhere along the way, Ezekiel had wandered away, and he failed to notice.

Boone had, though, and he'd blistered Moses with his tongue. Everyone except their mother went outside to find the boy before he fell into peril. There were wild critters who could do harm to a small child, hills and creeks to fall into and other dangers. He hadn't gone far, though, and when they located him, the relief had been sweet.

Moses thought he'd faint with joy the kid hadn't come to any harm under his watch. He'd scooped up the wiggling child in his arms and ran with him back to the house. Boone had apologized for his harsh words, admitting he'd been scared. By the time they came into the house, dark had fallen, and their father had died.

But Moses never forgot.

In his fitful sleep, he dreamed of how Boone returned from the war, grim faced and hollow eyed. He recalled how upset his mother had been when they got the letter that Boone was dying after being shot, then another that said he was to be hanged for a crime he didn't commit. So, with Ma's blessing, Moses had set out for distant Texas, hoping he could do something to save his oldest brother and to bring Ezekiel home if he failed. Ma hadn't gotten over missing Boone, and she had worried herself near sick when Zeke took off to find his brother in Texas.

They woke one morning to find Ezekiel wasn't in his bed or in the cabin. A search of the property yielded nothing, and just when Ma figured she'd best send word to her other children, the ones grown and married, who lived nearby, they found the note.

"Gone to Boone," Ezekiel had scribbled. "Heading out for Texas to find him. He ought not to be alone so far from home, and I am seeking my fortune. I will write when I can and might come home depending on how I find both Boone and Texas. All my love, Ezekiel Adam Wilson."

Terrible dreams haunted his mind, images that never happened, Boone swinging from the end of a rope, him being bitten by the rattlesnake in the corral when he'd been thrown, Mattie jeering at him instead of promising her love. Images of wild horses, fire on the range, and gunfire flashed through his brain, and he struggled to erase them, relatively sure none were real.

Moses roused and couldn't remember what had been true and what was not. He lashed out, hands curling into fists, legs trying to swing over the bed so he could rise. Then a chill hit, and the fever heat yielded to a terrible cold. He shivered hard with it, shaking and pulling the covers tighter.

"Hush, it'll stop soon," a soft and feminine voice said.

For a hopeful moment, he thought it might be Mattie and then realized it was Rachel. She took his hand and held it, her skin warm against his. "I'm here with you."

"Where's Boone?" he asked.

"Boone was dead on his feet from staying up with you for the last few days," Rachel said. "His back was troubling him, so I made him go to bed for a while to get some sleep, Ezekiel too. They'll get down sick if they don't rest. I've got some beef broth if you think you can take some."

"Ain't it starve a fever?" he mumbled and opened his eyes.

A small smile lit her face. "That's what they said about Boone, and they near starved him to death until I took over his care," she said. "You'll be better if you can get a little down."

The last thing he wanted was food, but he nodded and would try. She managed to get a few spoons down his throat before he shook his head and closed his eyes. He didn't go back to sleep, though, but lay in a lethargic state, listening.

"How is he?" Moses recognized Boone's voice.

"He took some broth," Rachel said. "He had a bad chill, but it's passed now."

"Go on back to the children," Boone told her. "And you rest a spell, you hear."

"I haven't done anything but sit here with Moses. I'm fine."

"And I want you to stay that way, honey. Is Ezekiel still asleep?"

"He went out to see if he could cut some cedar branches," Rachel replied. "It's Christmas in a few days, so he thought it might be festive if we had a little greenery for the mantle. He was talking about heading to Laredo, too, to fetch some peppermint sticks and trinkets for the children."

"That's good of him," Boone said. "I ain't feelin' merry myself, not with Moses so sick. I fear he's gonna…"

"Don't say it," Rachel cut him off. "You mustn't give up hope, Boone."

His brother grunted. Moses cracked one eye open to see him kiss his wife, then put a gentle hand over her rounded stomach. "Go home and take care, woman."

Over the next few days, Moses drifted in and out. He suspected that his fever climbed higher and that his condition had worsened. When he was awake enough to tell, he couldn't get comfortable no matter how he tried. Sometimes, he thought he sipped more willow bark tea, but he couldn't tell that it did any good at all. The aromatic scent of fresh cut cedar worked into his consciousness, and he squinted to see the boughs on the mantlepiece for Christmas.

Best he could tell, Boone was there most of the time and Ezekiel often. Once, he thought he heard Liam's voice, but although he tried to rouse, he couldn't manage nor make out what the boss might have said. Another time, he heard Mac's distinctive Scots burr and Deacon Lee's smooth Southern voice in the room. Maybe he was delirious again, for he thought he heard his mother's voice lifted in prayer. Another time, he could have sworn he heard her singing 'Amazing Grace.'

"I want to see Mo Mo," a young voice cried. Moses struggled to rouse at the sound of his niece's voice. "He needs me!"

Boone did his best to stop the little girl, but she maneuvered around her daddy like greased lighting and rushed to the bedside. She put one small hand on Moses' left arm, and he opened his eyes.

"Howdy, Miss Mima," he managed to croak.

Mima kissed his hand over and over. "Oh, Mo Mo, you feel like fire. Mama says you have the fever. I wanted to take care of you, but they won't let me."

For her, he rallied with all the strength he could. "Your

daddy's doing a fine job of that, Mima. Just you pray for me, hear?"

Prayers would come in handy, more so if he died, which is what he'd begun to expect. From what he overhead, so did everyone else.

"Our Father who art in heaven," Mima began, and Boone picked her up.

"You can pray for your uncle at our cabin," he said. His voice sounded thick, as if he had unshed tears caught in his throat.

Moses knew when his brother returned because Boone placed a fresh, wet compress across his forehead. It felt wonderful until the heat leached any comfort from it. He had a coughing bout, one that shook him so hard he tried to sit up to ease it but couldn't. Without asking, Boone's arms supported him to lift him upright till it passed. When he laid him back against the pillows and propped him up, he put a new compress on his head. It had become difficult to draw a breath, and each time he did, pain slashed through his chest. Each one he took required a conscious effort, and Moses wasn't at all sure how much longer he could continue.

"Boone," Moses said. He wanted to thank his brother and more, but he had trouble finding the words to speak. "Boone."

"Hush, Mosey," his brother said. The old nickname dated to their childhood. No one had called Moses "Mosey" for years. As a little fellow, he had tended to ramble or mosey off the path on the way to school or the cornfield or the tobacco patch. Their father had first called him that, and the nickname stuck for a few years. Until now, he'd all but forgotten it. "You save your strength."

"Boone, am I gonna cash in?" He had to ask. He needed to know.

"Mosey, I surely hope not," Boone said.

"I don't want to give up the ghost, Boone. I need my

boots."

His brother grasped his hand and held it tight. When he didn't answer, Moses glanced at him and saw Boone's shoulders shaking. He realized his brother held back sobs, and when he squinted hard, he saw the glint of tears tracking down his cheeks.

"I reckon you'll live to bury us all, and you don't need your boots. You ain't gonna die with them on or without." Boone's forced hearty tone was fake and warned Moses that he probably would die.

If he could summon the energy, he might weep too, but he used the breath he hauled up from deep within to say, "Will you sing to me?"

As a child, their mother sang to them all every night. As each child grew older, another took the coveted spot in the rocking chair. Times he'd been sick as a boy, Ma sang, and it had soothed him. If Mattie was here, he reckoned she would, but she was far away in San Antonio, and Boone did have a sweet voice.

Boone began to sing, his voice low and soft, although he didn't let go of Moses' hand.

Moses shut his eyes and let the music drift over him, thinking about it instead of how awful he felt or how likely he was to die.

The first songs were ones learned at Ma's knee, old ballads, although Boone skipped the more rollicking tunes. He sang the 'Bard of Armagh' and then switched to hymns.

"Shall we gather at the river," Boone sang, and Moses thought of the Rio Grande at Laredo, then of the many rivers he'd crossed to get to Texas.

Maybe Boone thought he'd fallen asleep, but the next song he sang worried Moses because it was the soulful and sad 'Nearer My God To Thee.' It had been one of the hymns sung at his father's funeral at the graveside, and it brought back sad memories.

The day was cloudy and cold. A sharp wind blew across the small burying ground, making everyone shake and shiver. Ma stood proud, her back straight as a ramrod on a rifle. The children gathered about her. Boone, just 15 years old, stood beside her. The family and those friends, the neighbors who'd gathered to pay their respects to Robert Wilson, watched as his simple coffin was lowered into the newly dug grave, a raw slash in the earth that gave him the willies. The preacher read some verses from the Bible, something from Second Timothy that his father had always favored, about a good fight and keeping the faith. Then, someone began the song, and they all took it up. The sound of voices raised in song became louder than the wind, and since that day, Moses hadn't liked the song much. As far as he knew, none of them had sung it again unless it was in church.

Listening now, Moses recalled that his daddy died of lung fever, the pneumonia that now ravaged his own body, and took his breath. Ezekiel must have come into the room, for now, his voice blended with Boone's as they sang. Moses figured it was meant to be a comfort, to make him feel good about being nearer to God and going to meet his Maker, but it riled him instead. He struggled to fight against death.

He imagined a skeleton faced specter, the Grim Reaper, complete with a scythe, come to cut short his life, and he thrashed in bed, trying to escape. The harder he fought, the shorter his breath came, and he stopped. No need to hasten what was happening anyway, he thought, no reason to rush into death. He'd cling to life for as long as he could, and maybe, sometime, he'd manage to elude that old Reaper.

Their voices stilled, and he wondered why because, if he remembered right, the song wasn't over. Then he heard a commotion outside on the dog trot. Rachel's voice mingled with others. There was a frenzy about their talk, but he couldn't make out a single word they said.

For all he knew, maybe he'd died and just didn't realize

it yet.

Boone let go of his hand, so Moses thought that might be what had happened until someone else took his hand. He thought it was a woman because the touch was gentle and light. The sweet scent of lavender drifted into his consciousness. Someone kissed him on the forehead and then on his mouth.

"That's no song to be singing. We're not at a funeral, and there's not going to be one. Moses will live."

He knew that voice and would recognize it anywhere. Moses fought to open his eyes in a half-slitted gaze. Mattie leaned over him, still wearing a woolen scarf and coat, her pretty features taut with worry.

"Mattie?" he said. He must be out of his head with fever now or dead because it couldn't be.

"*Ja*, Moses, it's me," she said. "Hush, man, hush and rest. I'm here, and I won't be leaving."

Moses liked that notion well and thought it might be a sweet dream. Boone came to the opposite side of the bed and took his other hand. Moses strained to turn his head and noted his brother's expression wasn't as quite as grim.

"I'd about given him up. I've been caring for him as best I can, but I've feared he's on his deathbed." Boone said. "Do you think you can pull him through?"

"I do, and I will," Mattie said.

Maybe, just maybe, he wasn't about to die, and even if he did, Mattie would be here.

Boone had been, he thought, through a fever haze, had been and would be.

At least if he did die, he wouldn't be alone.

CHAPTER FIFTEEN

Boone clung to his brother's hot, dry hand as if that could anchor Moses to life. If he could battle death in a fair fight, he would, either with his fists or with his pistol, spitting lead and fire. Against this illness, though, he had no weapons and no power but love and prayer. He'd never seen one of his own ailing this bad or felt as helpless. For the past six days, ever since Moses became so sick, Boone had been at his side most of the time. He'd slept a little, but only because Rachel insisted and ate little, living on coffee and a few cigarettes. Rachel scolded him to eat, and he tried, but when he did, it knotted his belly something fierce.

He could recall when their daddy died. Pa had been sick, too, but somehow Moses' condition seemed worse to Boone. Ezekiel wanted to ride for a doctor, but there was nothing one could do, not really. In his lucid moments, Moses wanted Mattie, and if he could, Boone would bring her, but the trip would take longer to make than he feared his brother had.

Liam came and went often to check on Moses. Christmas loomed, and though he'd lost track of the days, Boone thought it might be Christmas Eve. Most of the hands, even the newest ones, gathered out on the passage between the two cabins and waited for news. He valued their support, but it disturbed him, too, because it felt like a deathwatch.

When his little daughter burst into the room to pray for Moses, Boone thought his heart would break. Both his children adored their uncle, and he wasn't sure how he'd tell them if the worst came to pass. He'd rather they keep a distance now, though, for he didn't want either to fall sick or Rachel either. For himself, he didn't care, and Ezekiel refused to be banished. Boone appreciated his company and help more than he could say.

He'd lost track of whether it was day or night. Moses grew steadily worse. Unless he kept his brother propped up against a mountain of pillows, he gasped for air and could barely breathe. He had trouble enough, even with the pillows, for the last few hours. Moses wavered in and out of consciousness, although he rallied enough to ask if he might die. Boone lied through tears that trailed down his cheeks, and when Moses asked him to sing, he obliged. It seemed to be about all he could do for him.

Boone had used the old nickname, Mosey, from long ago without thinking. He worried about a letter he might have to write home with the sad news and understood for the first time how Ezekiel must have felt after Boone had been shot. He'd been bad, yes, but he didn't think his condition had been this dire, but he wasn't planning to ask Rachel.

At first, he sang the old songs Ma had sung to them, but then, as his spirits plummeted and his concern increased, Boone changed to hymns because they offered him comfort. He hoped they did the same for Moses. Ezekiel, who had been denying that the outcome of Moses' illness might be anything but recovery, stirred from where he'd been dozing and joined him in the last song, 'Nearer My God To Thee". They were near the end when the door opened, and Mattie Baumann walked through the door, Liam behind her.

Boone's voice trailed to a halt, and he thought he must be seeing things.

Moses stirred and responded to her voice and he thought maybe there might be a chance, now.

Liam insisted that Boone go get some rest and all but

shoved him through the door. Outside, the hands clustered around him, asking questions, offering kind words, but Boone couldn't concentrate.

"There's been no change," Liam told them. "Let Boone pass. He needs some food and rest."

Boone walked through his door into the cabin. It was dark, and night had fallen over the ranch, but he had no idea if it was eight o'clock or midnight or three in the morning. Rachel, clad in a nightgown that revealed her growing abdomen, sat in the rocking chair, asleep. He sat down at the table, making as little noise as he could so he wouldn't wake her. He put his head down, pillowed on his arms on the wooden table, and Boone, who never cried, who stayed as sober as a hanging judge, wept. He choked down the sobs, hoping Rachel wouldn't hear, but she did.

"Boone?" she asked, her hands rubbing his shoulder and back. "What is it? Is Moses gone?"

He lifted his head. "Naw, not yet anyway. Maybe he'll live. I don't know, but Mattie's here. I don't know how or why, but she's here."

Rachel stroked his hair with a tender hand. "You should know what a woman's love can do, Boone," she told him, referencing her stubborn refusal to accept that he would die from a gunshot wound to the chest. "Are you hungry? I made the frijoles you like and kept them warm."

"I don't know if I can eat."

"You need to," she said. "Eat and get some sleep, or you'll be down in bed, too. That won't help anyone, especially not Moses, and it'll worry me something awful if you don't."

His inclination was to go back and sit with Moses, but her plea reached him. For Rachel, he'd do about anything, and to save her worry, he'd force down the food and do his best to sleep.

"All right," he sighed. "Fix me a plate."

Boone downed most of it, noticing it tasted better with every bite he took. Once he'd eaten, the heavy fatigue increased, and he stumbled to bed, not bothering to take off any more than his trousers. He woke once, hearing the little ones chattering in the other room and Rachel shushing them. Although he meant to get up, he figured that if they were cheerful, nothing had happened to Moses, and he drifted back to sleep. When he woke again, his eyes burned from the stench of raw onions, and he could smell frying onions, maybe with garlic. That puzzled him enough to crawl out of bed and put his pants on. From the light that seeped into the cabin's rear room, he thought it morning.

"Rachel, why are you cooking onions this time of day?"

She paused, stirring onions around in a large iron skillet. "They're for Moses."

"What in tarnation?" Boone asked, annoyed. "He can barely get down beef broth, let alone eat onions."

"It's for a poultice," Mattie said. Until she spoke, he hadn't realized she was in the room. "I've known it to help those sick with *lungenentzündung,* lung fever. It helps get all the nasty infection out of the lungs. I think it will help."

Despite sleeping, his brain remained tired and fogged. A dim memory of Ma talking about the same remedy flickered, then faded. "It might," he said. "I reckon it's worth a try. Is he any worse?"

"He's not," Mattie said. "Ezekiel is with him now. He's taken a few sips of water and said a few words."

Boone wanted to be encouraged but didn't dare. "Fever down any?"

Her optimistic expression wilted a little. "Not yet," she said.

"He can't last much longer unless it breaks." Sometimes, a man just had to speak the harsh truth, but he regretted it as soon as the words were out. Rachel glared at him, and Mattie's face fell.

He thought she might be about to cry. Boone attempted to temper his words. "I want him to live more than almost anything."

"So do I," Mattie said. "I spent the last six days being jolted in a wagon over rough country in freezing temperatures, for Moses' sake."

He asked the question he'd been holding. "How did you know to come? Moses asked for you, but I didn't figure there was any way we could fetch you in time."

Mattie lifted her chin high. "I had a feeling something was wrong," she said. "I felt I had to come to Moses, and so I did."

Boone couldn't imagine the petite and pretty young woman making the trek from San Antonio alone. Last he could remember, she didn't even ride. "How did you get here?"

"Your friend, Phineas Dawson, brought me in a covered wagon. I believe he's still here, over at Liam's."

A low chuckle escaped Boone's lips. "You got my old pard to bring you to see the man you love because you thought something was amiss?"

"I did, and he was my last resort," Mattie said. "I tried to convince my family I wanted to spend Christmas with Maggie and her family, but they wouldn't believe me. I asked Gunther Hammerschmidt to bring me, but he refused. I went to Dawson's Mercantile and well, Phineas offered. I arrived late yesterday, and as soon as Liam told me about Moses, I came here."

"I thought that banker expects you to wed him?"

"He very well might, but I won't," Mattie replied. "Moses and I are promised to marry."

If he lives, Boone thought but didn't say so aloud.

"These onions are ready," his practical Rachel announced.

Boone glanced around and realized his children weren't present. "Where's the babies?"

"Liam took them to Maggie's so she can mind them," his wife replied. "They shouldn't be here for this. I've not seen it done, but I've heard it can be messy."

"It can," Mattie stated. "Besides, I'll need you to help, Boone, Ezekiel too. I might need some of the ranch hands, too, if they're still here."

"I'll do anything that might help," Boone said and meant it.

"Then let's get started."

Mattie took a large square of cheesecloth she begged from Rachel and spread it on the table. Then, she folded it over several times. Rachel had stirred a little flour and oil into the fried onions and garlic so Mattie spread it over the cloth. The vegetable mass steamed, and the aroma was rank in Boone's nose. He watched as Mattie slid a tin plate beneath it and carried it across to the other cabin.

"Start another skillet of onions," she told Rachel on her way out of the door.

Moses lay abed, half-propped up against the pillows. His eyes were closed, and his breath shallow. The room reeked of sickness, an odor that would soon be banished by the powerful onion smell. Boone said a silent prayer as Mattie directed them to stand by as she undid Moses' nightshirt.

"The poultice is still very hot," she said. "I'll let it cool a bit so it won't burn his skin, then I'll put it on his chest."

"What do we do?" Ezekiel asked.

"We wait," Mattie said. "The poultice should bring up a lot of the mucous and lung infection. Moses will need to sit upright for that so he doesn't choke on it. That's where I need your help. I'll need a basin, too, to catch the flow, or it'll foul the bedclothes."

Boone took a position on the far side of the bed. He touched his brother's face and winced at the fever heat. Moses cracked open one eye and looked at him. His lips moved in the shape of Boone's name, but he made no sound.

"Mosey," Boone said. "Mattie's here with a cure for what

ails you."

His brother moved his head in a slight nod and, this time, said in a whisper, "Hope so."

So did Boone.

"It's an onion poultice for your chest," Mattie told Moses. "I know it smells, but it will help clear out your lungs. It'll be very warm when I put it in place."

She laid the folded cloth on his chest, and Moses winced. Then he closed his eyes again, and they waited. Twice, Mattie sent Ezekiel for a fresh poultice. Rachel, who remained in their cabin, continued to fry up onions with garlic. An hour passed, then two with no results, and Boone's faint hope began to fade like the light at the end of the day.

He craved a smoke bad, knowing it would calm his jangled nerves, but he resisted and stayed in place. If there was any chance at all that Moses could recover, he was committed. The quiet bothered Boone, and he wondered if he should sing. Zeke must not like the silence either because he began to say their mother's favorite Psalm, Psalm 91. After the first few lines, Boone joined him.

Before the third poultice grew cold, Moses moved. He became agitated, thrashing against the sheet as he made small sounds of distress. Mattie watched, her face as calm as an angel carved from stone.

"Lift him up now," she said. "Help him into a sitting position and hold him there."

She placed a granite ware pot in Moses's lap and spoke to him.

"Moses, *liebling,* the onions will make you cough up the nastiness in your lungs, but I'm here, and so are your brothers."

Moses coughed a little and then began to hack. It hurt Boone to hear because he knew it must hurt. About the time Boone had all but decided his brother was going to cough up a lung and then likely die, a vile spew shot from Moses' nose and mouth. Blood-streaked green and yellow mucous poured out with some blood. There were hard white pellets in it that reminded him of sleet. It had a foul stench from the infection, and Boone's stomach rolled, but he held steady.

The thick sludge filled most of the pan before Moses stopped coughing. Already pale, he went whiter and slumped back. Alarmed, Boone leaned closer, but his tension eased when he saw the rise and fall of Moses' breath. "Put him back on the pillows," she said. "I imagine that tired him."

She thrust the basin at Zeke, who gulped and took it outside to empty, then clean. Thankful the task hadn't fallen to him because he was sure he would have puked, Boone sat down hard in a chair beside the bed. Mattie removed the poultice and set it aside. Then she washed Moses' face with a clean rag and bathed his forehead and neck with cool water.

"Will you sit with him while I see if the coneflower tea has steeped?" Mattie asked. "If he wakes and can take it, give him a spoon of honey."

Boone nodded. Once she'd gone, he continued to bathe his brother's fevered brow. His skin still burned with heat but Boone wanted to think it might be a little less hot. The silence in the room felt heavy and so he started talking, babbling about their boyhood and Kentucky. He'd lost track of the days but knew it was very near to Christmas.

"I always loved those stack cakes Ma would always bake," Boone said. "And I'd be hard pressed to say if I liked the ham or the goose best. Some years, she'd bake a ham and sometimes a goose or a big piece of pork loin with dressing. The church house would be bright with candlelight for the Christmas Eve service and all decorated with greenery from the woods. Pa used to shoot down some mistletoe, and he'd used it as an excuse to kiss Ma every chance he got. It's near about Christmas now, Moses, and I don't even know what Rachel means to cook. Ezekiel went into Laredo one day to get candy for the little ones, and I don't know what else. Before you took sick, I figured on maybe having a shooting match on Christmas, but I don't have the heart for it now. Mosey, the Christmas miracle I want to see is for you to beat this fever."

His brother opened his eyes and fixed a clear gaze on him. He coughed a little.

"Thirsty," he said.

Boone poured some water into a tin cup and held it to his lips. Moses drank, and then, as he'd been directed, he got him to take a spoon of honey.

"Write Ma," Moses said with effort.

"Write her about what?" Boone countered, afraid his brother would say to tell her about his death.

"Tell her I'm getting married," he replied. "Write her about Mattie."

Encouraged by the lucid thought yet concerned Moses might tax his feeble strength, Boone nodded. "I will, and I'll do you better than that. Once you're up and on your feet, I'll pay for the wedding picture, and I'll send one to Ma."

The faintest ghost of a smile touched his brother's lips. "I'll hold you to that."

During the long afternoon, Mattie dosed Moses with various teas and bathed his head with cool water. She made lemonade, too, the sweet drink he'd liked so well when he'd hurt his ankle last summer. Moses managed to get it all down. Although Mattie, then Rachel, urged Boone to take a rest, he wouldn't. He and Ezekiel remained, sometimes smoking across the room but mostly at Moses' bedside as if their presence could keep death away.

Boone stepped out near sundown for air, needing a break from the fetid sick room. Some of the hands were still waiting, and he spoke with them, although he scarcely knew what he said. It was a glorious sunset, the colors vivid and bright in the western sky, and he lingered, admiring it.

"Boone, come quick," Ezekiel shouted, and he rushed inside, tripping over his feet in the process and falling to his knees on the porch floor.

It might be the end, Boone thought and tried to prepare to accept it but couldn't. Mattie sat on the edge of the bed, facing Moses. She had both of his hands locked in hers, and her shoulders shook as she wept.

He stepped around her to see and stopped short. His brother's face was wet with sweat, and his eyes were open. Although very weak, Moses turned his head toward Boone and tried to smile.

"His fever broke," Ezekiel said in a jubilant tone. "Boone, his fever broke."

Now he understood why Mattie wept, not from sorrow but joy. His legs threatened to buckle, and if he didn't sit, Boone figured he'd fall out on the floor. He sat down hard in a chair, his cheeks damp with tears.

"Get Rachel," he said.

"I'm here, Boone," his wife said and came to him. He buried his face against her shoulder and savored her closeness. "I've asked that Jim, one of the new hands, to tell Liam to bring our children home for Christmas."

"When is Christmas?"

She laughed. "Tomorrow."

The miracle he'd wanted had been delivered, and Boone offered a silent thanks to God that his brother lived. Then, because he knew he needed food, a wash, time with his family, and sleep, he rose to go home.

He leaned down over his brother, and for the first time since Moses was about six years old, Boone kissed his forehead.

"Merry Christmas, Mosey," he said.

"Merry Christmas."

The Wilsons would keep Christmas, after all.

CHAPTER SIXTEEN

Before he opened his eyes, Moses could smell the sweet aroma of fresh cedar and remembered that it was Christmas. It took effort to turn his head to see who might be at his bedside, but when he did, Mattie was there, her golden hair in braids wound around her head. Her eyes were closed, and he thought she might be asleep. Rather than wake her, he collected his thoughts and tried to remember how he'd come to be in bed.

Moses remembered being sicker than he'd ever been but only in snatches, the fiery heat of his fever, the shuddering cold of chills, and coughing so hard he thought his body might tear into two. His chest still ached, and if he could, he'd rub it. Boone had been there, he knew, almost every time he roused. Ezekiel and Rachel had often been at his side, too. If it hadn't been a fever dream, Boone had called him 'Mosey,' his old boyhood nickname, one not used in many years. He'd longed for Mattie, and after a very long time, she had been there, her soft voice offering comfort and her gentle hands providing aid. And, if he hadn't dreamt it, Boone had shaved him, which seemed odd, but he was sure it had happened.

Propped against pillows, he was comfortable, if weak, warm, and without any complaints. Guessing by the light outside the room's one window, he guessed it to be early morning. Best he could tell, no one else was in the room, but he thought he heard voices from across the dogtrot raised in joy and song.

A bit later, he heard Boone's heavy tread in boots cross the outdoor space, and the door opened. His small niece, Mima, burst into the room despite her daddy's hushed admonition to be quiet. "Hush, Jemima Ann," Boone said, using his daughter's full name. "If he's asleep, don't wake him."

She sashayed to the right side of the bed and stood there, Boone behind her. When Moses turned his head, she grinned. "Happy Christmas, Mo Mo," she told him.

"Merry Christmas, little gal," he replied.

Before Boone could stop her, she climbed onto the bed like a young monkey and knelt facing him. She leaned over and kissed his cheek, then picked up his right hand and kissed it, too.

"I worried when you were so sick," the precocious little girl told him. "I'm glad you didn't die, Mo Mo."

"Me, too."

At five, Mima possessed a maturity and vocabulary beyond her years. Her devotion to her uncle ran deep, and they were bonded.

"Don't devil your uncle," Boone said. "He's powerful weak, and needs rest to get better."

He reached for the girl, and she curled up beside Moses in the narrow space.

"She's all right for a spell," Moses told him.

With a sigh, Boone pulled up a chair and sat. "Be easy with him, Mima."

"She's good medicine," Mattie said, rousing. "Good for his heart."

Moses shifted his head to see her. "Mattie."

She put the back of her hand against his forehead and smiled. "Still no fever. Do you want some water?"

He nodded. He sipped his fill from the tin cup she held and sighed. The simple act wearied him, and he closed his eyes.

"Rachel has a notion to bring dinner over here to eat,"

Boone said. "Not that Moses can have much but broth just yet, but she didn't want him to feel left out. Reckon that's alright, or will it tax him too much?"

"It'll be good for him," Mattie said. "Who's coming?"

"All of us Wilsons, plus Liam, Maggie, Grace, and the baby, Phineas Dawson, too," he said. "Ten or so. I wouldn't turn any of the hands away if they show up, but we cain't have them all."

"Moses'll be fine," she replied, and Moses smiled a little. He'd rather be with them than alone so it would make his Christmas a good one, despite his health.

"What's Rachel fixing?" Moses asked.

"Z shot a turkey," Mima said. "We're having turkey and mashed potatoes and cornbread and leather britches beans and sweet 'taters and noodles and an apple cake for dessert."

He hadn't realized he was hungry until his stomach indicated some interest, although he knew he couldn't eat such hearty fare yet.

Mattie must have read his mind because she said, "Don't fret. There'll be plenty of broth for you, maybe a few noodles if you can take them. I plan to make some vanilla pudding for you, too, soon as you can have some."

"I could eat a bite now."

Boone lifted his daughter from Moses' sickbed. "Baby girl, let's go see if we can beg some broth from your mother so Moses don't starve."

She protested till Moses said, "If you bring it to me, you can sing me a Christmas carol."

Mima grinned. "I will!"

In the sudden quiet, Moses asked, "Where's Zeke?"

"Sleeping," Mattie replied. She pushed back his tangled hair from his forehead. "He's been distraught, not just because you were so sick but because he thinks it's his fault."

Perplexed, Moses asked, "Why?"

She straightened his covers and tucked them tighter. "You already had a cold when you went to find him in the snowstorm, and he thought you probably wouldn't have taken pneumonia if you hadn't already been sick."

"Likely, I'd came down with it anyhow."

"That's what I told him, and Boone said the same."

Moses mulled it over. He would never forget searching for his youngest brother in a driving blizzard and fearing the worst. The joy when he'd found Ezekiel alive remained. They'd both been cold, near frozen to the bone, but made it home. Neither had mentioned the fact they'd had words before Zeke rode out foolishly into the weather because it didn't matter. As brothers, the Wilson boys had sometimes argued and fought, but at the end of the day, the love remained.

He left the subject and would tell Ezekiel the same if it came up. He inhaled and cringed. The stench of sweat, sickness, and onions permeated his nose, and it wasn't pleasant.

"Mattie, I stink."

"When you're stronger, we'll wash you and get a clean nightshirt on you."

"I can't bear it – gotta be now."

"I'll help you in a bit," Boone said as he and little Mima entered the room. The child carried a steaming cup of broth, clasped in her hands with care. "Let's see if you can get this down first."

"I want to give it to Mo Mo," Mima said.

"Whoa, now," Boone said. "I believe you promised your uncle a Christmas song. I reckon it'd be best if you were to sing it while Mattie helps him with the broth."

Moses all but sighed with relief. He knew he couldn't hold the cup in his weak hands but thought maybe he could sip it like the water. Mattie, however, was taking no chances, and she gave it to him using a spoon. It took longer, but it proved easier for him. The warm broth tasted grand, and he swore he could feel it giving him strength as it went down.

As he took the sustenance, his niece stood at the foot of the bed, hands folded, and sang 'Joy To The World' in her high, bright voice. She had Boone's gift for song, he thought, as she sang all the verses without missing a word or note. Moses savored the music along with the broth.

He finished the broth long after she ended the song and launched into another. When he couldn't down another drop, his belly tighter than a tick on a hound dog, Mattie wiped his mouth and kissed his forehead. "You should rest now," she told him quietly.

"I will as soon as Boone cleans me up," he replied.

Mattie protested, but Moses persevered. It wouldn't be proper for her to do the task, not when they weren't yet wed, so she took the little girl and the empty cup back to Rachel after admonishing Boone. "Be gentle, and don't tax him too much. He's very weak."

Ezekiel emerged from the bedroom, sleepy-eyed, as Boone began stripping off the reeking nightshirt that he wore. There was no other, so Zeke brought out a clean, spare cotton shirt that would serve. After heating water over the fire, Boone scrubbed Moses' face, neck, and chest with a little soap. He didn't use the harsher lye soap that served for every day but sent Zeke to borrow Rachel's bar of castile soap. Although Boone's hands were gentle during the task, he was also quick and had the clean shirt on Moses before he could become chilled.

"Are you warm enough?" Boone asked as he tucked the covers and quilt back around Moses. "I don't want you to take a chill."

"I'm good," Moses replied, resisting the urge to shiver. Boone shot him a look and stirred up the fire, adding more wood.

As the room warmed, he became drowsy and closed his eyes.

"He alright?" he heard Zeke ask.

"He'll do," Boone said. "Fever's still gone, but he's weaker than a just born kitten. He's lively for a near-dead man, that's for sure. I can't keep him from talking, but he did get some broth down. Sleep'll do him good."

"I still feel it's my fault he was taken so bad," Ezekiel said. "If he'd died…"

"It ain't," Boone told him. "And he didn't, thanks be to God."

Listening to his brothers eased him, Moses thought as he fell asleep.

He had no idea what time it was when he woke, but they'd moved the table over from Boone's so that two tables sat before the fireplace. Both were set and laden with various dishes. The aromas wafting his way smelled delicious, but Moses didn't figure he could partake of much more than broth. His brothers, Rachel and Mattie, along with the Raffertys plus both Deacon Lee and Mac, gathered around the table.

Liam had paused at Moses' bedside to grasp his hand and wish him well. "Glad to see you're on the road to recovery," he said. "You had Boone fretful as I've ever seen him and the rest of us concerned. Then Mathilde shows up out of the blue to keep Christmas, but once she heard you were sick, she hightailed it over here, and we've hardly seen her since."

"She's been taking care of me," Moses told him. "And she does a fine job of it."

He wanted to add that they had promised to marry but didn't. Mattie wanted to be the one to inform her family, so he respected her wish. If he had his way, she wouldn't be returning to San Antonio. Instead, they'd be married and live on the ranch.

Mima showed him her new miniature quilt for her doll and new hairbows in rainbow colors. Rob had a new top that

Ezekiel had carved for him, as well as a wooden train he could pull on a string. Both children had some candy from town. Although apparently gifts had already been exchanged prior to dinner, Boone brought a new lariat for Moses, and Zeke gave him a whetstone to sharpen his knives. Rachel and the children presented him with a new handkerchief, but his favorite present of all was a new shirt, handmade by Mattie, and a copy of Mark Twain's book, *Roughing It.*

"I'll have time to read it while I'm convalescing," he told her. "Thank you, Mattie, and I'll keep the shirt for my best."

He'd bought a string of green glass beads for her, but he didn't want to present them in front of the gathered families. Moses also had bought her a pair of soft kid gloves and asked Ezekiel to bring them from his room.

Although the meal awakened Moses' appetite, he ate very little, more broth and some mashed potatoes with gravy. Mattie spoon-fed him again, and he had two tiny bites of apple cake. While those gathered sang more Christmas carols and young Mima curled up beside him, Moses became drowsy. He was full and tired. Although he enjoyed the company, his feeble strength faded fast, and he needed sleep.

Moses dozed off more than once, and when Boone noticed, the celebration concluded.

There was noise and a rush of activity as one of the tables and chairs were moved back across the dog trot, dishes gathered, and people departed. Most of them paused for a word with Moses, although by then, he was so weary he did little more than nod. Afterward, he couldn't have named those who shared a word if his life depended on it.

Mattie was the last who lingered. She leaned over him, kissed his lips, and said, "Moses, I'm going home with Maggie's family so I can get some sleep. But I'll be back come morning."

He nodded. "I hope so."

Her smile brightened the room as she told him, "I love you, Moses Wilson."

"Love you, Mattie."

Then she was gone, in a swirl of cold air from the door, and then silence. He thought at first that he was alone, but when Moses opened his eyes into mere slits, he saw both his brothers remained. Boone sat down in the chair by the bed, and Moses turned toward him. For the first time, he noticed how exhausted Boone appeared and that the faint worry line that divided his forehead had returned.

"I'll do, Boone," he said. "You ought to go get some shut-eye yourself."

"I'm fixin' to do just that, but Ezekiel will be here, and if you need me, he'll fetch me back. How'd you feel?"

"Frail as a little old lady," Moses said in what he meant to be humorous but was true. "Tired and sleepy, otherwise good."

Boone laid a hand across his brother's forehead. "I'll be back. Don't relapse on me, Mosey. I don't think my heart could stand it."

Moses had about run out of steam, but he attempted a grin. "Won't."

Sleep claimed his weary body, and over the next few days, he slept more than he was awake. When he wasn't sleeping, he ate cups of broth, noodles, and a few thin slices of meat. Mattie, true to her word, came daily and scrambled him some eggs. They were about the best thing he'd ever tasted, and the first day he managed a biscuit slathered with butter, he could almost swear he'd died and gone to heaven. When she made the promised vanilla pudding, he savored every sweet bite.

On New Year's Day, with the help of both his brothers, he took a few slow steps to a wooden chair with arms that Boone had found somewhere. He might have even fetched it from Laredo, Moses wasn't sure, but he sank into it with a sigh. If it had been any further from the bed, he would likely have fallen face down on the floor. The effort, even with assistance, robbed his breath and brought a wave of weakness. For a few moments, he saw nothing but bright and thought he might faint. Boone realized it and pushed Moses' head down.

"Try not to swoon."

"I'd rather not," he told him. "I would care for a cup of coffee, though."

So far, the women had plied him with teas, and lemonade and water, even a little apple cider, but he craved coffee.

Boone draped a blanket across Moses' shoulders and eyed him. "They ain't let you have any? You ought to have asked before now. I reckon the ladies don't understand cowboys live on coffee."

"I'll fetch it," Ezekiel said.

"Better yet, I'll make a pot," Boone told him. "I could use a cup or two myself. Anyone feed you yet?"

"Mattie ain't here yet, but Rachel gave me some of that gruel," Moses said with a shudder. He'd got tired of the thin oatmeal days ago. "I could use some vittles."

"I'll fetch over a piece or two of land trout," Zeke said, using the cowboy nickname for bacon. "Or I will if the littles ones haven't ate it all. Liam's roasting a hog for everyone on the ranch today. I imagine Mattie's helping to make the food to go with it. She'll be here directly."

Moses' belly rumbled with anticipation. He could use some solid meat to help gain his strength back, and roast pig sounded good. Much as he craved the food, though, he wanted Mattie at his side more.

He munched down the two pieces of bacon Ezekiel delivered along with some cornbread, then savored the hot, strong coffee. Together, they revived him from the trek from bed to chair. Moses could hold out until it was time to eat roast pork.

After that, he doubted he'd be much good for anything but a return to bed.

When Mattie arrived, her smile emerged like the sun on a cloudy day.

"You're out of bed," she cried as she crossed the room to him. "You look more like yourself, Moses. How do you feel?"

He'd come to dislike the question, but he understood why everyone kept asking it.

"It's grand to be out of bed," he said. He didn't mention he remained debilitated and puny. "Looking forward to some roast pig here afterwhile."

She sank to the floor as her skirts belled out around her and rested her head on his knees.

"I'm so pleased to see you looking better," she said. "I've been worried to death, Moses."

He laid his hand on top of her head. "Dear heart, I'm alright."

"You will be," she said.

After the tender moment, she rose and bustled around the room. She stripped the bedding and tossed it into a pile. Then she remade the bed with fresh sheets and clean covers.

"What do you plan to do with the dirty laundry?" he asked, curious because until he fell sick, he'd been helping Rachel on washday, but he wouldn't be able to do that for some time to come.

"I'll take it back to the house, and we'll do it with the ranch's wash."

"Where did the clean bedclothes come from?"

She smiled and displayed her dimple. "From my trousseau," she told him. "I'm sure my parents are fit to be tied, but I brought most of it with me. If you'd died, I suppose I would have had to haul it all back to San Antonio, and one of my sisters could have had it someday."

"Wouldn't you have kept it for when you wed?"

Mattie raised up on her knees so that they were face to face. "Moses, if you'd died, I wouldn't have ever wed. I don't want any man but you. I'd been a sad spinster, and that's a fact."

He had to kiss her and removed his hands from where they'd gripped the chair. Moses put his arms around her and hoped he wouldn't topple to the floor, then kissed her. It marked the first time he'd really bussed her since becoming ill, more than a mere brush of his lips but not quite a deep or passionate kiss. He stopped when his head whirled with a wave of dizziness, and he had to catch his breath.

"We couldn't have that," he told her, and she shook her head, smiling.

"No, we certainly could not."

If he'd been just a bit stronger, he'd been tempted to take her onto his knee, but Moses knew he lacked the strength, so he didn't. Instead, remembering the day, he said, "Happy New Year, Mattie."

"It will be," she told him. "1876 and a brand-new year. It's the year I'll be your bride."

With no idea when exactly they would wed, where they would live, or how it would happen, Moses grinned. They'd be married, and for now, that was enough of a joy.

The details could be settled later.

CHAPTER SEVENTEEN

Each morning when she woke in the tiny upstairs room at Maggie's, there was a moment when Mattie wondered where she was. Then, she would remember and think of Moses. Although she spent each day at his side, she came here to sleep. It wouldn't be proper to stay in the small cabin Moses shared with his younger brother. Boone and Rachel had no beds to spare. If it was early, Mattie would start breakfast, but today, she'd slept longer. The aroma of coffee and bacon floated upward. She could hear Grace chattering to the baby, who made wordless noises, along with the sound of Liam and Maggie's voices.

She dressed and descended into the kitchen. Her sister and her husband stopped talking.

"What is it?" she asked, her heart in her throat. "Is it something with Moses?"

There was always the fear of a relapse.

"No, he's doing well, no change that I've heard," Liam said. He held up a sheet of paper. "It's just that there's a letter from San Antonio, from your mama and daddy. They insist you must come home now, that you can't stay on the ranch any longer."

Fear faded and became annoyance. "I won't go, Liam."

Maggie wore a sad expression. "You might read the letter first."

"It won't change my mind," Mattie said, but she took the

letter Liam offered.

She recognized the handwriting as her brother Freddy's, for he had a fine hand, but the words and tone were her mother's.

> *Daughter,*
>
> *You acted in haste and in poor judgement in leaving San Antonio in the manner that you did. You must return home immediately to correct this folly. You endangered both your life and your reputation. It is common knowledge that Phineas Dawson took you to the ranch and that you spent days alone in his company without a chaperone. That is not acceptable, not socially or morally. Nor is your wild rush to visit that ranch or that cowboy. Gunther is quite upset, but he has offered to set out with a team of horses and a wagon to bring you home. Unlike Mr. Dawson, he will bring along a chaperone. Gunther's desire is to wed you upon your return. It seems the only way to stop the wagging tongues and to restore your position in society.*
>
> *You have brought shame on your family and endangered your chance at a good marriage. Were Gunther not possessed of a forgiving nature, you would have lost any chance to return to San Antonio in good standing.*
>
> *Gunther plans are to follow after this letter was sent, so he should arrive very soon at the ranch. I urge you to return with him and to become his bride. Toward that end, I have asked my dressmaker to sew a gown from ivory silk and to trim it with the finest Honiton lace. I will take care of other details before your return.*
>
> *I warn you if you do not choose to return or to marry Gunther, we shall cut you off entirely. You will be disowned, and you will not be welcome in our home. We*

will consider you dead in every sense but the physical.
    I shall hope to see you very soon and that you will
have regained your senses.
    Your mother, Frau Ilse Baumann.

Mattie read it once, with disbelief, then again with both anger and sorrow. She threw the letter down on the table and said, "If he comes, it will be a wasted trip."

"But Mattie, they'll disown you!"

"Papa gave me his blessing the day I left!"

"Well, it would seem Mama has changed his mind. And they will shut you out!"

"That makes me very sad, Maggie, but I won't marry Gunther for any reason. I loathe the man, and I'm promised to Moses. Besides, didn't they say the same when you told them you were marrying Liam?"

Maggie turned crimson. "They did, but…"

"But you still married him. Do you regret it?"

"I don't, and you know it, but Mattie, it was different because Liam owns land. That was what brought them around in the end."

Mattie stared at her sister. Either she didn't know what the men had discussed, or Moses had lied, and she would stake her life that he told the truth.

"So, they wouldn't mind so much if Moses owned a ranch or was part owner of one?"

Maggie shifted the baby in her arms so he could nurse, then said. "They might not, but he isn't."

Liam glanced over at Mattie and cleared his throat. "Well, actually, he is, in a way."

Mattie smiled, and her sister stared. "What are you talking about?"

"I invited all of the Wilsons to buy into the ranch if they

wanted," Liam said. "I did so last fall, and they've agreed. We haven't hammered out the exact details yet, but I'd say we have a gentleman's agreement in place. This place is large, but it could be bigger, but that takes more investment, which is what they will provide."

Maggie frowned. "I didn't know anything about this."

"Well, my love, you were with child and then having our son," Liam said. "Do you object to the idea?"

"Well, no, I don't."

"Then we have time to talk about it later. Right now, I think the first order of business is that this Gunther person – "

"Gunther Hammerschmidt," Mattie supplied. "He's a banker."

Liam's expression changed. "*That* one? No wonder you loathe him. Anyway, if he is truly en route, he could be here almost any day. We need to be prepared. The last thing we need here on the ranch is a fight."

"Moses isn't strong enough yet for any trouble or commotion," she said. "I don't want him to get worked up or worry over this."

"We have to tell him, Boone, too," Liam said. "They can't be blindsided by this."

"Tell Boone what?" Boone said. He stood in the doorway and had arrived in time to hear the last few comments.

"It'll be faster if you read the letter," Liam told his top hand.

Mattie poured two cups of coffee and handed one to Boone. She knew how fond he was of the beverage and figured he could use the fortification.

"What the deuce?" he said once he'd finished the letter. "That old dog ain't gonna hunt."

"No, it won't," Liam replied. "But if he's on the way, we need to be ready, Boone."

He sipped the coffee, eyes narrowed, and a stern expression on his face. "I'm up for whatever needs done. I'll turn him around like a stampeding herd, then send him back to San Antonio or put him in the bone orchard if necessary. He won't be getting anywhere close to Moses or Mattie."

Maggie gasped, but Boone's words gave Mattie a warm feeling.

"Let's hope it doesn't come to putting him in the ground," Liam said. "That could cause trouble we don't want. He won't be staying or be welcome, but I think there's other ways to settle this."

"I'm listening," Boone said.

"If Moses and Mattie get married before he comes, there's no question of her returning," he said. "And if we go ahead with the partnership, in time her folks may accept the marriage. They weren't keen on me, either, but when they learned I owned the ranch, they changed their tune. That, and when Grace was born. A grandbaby can be a considerable inducement."

"I'd marry Moses today," Mattie said. A wild rush of joy filled her mind, blowing away her despair.

Boone finished his coffee and put the cup down. He smiled at her.

"I reckon you would, and I don't doubt he feels the same, but he can't sit up for more than a few hours at a time or stand up. You'd have to go to Laredo to wed, even with a judge the way Rachel and I did. It's gonna be quite a while before he can mount a horse, let alone ride, even in a wagon that far."

"A preacher or Judge Masters might come here," Liam suggested.

"He might," Boone said. "Mattie, are you willing to get married today or tomorrow if we can work it out?"

She nodded, almost afraid to hope.

"Then let's go talk to Moses," he said. "Liam, can we

borrow that letter?"

With the letter tucked into his pocket, Boone strode back to the cabins with Mattie at his side. Her thoughts were jumbled, but halfway there, she came to a halt.

"Am I going too fast?"

"No, Boone, not at all," Mattie told him. "I just think we have to be cautious how we tell Moses about all this. He's still weak, and I don't want to upset him. I worry about him having a setback anyway – some patients do."

In her rounds with Frau Zieff, she'd seen it more than once. If the recovering individual did too much or pushed too soon, they became ill again. Sometimes, they became sicker than before, which in Moses' case might prove fatal.

"He'll be over the moon to marry you," Boone said in the gruff yet sweet way he sometimes had. "Might be awhile before you can honeymoon, if you know what I mean, but he won't mind."

Mattie felt a hot blush stain her cheeks. "I wouldn't either."

"If this is what's best – and that's how it seems – we'll make it happen. You're already family to me, Mattie, and you brought my brother back from the edge of death. I doubt he would have survived if you hadn't come. Let's go share the news."

Moses sat in the chair before the fireplace, where a low fire burned to keep the cabin warm and cozy. The Mark Twain book he'd received for Christmas was in his hands, but he'd been dozing. He stirred as they entered and grinned when he saw Mattie.

"Good morning, pretty girl."

She took the book from him, marked his place, and put it up on the mantle.

"Hello, Moses." Mattie kissed his forehead and pushed a stray lock of hair back from his face. It wasn't just an affectionate caress but a way to judge whether he was feverish. His skin, though, was warm, not hot.

"I was beginning to think you weren't coming today," he said, his tone a little petulant.

Before she could say anything, Boone did. "There was a hullabaloo over at the main house that required our attention."

He brought over a chair for Mattie and one for himself. Boone sat down backwards in it and sighed. "Now, don't you get your drawers in a knot over this, Moses," he said. "You gotta promise me you won't get riled up 'cause it wouldn't be good for you."

Moses' face went paler, something Mattie wouldn't have thought possible. "What's the matter?"

"Ain't no easy way to tell you, so I'll just say it outright," Boone told him. "That German banker, Gesundheit or whatever his name is, is coming to the ranch, will be here in a day or so. He's coming to fetch Mattie home, and over in San Antoin, her ma is planning a wedding, one that don't include you."

A harsh cough shook Moses' shoulder, and he rubbed his chest with his free hand. Mattie held the other. "Don't fret," she said. "I'm not going, and I'm not marrying anyone but you."

"Mattie…" Moses' voice was low and sad. "I don't understand a bit."

"My parents are angry," she replied, pausing to select her words with care. "Vati, Papa, gave me his blessing when I left, but it seems my mother has changed his point of view. They wrote a letter asking me to come home and telling me that Gunther Hammerschmidt is on the way to fetch me."

Moses' eyes grew huge in his face, slenderer than she'd ever seen it.

"If you aren't fixing to ride off with him, why are you telling me?"

"Because her folks have said they'll cut her off, Moses," Boone said. "Her ma's having a wedding dress made, and I imagine that man's going to pitch a fit when she says she won't go."

"Promise me you're not," Moses spoke in a harsh whisper.

"I'm not, *Liebling,* not now, not ever."

She watched his face and saw the moment he realized why there was an issue.

"What happens when he shows up?"

Boone laughed, but it wasn't with humor. "I told Liam I'd do whatever it took to send him back to town, turn him and party like a stampeding herd, or put German George in the ground. Liam wasn't fond of the idea, figuring it'd bring trouble to the ranch."

"You could hang for it, Boone," Moses said. "I ain't in no shape to head off another hanging."

"You won't have to – Liam's got a plan, and it'll work."

"Tell me," Moses croaked as his hand tightened around Mattie's.

"If he shows up and she's already married to you, there ain't much he can do," Boone said. "Even less when he finds that the Wilson boys are partners in the ranch."

Moses stared at first Mattie, then his brother. He shook his head and cleared his throat.

"My brain ain't working right," he said. "I cain't quite picture it. Is that coffee still hot?"

Mattie rose and pulled the pot from a hook over the fire. "It is."

Without waiting for him to request it, she poured him a cup and added sugar. He grasped it tight. "We're getting married sooner rather than later," she told him. "I'm willing, Moses."

He sipped the brew. "Mattie, I'll marry you whenever you want, but I spend most of the day and all the night in bed. I can't walk across the room without help, and my legs are wobblier than a newborn calf. Ain't nobody on the ranch who can marry us proper, and I sure couldn't take the trip into town."

"Naw, but if a preacher man or Judge Masters came out here, you could manage," Boone told him. "Where's Ezekiel?"

"Working, far as I know. You're the top hand, not me."

"He should be down at the corrals where they're breaking a colt. I'd best fetch him so he can head to Laredo."

"Boone, you're serious about this?"

"Serious as an undertaker at a funeral. We'll plan on maybe a little wedding tomorrow if we can get someone here to do the honors. You can still have a big shin-dig later when you have your strength back."

"Is it gonna be alright for you, Mattie?"

"Oh, Moses." His sweetness and caring concern made her want to cry tears of joy. "Yes, yes, yes. I told you I brought my trousseau or most of it. I also brought a dress I made that I figured I could be married in one day. It's not white or fancy, but it's pretty."

Boone smiled. "I reckon I'll mention all of this to Rachel, then go find Zeke. It's early enough, yet he can make it easy into Laredo today, and if he can't bring someone back tonight, they can get here first thing in the morning. If he cain't, I'll go myself. You'd best rest, Moses, to be a bridegroom come tomorrow."

He stood, put the chair back at the table, patted Moses on the shoulder, and headed out the door.

Alone for the first time since their wedding had become imminent, Moses reached for Mattie and, with effort, stood. He locked his arms around her and held her close. She rested her head against his shoulder and let one of her arms encircle his neck. There was no need for words, just a powerful sharing of love. Moses held her in his arms for at least ten minutes, then said, "I'd like to kiss you, but I reckon I'd best sit down."

"There'll be plenty of time for kisses and more," Mattie told him boldly. "I can wait."

"I'd rather not, but I do believe I'll have to," he answered.

He settled down into the chair, and she tucked a blanket around his knees.

"Are you hungry?"

"I am, a bit."

Mattie realized she'd never eaten. The letter had slammed her before she'd had time.

"So I am," she said. "How about biscuits and some bacon?"

Maybe she should make soup, but that would take time, and they needed to eat now. He'd graduated to regular food a few days early.

"That would do, especially with a little gravy," Moses said. "Are you happy?"

She wasn't sure if she had words to describe just how happy she was. Joy filled her heart and wanted to burst out through her fingers and toes. "I am," she told him. "I truly am."

It might not be the wedding she'd imagined, and she wished Gunther wasn't headed for the ranch, but she was happy despite it all.

CHAPTER EIGHTEEN

In Kentucky, he'd stood up with his brother Jacob when he married his Sally Ann. Boone already had a wife when Moses arrived in Texas. If he'd been asked to speculate, Moses would have said he would be wed in the same little country church where his parents had said their vows. That would have been before he followed two of his brothers to Texas or met Mattie.

If he wished anything now, it was that their mother, Jemima, could be present at his wedding and that he wasn't weak from nearly losing his life to pneumonia. Though he longed to make Mattie his wife in every way, to make sweet love to her in the quiet of night, he could wait until he grew stronger.

After their midday dinner of bacon and biscuits with the requested gravy, Boone returned.

"Ezekiel headed for Laredo," he said. "His notion is to come back early in the morning, and the two of you can get hitched as soon as the judge or parson gets here."

Moses nodded. Weariness had settled on him, heavy as the blankets. "I'll be ready if you'll help me wash and shave and get dressed tomorrow."

He hadn't worn normal clothing since he took sick, and imagining putting on trousers, shirt, and all seemed like a difficult task. He figured he could manage it with Boone's help.

"Yeah, I will. You about ready to go back to bed? You're gonna need to get some rest."

"I reckon so, but Boone, let me try to walk it. I want to stand up to say my vows tomorrow."

He read the hesitation in his brother's face and realized he'd scared him when he came so near dying. Despite the sober expression Boone often wore, he cared deeply for his family and always had. "You can try, but I'll be right here in case you falter."

Moses strained to rise, using the arms of the chair to help him stand. Once on his feet, he took a small step, then stopped. He swayed, tottering a little, and Boone caught his arm to steady him.

"Whoa, go easy," his brother said.

"I am." For all his bravado, dizziness plagued him, and he wasn't sure if he might not go down before he reached the bed. It was eight steps away, and he managed four before he asked for help.

"Boone."

"I got you." He provided his arm for support. Once there, Moses sat down heavily on the bed, face wet with sweat. He managed to get into bed, his head and shoulders up on the pillow. If he lay flat for long, he still started coughing. "Tell me you ain't gonna swoon."

"I'm not," Moses replied, but it'd been a near thing.

Without complaint, Boone tucked the blankets around Moses and wiped his face.

"Thank you," he said, then admitted the truth. "Boone, I don't feel so good."

Worry furrowed his brother's forehead. "What's the matter?"

"I'm just awful tuckered out," he said, trying not to sound whiny. "Besides that, the bacon and biscuits aren't sitting too well in my belly."

He should have known better than to chow down such food, not when he'd been limited to soups and stews and lighter fare.

"Are you gonna puke?" Boone, the oldest of a large family, asked with resignation.

"I surely hope not."

Moses didn't. After he'd rested awhile, his stomach eased, and he fell asleep. He woke to find Boone still there and asked, "Where's Mattie?"

"The women are fussing over what to make for your wedding feast," Boone said. A cigarette in his hand wafted smoke toward the ceiling. It smelled good, but Moses figured his lungs weren't ready for tobacco. "Rachel was all fired up to do a bunch of cooking, but I'd rather she didn't. She looks ready to burst now, and it's still two months till she says the baby will come. I worry about her, Moses."

"I don't reckon I can eat much of a feast anyway."

Boone laughed. "They're still gonna make one. Last I heard, Rachel was baking a wedding cake. They couldn't choose between the traditional one with currants and raisins or a Queen Cake. I believe they decided on the Queen Cake. Liam said they could have a roast off the last beef he slaughtered, the one hanging in the smokehouse, and Mattie plans to make noodles to go with it. Something was said about baking some light bread, too and cooking some leather britches beans. I think Liam told them that was enough, but they're all over there at his place, planning and cooking. Mattie said to tell you she'd be back in a bit."

Moses nodded. With all the preparations for the wedding, he remembered something.

"I got her a ring back when I went to San Antonio last fall. It's in the other room with my gear. Can you find it?"

"I surely can. Liam told some of the hands to bring over Mattie's two trunks, and I figured they could put them in the bedroom for now. Until you're stronger, we all thought the bed should stay here, but Zeke's moving back to the bunkhouse after he gets back."

That relieved one worry from Moses' mind. Although he wouldn't be intimate with his wife very soon, he'd wondered about sharing space with his brother. He preferred having Mattie all to himself, and he was glad.

"He don't mind?"

"Heck, no, he'd rather not be subjected to a pair of lovebirds," Boone said, with amusement.

Ezekiel surprised everyone by returning to the ranch around sundown, bringing with him Judge Ike Masters, the same judge who had officiated at Boone and Rachel's wedding. He had also been the official who pronounced Boone to be innocent of murder and ordered him freed from jail. Since Mattie would spend one more night under Liam's roof, the judge came to sleep in Ezekiel's bed after a late supper at Maggie's table.

"I brought the judge rather than a preacher because tomorrow's Sunday, and they'll all be in church," Zeke told his brothers over a plate of frijoles. Moses managed a few refried beans, but he didn't dare eat any of the tamales Ezekiel had also brought. "Besides, he was willing when he heard it was for you, Moses. Seems like he's fond of us Wilsons."

Early in the morning, despite Boone's protests, Rachel came over to sweep and clean the cabin. Since it was the middle of winter, there were no flowers to be had, but she brought over the dried flower bouquet she'd been married holding. Boone, true to his word, helped Moses wash, although neither figured he could stand a full bath. He shaved him as well, urging the younger man to save his strength for the ceremony.

Moses dressed in the new clothes he'd bought to visit Mattie last fall, black wool pants, the pinstriped shirt with a black string tie, and a frock coat loaned by Liam. He donned boots for the first time since he became ill and then sat in the chair by the fire, reserving his energy for the ceremony. Boone, who would serve as his best man, had the ring for Mattie in a vest pocket and hovered over Moses with concern.

At ten o'clock in the morning, all the hands and ranch residents arrived and lined the room. Ike Masters took a position before the fireplace, and Moses stepped into place, Boone at his side and Ezekiel just behind.

Maggie and Rachel entered together, their children just behind. Each woman wore her best dress, and Mima wore hers too. They took a place opposite Boone and Zeke, then Mattie stepped through the door. She wore a navy blue dress, the one she'd told him she had made, simple yet lovely. It had a high waist, four buttons down the front, and a long, full skirt. A lace fichu collar was pinned in place with a cameo brooch, and she wore her long hair down.

Moses gazed at her, lovestruck. He'd always found her to be pretty, but today, Mattie was beautiful. Her hair cascaded in natural waves past her waist, as bright as corn silk. The dark blue of her dress accented her eyes, and she wore a smile as she walked toward him, Rachel's dried floral bouquet in her hands.

Boone sang the sweet love ballad, 'Annie Laurie,' as she came toward Moses, the sole music. She paced her steps to the song, and when he'd finished, Mattie stood beside him. She handed the flowers to Rachel. They turned to face each other, and he took her hands in his. A powerful rush of emotion swept through him, and he thought he might shed a few tears. Mattie spoke her vows first, her voice soft and tender.

"I, Mathilde Anna Baumann, take thee, Moses Robert Wilson, to be my wedded husband, to have and to hold from this day forward, for better, for worse, for richer, for poorer, in sickness and in health, to love and to cherish, till death do us part according to God's holy ordinance. I pledge thee my faith, my love, and my life."

Their eyes met as she said her vow. Moses held her hands

tight, and when he thought his knees might buckle, Boone grasped his elbow and stayed him. He repeated the vow and managed to keep his voice strong.

Once each had spoken, the judge said, "By the power invested in me by the state of Texas, I pronounce you husband wife in the eyes of the law, by God, and before man. You've had a hard row to hoe, I hear. Moses, you may kiss your bride."

He slid the slender gold ring onto her left hand with a smile.

In those moments, he forgot how sick he'd been and didn't remember his current weakness. Moses took his bride into his arms and kissed her soundly. He'd kissed her many times, but this time, it was different. She wasn't a girl he courted any longer but his wife, now and forever. Moved and happy, he hugged her close. It was a miracle she'd come into his life and a joy. She was now his wife.

She kissed him back, her eyes wet with happy tears. "I love you, Moses," she said, soft for his ears alone.

"And I love you, Mrs. Wilson."

Their family and friends who had gathered cheered. Boone spoke into his ear, "You ready to sit?"

Moses was and nodded. He sank into the chair, guided by his brother's hand.

His niece ran over. She hugged Moses, then she turned to give Mattie a hug. Someone must have explained that she gained an aunt because the little girl said, "Aunt Mattie and Uncle Mo Mo." Moses laughed and put her on his knee for a moment. He kissed the back of her neck and then released her. Someday, they would have a child, a cousin for Mima and Robert, he realized. Back home in Kentucky, there were more, but he doubted they would ever meet any children he and Mattie might have.

The table had been moved so that he sat at it, and Mattie sat at his right side. Boone and Ezekiel joined them at the table, along with Liam, Maggie, and Judge Masters. Rachel took their children, along with Grace and Seamus, across to their cabin to eat. The hands retreated to the bunkhouse where Cookie had promised a spread in honor of Moses' wedding.

That roast beef tasted wonderful in his mouth, but Moses liked the noodles his wife made best of all. They were rich and thick with the beef broth they had soaked up. He ate sparingly but tasted the green beans and enjoyed a small slice of bread.

He and Mattie cut the cake together, then shared a few bites. It was sweet, and he appreciated it as well. Compared to what everyone else ate, Moses had little, but he didn't want to chance being sick.

Jubilant, he still grew tired, and after a couple of hours, he knew it was time to rest his weary body. A quick word to Boone and his brother cleared the room of everyone except himself, Ezekiel, and Mattie.

"I wish you well," Boone told him once Moses had been settled into bed. With his brother's help, he had taken off his wedding finery and returned to his drawers with a nightshirt. "I hope you're as happy as me and Rachel are. Unless you need something, we're all going to leave so you can be with your bride."

He exchanged a glance with Mattie and said, "I believe we're good, Boone, but thank you. I appreciate everything you've done for me, Ezekiel, too."

"You're my brother," Boone said as if that was explanation enough and it was. "I'll write Ma the news, and when you're able, I will pay for that wedding picture to send her."

Moses shook his head. "What picture?"

"I reckon you don't recollect, but I told you when you were sick that I'd pay for the picture, and I will," Boone told him. "I'll take care of the judge, too. Liam drew up the papers for the ranch, and I'll need your signature, but it can wait."

He had no memory of the promised photograph, but Moses wanted to sign.

"Let me sign it today, Boone. Then Judge Masters can take it back and get it filed so it's proper."

Boone demurred, but Moses insisted. He signed where directed, the pen heavy in his hand, but his name was legible.

"Holler for me if you need anything," Boone told him.

"Congratulations," Zeke added.

Mattie saw them to the door. Moses watched from the bed as his brothers hugged her and he heard Boone say, "Take care of him, Mattie."

"I will," she replied. "I always will."

Alone as husband and wife, he patted the bed. "I cain't do much else but come lay down with me."

"I will, later," she told him. "You need to get some sleep. You've done more today than you have since the fever broke. I don't fancy being a widow before I am barely a wife so you rest."

"What are you gonna do?"

She grinned. "I'm going to settle in, Moses. This is my home now, too, and I want it to look like it."

He was becoming drowsy, but he remembered her family's home and wondered what she intended to do. This humble two-room cabin must seem small, he thought, after the house where she'd been raised. Moses hoped she wasn't disappointed. One day, he'd built her a larger house. Boone had expressed interest in doing the same for Rachel.

When he awakened, it was near dark. A coal oil lamp burned on the table, and she'd built the fire up. As Moses looked around, he saw she'd hung curtains at the window. There were some vases and such on the mantlepiece. Everywhere he looked, she'd added homey touches from her trunks. She'd hung a calendar on the wall, too. All of it transformed the simple place into a home, and he liked it, very much.

"Husband," she said, and he realized she sat beside the bed. He decided he'd buy her a rocking chair the very first chance that he had.

"Mattie, you shouldn't have let me sleep so long."

"You needed it," she told him. "Are you thirsty or hungry? There's coffee made, and Liam sent over some milk if you'd rather. I kept some beef and noodles warm for you, too."

Moses wasn't hungry, but he ate a little to please her, then said, "Come to bed, Mattie."

She cleared away the dishes. "It's early yet."

"I want to lay here with you in my arms," he told her. "Cain't do much else, not yet, but I'd like to hold you."

Mattie nodded. He noticed she had braided her hair into one long tail and that she no longer wore her wedding gown. Her simple calico dress suited her, but as he watched, she walked into the bedroom and returned in a white nightgown. Although it covered her from neck to ankles and was modest, it fired his imagination. Nobody besides a husband would see her this way, and he enjoyed the privilege.

He made room for her in the bed, and she slid beneath the blankets. Moses put his arms around her and said, "Mattie Wilson, I love you."

Her smile provided all the answer he required, and he savored the moment, happier than he could ever remember he'd been.

CHAPTER NINETEEN

The day after their wedding, it turned colder and rained, but there was no snow. The falling rain beat a rhythm on the roof and provided a cozy feeling. Mattie lit the coal oil lamp early to banish the dim shadows from the room and made a pot of potato soup flavored with a little bacon. Moses managed the short distance from the bed to the chair with her assistance. Neither of his brothers appeared during the day, and Mattie was thankful for the time to spend with her husband without distraction. As much as she liked Boone and all the Wilsons, they needed some private time to adjust to marriage. Although they couldn't be intimate in every way, Mattie couldn't stop touching Moses. She stroked his hair and caressed his cheek as she passed by him, delivered kisses, and held his hand.

They talked to pass the time. Mattie shared stories from her childhood, and Moses offered memories from his. When conversation slowed, he read a book, and so did she, then they would discuss what they had read. He had been whittling a wooden bear for young Robert before Moses took ill, and he began working on it, slow and with great care. The boy would turn two later in the month.

Neither said a word about Gunther Hammerschmidt or the fact he would arrive at any time. Mattie thought a great deal about it, though, and was more than a little worried. She didn't want any commotion but feared he wouldn't leave without a disturbance. Boone had left the letter in her keeping and she read it over many times. Her heart ached when she thought about her parents cutting all ties and hoped that once they received news of her marriage, they might relent.

"My family is yours now," Moses told her, aware that the rift caused her pain. "You're a sister to my brothers now."

He was lying down, resting against the pillows and she cuddled up beside him. "How many sisters do you have?"

"Nary a one," he said. "Ma had all sons."

Mattie had three sisters, Maggie and the young ones still at home, and her brother, Manfred, who preferred Freddie. The Wilsons had five brothers in the family. "Do you miss your other two brothers?"

"I do, some," he told her. "Boone's the oldest, and he stepped into our daddy's shoes when he died. He's eight years older than me and twelve years older than Zeke. I always have been close with Boone and Ezekiel, more since we've been here in Texas today. We've been through a lot, but I'd like to see Jacob and Garrett again, too. Boone meant to go home to Kentucky once he recovered from being shot and didn't get hanged, but Rachel was in the family way, so he couldn't."

"So, none of you went back," Mattie said. She found their sense of one for all, all for one reminiscent of 'The Three Musketeers.' She'd read an English translation of the story and been captivated by it in school.

"Naw, it didn't seem right to leave Boone or Zeke behind," Moses said. "And now Rachel's fixing to have another child sometime in March."

Rachel had confided that to Mattie, but Mattie, who had observed Frau Zieff at work, doubted it would be that long. "I think she'll have the baby sooner," Mattie told Moses.

"Why do you think that?"

"Her belly's dropped," she explained. "That happens

usually a few weeks, no more before birth. If I were to make a guess, I'd say she might have it almost anytime."

Moses frowned, so she asked, "What's wrong?"

"Boone's worried now. If Rachel has that child sooner, he'll be beside himself. He's had enough on his plate, fretting over me. I noticed he's got a few gray hairs now, and he ain't but thirty-one years old."

She wanted to offer reassurance that all would be well, but since she'd been present when Rachel miscarried in the summer, Mattie didn't dare. Rachel had bled so much that both she and Maggie had feared they might lose her. She might deliver without complications, but there were no guarantees she would. Many women died giving birth or afterward.

"Did Ezekiel mind going back to the bunkhouse?" she asked, to change the subject.

"Not much, I don't think," Moses replied. "This time of year, it's not so crowded, but come spring, Liam will bring back more of the hands for the drives."

Mattie didn't ask if he would have to go, but she hoped that now he was partners in the ranch, maybe he wouldn't. If he did, she would miss him so.

They had four days of married bliss before Hammerschmidt arrived, driving up as if he belonged on the ranch in a covered wagon with a team of horses. Mattie had gone outside to fetch water from the well, or she wouldn't have seen his arrival. She stopped, empty bucket in hand, and then turned around. Without running, she hurried back to the cabin.

"That didn't take long at all," Moses said from where he sat near the fire. He had insisted on getting dressed in his usual work clothes so he looked hale and healthy, much more than he was.

"I didn't get to the well," she replied. Her heart pounded, and she struggled not to breathe hard after her rushed return.

"Gunther is here. I saw the wagon pull up by Liam's house."

"Shoot fire and save matches," Moses exclaimed.

"It's not like it's a surprise. We knew he was coming."

Mattie knew just how Moses felt, though. Gunther's arrival still came as a shock, and she dreaded how he'd respond when he learned she wasn't returning with him and that she was married.

Ezekiel exploded into the cabin without knocking. "That German is here!"

"Does Boone know yet?"

"He does. He's heading over here now. We were down at the corrals."

Zeke had run, but Boone rode up on Sprat. Once he'd tied the horse to the porch rail, he came inside. "I reckon you heard," he said. "Guttersnipe is here."

Mattie had noticed he'd taken to calling Gunther anything but his name and admired it. It removed most of the menace and made him into a joke.

"I saw the wagon."

"We'd best get up to Liam's and get this over with, then. Are you ready, Mattie?"

She hadn't realized she'd have to face her former suitor. From the stricken look on Moses' face, neither had he. "I suppose so, but do I have to see him, Boone?"

He sighed hard. "Man like that is never gonna accept the news unless he hears it straight from your mouth, and even then, he won't like it. I'll stand beside you, and Liam will be there. I sent most of the hands that way, too. Ezekiel, will you stay with Moses?"

"I will."

Moses used the arms of the chair to stand. "I want to be there, Boone."

"I know you would, but you ain't fit for it. Have you been

out of this cabin in weeks? No. Can you walk up there without fainting in the mud? Likely not. You ain't even walked farther than the bed to the chair, and that's with help."

"It's my place as Mattie's husband to be there."

"If you hadn't nearly died, yeah, it would, but use some sense," Boone told him. "If you push too hard and take a turn for the worse, we might not pull you through this time. I don't suppose you want to make her a widow?"

His face remained set with a mulish expression, but Moses sat back down.

"Why'd you have to make sense?" he muttered.

"Because I'm smart," Boone said with the ghost of a grin. "Let's go before the son of a buck heads down here. I don't want him upsetting Rachel or you. If he did, I might have to shoot him, and that would prove a mistake, most likely."

"Might solve the problem, though."

"That's already done. Mattie?"

She kissed Moses and took off her apron. "I'm ready, Boone."

He nodded. "Zeke, boost her up behind me once I'm mounted. I ain't taking the time to walk."

It wasn't far to the main house, but Boone urged his horse to a canter. They arrived to see Liam on his front porch. Maggie peered from the front door, Grace at her knee and the baby in her arms. Gunther stood in front of the house, waving his hands about in a wild pattern.

Boone dismounted and eased Mattie to the ground. He led her around the wagon but stopped several feet from Gunther. At that distance, they could hear what was said.

"I've come for my bride, Liam Rafferty," Gunther said. "I won't leave without her, and we're heading back to San Antonio within the hour. Don't vex me. It's been a miserable trip, and I'm in a bad temper. Where's Mathilde?"

"I'm here," she said, although her voice emerged more than a little shaky.

At the same time, Boone spoke. "If you mean Mrs. Mattie *Wilson*, she's right here."

Gunther whirled toward them. When he did, Boone pushed back his coat and let his hand rest on his Griswold revolver. When the German banker took a few steps in their direction, he pulled it from the holster. "I don't recommend you come any farther, Hammerschmidt."

"Step away from the woman, cowboy," Gunther said. "Mathilde, get your things and get in this wagon."

"I won't be going anywhere, especially not to San Antonio," she said. Her voice was stronger now. "I'm married now, and this is my home."

Gunther snorted. "I don't believe such lies. Surely you wouldn't marry a cow hand."

Mattie lifted her left hand to display the wedding ring. "I could, and I have."

"Is this your man?" he asked with a sneer, glancing toward Boone.

Boone locked his steely gaze on Gunther. "I'm his brother."

"She's not married," Gunther said with a cocksure confidence that irked Mattie.

Liam spoke for the first time since she had arrived. "She is, Hammerschmidt. I was a witness to her wedding. Judge Ike Masters, out of Laredo, performed the ceremony. She's wife to Moses Wilson, one of my partners in this ranch."

"I want to see the marriage certificate, then." Some of the bluster had vanished from his voice, though. His sour expression indicated he thought it could be true.

"I've seen it," Liam said. "And signed my name as witness. You don't need to see it, but you do need to get off this ranch."

If he had her marriage certificate in hand, he'd tear it up,

Mattie thought. Then he would try to claim it never existed.

Gunther smiled, but it was an evil, terrible expression. He barked out a few words in German, and four armed men climbed from the back of the wagon and stood.

"And who will make me go?" he asked.

Ten ranch hands came up from where they had waited, all with pistols or rifles at the ready, and ringed the wagon.

"We will," Deacon Lee, Boone and Liam's old friend, said. "And the law will be here from Laredo."

That much had to be bluff, Mattie thought, but when Gunther's arrogant expression faded, she figured he believed it.

Mean natured, though, he wasn't going to go without slinging some insults and having the last word. "You're a wicked woman, Mathilde, with low morals, and I am glad now to be free from your whiles," he said in a venom-laced voice. "You've turned your back on your family and society. You won't be welcome again in San Antonio unless it's in the lowest dives. How many of these ignorant, thick-headed *Dummkopfs* have you taken into your arms? And where, if you are wed, is your husband? Why is he not here to defend you? I think perhaps you don't have a husband after all."

Before anyone could say a word, Moses spoke into the heavy silence.

"I'm right here," he said and took a place beside his wife with Boone on his left. "You owe my wife an apology, and then I suggest you do as Liam asked and leave the ranch."

"Moses!" Mattie said, stunned that he had appeared. She wondered how he could have made his way from the cabin. He couldn't have walked. Ezekiel stood a few paces behind, and he grinned at her.

Moses held his Colt revolver and aimed it at Gunther. "Go now, or I'll shoot. I don't take kindly to anyone trying to interfere with my wife."

Gunther cut loose a flood of German from his mouth, most of it swear words that Mattie wouldn't repeat to anyone. Then he jerked his head, and his armed men climbed back into the wagon. Then he climbed onto the wagon seat and looked at them all.

"If any of you set foot in San Antonio, I will see that you're arrested, tried, and hanged for attempted murder," he said. "I will tell the Baumann's to consider their daughter, both their daughters, as good as dead."

He clicked his tongue and used the reins to get the team moving. The wagon rumbled through the ranch yard and turned back toward San Antonio. As soon as it headed away, Boone grabbed Moses before he could fall down, and Ezekiel took his other side. They steadied him between them while Mattie stood in front of him, crying and kissing his face.

"How in the name of everything holy did you get here?" Boone demanded with a sharp look toward Zeke.

"I brought him piggyback," Ezekiel said. "He was fit to be tied, Boone, and saying he'd walk here on his own if he had to, even if he swooned or died trying. He's heavy, and I thought sure my back would give out, but we managed."

"That's pure luck, and you know it," Boone groused. "You're a pair of idiots, stupid fools. He could have fainted anywhere along the way or right here in front of Guttersnipe. You look like you're about to go down now, Moses."

"I ain't so peart," he said.

"Liam, fetch him a chair," Boone said. "Mattie, tend your loggerheaded husband."

"I got one right here," Liam said and set down a chair. His brothers lowered Moses onto the seat and stepped back.

Mattie knelt on the ground, heedless of the mud, and hugged her husband. She should have been angry, and she was worried, but more than that, she was proud and moved deep within.

"'So faithful in love and dauntless in war,'" she said, quoting a poem by Sir Walter Scott. "'There never was knight like the young Lochinvar.'"

"Except for loco Moses Wilson," Boone said in a dry tone, but a smile played around his lips. "You all right, young Lochinvar?"

"Naw," Moses replied. "I reckon I'm about to swoon."

He did, but his brothers caught him before he crumpled onto the dirt.

Mattie cried out as Maggie handed the baby to Liam and joined her. After a wild rush of aid, Deacon Lee brought around a wagon, and they loaded Moses into the back. Once home, his brothers toted him inside, then stripped him back to his drawers and nightshirt. They tucked him into bed, Boone complaining the loudest. Mattie propped him on the pillows and waited to see if he'd rouse. He hadn't yet.

"What in the world happened?" Rachel asked, dashing over.

"Is Mo Mo sick again?" Mima asked, echoing the fear they all shared.

"He'd better not be," Boone said with a grim expression. "If he is, I'm gonna knock him winding when he gets over it."

Moses groaned, and his eyes fluttered open. Mattie, seated on the bed facing her husband, released a long sigh. "I ain't sick, Boone," he said. "I'm just so awful weak, that's all."

Standing on the opposite side of the bed, Boone shook his head. "You took a terrible chance, Moses. You ain't getting out of this bed for a couple of days, sick or well. I ain't giving you up to the ground."

Mattie took Moses' hand and held it. "Can you drink a little water?"

He nodded, and she rose to get some.

"Mattie, I'm going back to work," Boone said. "Send for

me if he takes a turn, though."

"I will," she promised. "Don't fret."

"Cain't help it," he said. "I near finished raising him and that one too."

He hugged her, then and left. Rachel lingered for a few moments, and so did Zeke, complaining good-naturedly that his back was probably broken, then they were gone.

Mattie brought Moses a drink of water. Then she crawled onto the bed beside him and put her head on his shoulder. "I love you, Moses," she told him. "If you didn't already own my heart, you would have got it with what you did, but Boone's right. You took too much of a chance."

"I'd do it again," he said. "You're my wife, Mattie, and I love you. I had to be there."

"You'd best not have a setback," she warned.

"I don't reckon I will, but I need to sleep a spell," he told her. "I'm awful tired."

"I'm staying right here," she said.

"Good."

She remained cuddled with him for a long time, savoring his nearness, then unwound herself without awakening him. Mattie took his place in the chair by the fire, buried her face in both hands, and wept. Part of it was a rush of love for this man and how much he'd risked for her sake. There was concern, too, but she also cried because her parents, her family, would now disown her. Like Gunther had said, they would think of her as if she were dead. Mattie grieved that and knew that part of the reason Moses had pulled the stunt he had was to make up for that.

He didn't have to, she reflected. She had no doubt of his love for her or what lengths he would go for her sake. But she was glad that he did, even as she prayed that he would have no ill effects from his gesture.

Other than spending three full days in bed, being cosseted and spoiled by her, he didn't.

As Boone had said, when it became apparent Moses wouldn't suffer a setback, thanks be to God.

CHAPTER TWENTY

Perry County, Kentucky
Near Hazard

The December skies were a heavy gray, and the clouds threatened rain or snow as the Wilson family gathered around the raw new grave in the family cemetery. Jemima, who had never ceased wearing black since the day she had been widowed, stood beside her second eldest son, Jacob. His three children, all daughters, ages ten, twelve, and fourteen, and clustered close to their father as the casket containing their mother was lowered into the ground. The rest of Jemima's family, save her three sons who lived in far distant Texas, circled the grave, faces somber and sad. As she so often did, she wished her oldest, Boone, were there. A mere fifteen when his daddy died of pneumonia, he'd been her rock, a steady older brother and sometimes surrogate father for the younger children right up until he left to fight in the War Between The States. Although he'd come home when many hadn't, he didn't linger but headed away to Texas, where he remained.

She'd thought for a time that he and her youngest, Ezekiel, would return home, and they'd written that they both would. Ezekiel had left home at fifteen to be with Boone, but Boone nearly died of a gunshot wound, then came close to being hanged for a crime he didn't commit. When the news came that her oldest son might be hanged, she'd sent Moses to Texas. Jemima had expected them all back, but Boone had married, and his wife was in a delicate way, so they couldn't make the journey. Although she had three granddaughters right there in Kentucky, in Texas, she had a granddaughter named for her, Boone's first child, and another boy. By now, there was likely another in Boone's family. She'd made up her mind that if they weren't coming home, she would go to them, but she was waiting for train travel to reach somewhere close to where they lived.

Jacob, her second oldest boy, had married young right before the Civil War ended. His bride, Sally Ann, had been sixteen, just a girl, but they'd been in love. Jemima didn't object to the wedding, suspecting they'd already been intimate. She had been wise enough to see that they were a matched pair, so better to bless the union and move forward. Sally Ann had proved to be a good wife to Jacob. Standing at her graveside, it still didn't seem possible she could be gone.

She'd delivered a stillborn child in the second week of November, and although they grieved the loss, Sally Ann had seemed well but weak. She succumbed to childbed fever and succumbed weeks later, leaving her daughters upset and Jacob heartbroken. The trio of girls, named Faith, Hope, and Charity, would live with Sally Ann's parents now. Jacob had declared he couldn't stay in Kentucky after losing his wife and that he meant to light out for Texas to follow his brothers.

The Wilsons had two ways to make a living, growing tobacco and raising horses. Until they lost most of a crop a few years earlier, Jacob had farmed, but now he split his time between the plow and the corral. It was no secret he'd hoped for sons to help him, but each time Sally Ann had a child, it was another girl, including the stillborn infant.

After his wife had been buried, Jacob lingered at his mother's home. Earlier, there had been food, plenty of it, but he couldn't eat much. Mourners had crowded into every corner, but as it grew later, they began to leave, first the neighbors and friends, then the family one by one. Jacob's daughters had gone home with their mother's people, taking their possessions with them. Jemima had watched as he kissed each one on the forehead and said goodbye. She hugged each one in turn and watched them go, but her son did not.

"Jacob, if you want, you can stay here," she told him. The four-room house, once a mere cabin, offered space now.

"I might take you up on that," Jacob said after a long pause. "Our place is going to be awful lonely now, and I'd be thinking I saw her everywhere. Fact is, if one of the others wanted it, they can move on in. I ain't figuring to stay, especially since Maude and Thomas took the gals."

"Stay in the cabin or stay in Kentucky?" Jemima asked. She'd learned to ask rather than assume, especially with her children.

"Neither one," he said. "Ain't nothing left for me here. I'm not rightly sure where I'd go, Ma, but somewhere. They got the railroad all the way to California, and I might like to see that country. Or I might mosey on down to Texas, find the others. I reckon I know as much about horses as they did when they skedaddled."

"I have it in my mind to go to Texas myself one of these days," Jemima said. She'd written in a letter to Boone, but until now, she hadn't spoken it aloud. "Railroad isn't finished there, though, and I think it's a hard trip."

Jacob rose, poured a cup of coffee from the pot on the cookstove. "It likely would be for you, Ma. You're an old woman."

She bristled at that. "I'm not but fifty-one years old," she told him. "That ain't exactly ancient, nor do I have a foot in the grave yet."

No sooner than she'd spoken the words, she remembered

they'd just buried his wife and regretted them. Still, there was no taking them back, so she didn't bother.

"You might be feelin' young, but I ain't," Jacob replied. "Are you thinking to go visit or to stay?"

"I ain't decided."

He laughed a little, first time since Sally Ann delivered a stillborn child and died. "What's Boone gonna think if you turn up in Texas?"

"I like to think he'd be happy to see me, Moses, and Ezekiel, too."

"He likely would," Jacob replied. "I'm still working out whether or not he'd be glad to see me."

"He would be surprised, but I think he'd be pleased."

"That's what I figure, but I ain't going anywhere just yet. I need a little time to study on it all. When you write, don't mention I might be heading in that direction."

"I won't, but I will tell him the sad news about Sally Ann."

Jacob nodded. "Do that. I'm turning in for the night. I'm wore out."

"Good night, then, son."

Although it was late, Jemima sat at the table in the kitchen. She wasn't sleepy in the least, and her mind brimmed full of possibilities. She would like to look on her boys' faces again, and Texas, though it sounded like a wild place, intrigued her.

With that in mind, she got down the last letter she'd had from Boone, read it again, and got out paper to write a reply.

> *December 11, 1875*
> *Dear Boone and all,*
>   *I am well, and so is most of the family, but I must write some sad news. Jacob's wife, Sally Ann, died the last week of November after delivering a stillborn child. She had the childbed fever, and it took her. Jacob is*

heartbroken. Sally Ann's folks took the three little girls to live with them, and Jacob is here with me, at the home place.

> *I hope all of you are in good health. I pray for that each and every day. I think of you all daily. I try to imagine what life in Texas is like. I probably have no notion of it, but when the railroads get close, I plan to come to Texas. I want to see all of you, meet Boone's Rachel, and love those precious grandchildren.*

> *If the Good Lord is willing, I will do that all one day.*

By the time she'd written that much, Jemima had become weary, so she put the letter away to finish on another day. Tomorrow was Sunday, and she would go to church even if Jacob didn't. It was not a far walk, and she needed the solace found there. After the service, she made the trek home while snow flurries fell. Although her custom was to have a big Sunday dinner, there was so much food left that neighbors had brought that she and Jacob ate cold fried chicken for their meal.

With one thing and another, Jemima didn't return to the letter for almost a week. She tried to think of things to share but had trouble. When her children all were near, they were part of the cloth her life was fashioned from, she thought. She knew each stitch, was aware of any rips or tears, knew when mending took place. With three of her sons and two grandchildren in Texas, however, she had no idea what happened in their daily life. By the time she wrote a letter, time had passed, and there was no space for any but the most vital news. Jemima didn't write about the flock of geese that came over or the two she roasted after Garrett shot them, about the fact the new pastor was a widower who seemed to have an eye for her, or that the milk cow went dry. Such details wouldn't matter much weeks or months later, she thought.

And although Boone was good to write, he seldom shared tidbits of their daily lives in Texas. Jemima had no idea when her granddaughter first walked or talked or what she said as her first word. She knew Boone was top hand but not what exactly he did. When her sons trailed cattle, she had no notion of what they faced or how many miles they covered. If they were sick or hurt, she would never know unless it was something severe. There were no detailed descriptions about the ranch, although he had written about the bluebonnets in spring and the heat of summer.

On the last Saturday before Christmas, after she'd baked some gingerbread, Jemima sat down to finish the letter but stared at the paper instead. She had awakened with Moses heavy on her heart and didn't know why. There had been something in a dream she had, something she could not quite remember, that disturbed her, but the thought of Moses lingered. Jemima worried. It wasn't usual for her to have such worry over one of her distant sons. Although she thought of them often, at least once each day, it wasn't with such trepidation and concern.

The four years, almost five since she'd seen Moses, were no longer important as she went about her daily work and prayed all was well. Although he was her second to youngest son, Moses had become her right hand in the years after the war, after Boone left for Texas. He'd been her confidant and her help. Just nineteen years old, when they got word that Boone was expected to hang for a murder he didn't commit, she hadn't hesitated in sending Moses to find out how his brother fared. By all accounts, it had been her Moses who tracked down the true events of the killing and caused Boone to be spared. Jemima had not regretted sending him, but she did miss him, just as she did Boone and Ezekiel.

She had never been prone to premonitions, not the way her Irish granny had been, but Jemima had a sense that Moses was in trouble. She couldn't pinpoint whether it was a sickness or an injury, but she felt it, and so she prayed. There wasn't anything else she could do. There was no way to head for Texas that didn't involve a long journey and no way to communicate. Even an expensive telegram would take time to arrive and to be answered.

Jemima got out the half-finished letter and continued,

> Is all well with Moses? I've been troubled on his account, so I pray he is well. There is nothing more I can do but pray, although I wish that there could be. Write me back as soon as possible to let me know how he fares so I won't worry more.
>
> We are getting ready for Christmas here. I will cook two hams, and all those near will come, including Jacob's three girls. I am hoping that will cheer him for he has been in despair since Sally Ann passed.
>
> I wish all of you the best in the new year, 1876. This nation will be a century old. That is something to ponder.
>
> I pray that we will meet again in this life, and if not, I take comfort that one day we will be together on that bright and golden shore called Heaven.
>
> All of my love, your mother, Jemima Wilson.

With the letter finished, she sealed it. Jacob or Garrett could take it to be sent on the next trip to town. She turned her efforts toward making Christmas as merry as it could be under the circumstances, baking, and cooking, and planning. Her heart wasn't in it, though, not for watching Jacob mourn and worrying about Moses.

The day came with snow, and although she had never

adopted the custom of a Christmas tree as many did, Jemima's house was decorated with cedar boughs and a few sprigs of mistletoe. She enjoyed having a houseful, but when they had all gone, the silence made her sad, remembering when her home brimmed full each day.

Between Christmas and New Year's, Jacob worked around the place, taking care of chores that had been neglected. He added to her diminishing woodpile and fixed the broken step that led up to the front porch. He made various repairs around the place and took over tasks she normally did, like feed the chickens and milk the cow.

For some reason, she didn't understand, her worry for Moses diminished, and she felt that perhaps the crisis, whatever it might have been, had passed. Jemima still longed to know how he did and waited for the return letter, that would take a long time. Her letter to Texas was likely not to arrive for a month, maybe longer so she resigned herself to waiting.

After New Year's Day, the new pastor, a man named Samuel Coffey, came calling. He'd visited in the past, but this time was different. Now, the Reverend came courting. He brought her a paper of pins and flat out told her he'd like to court her with the object of marriage.

"You're a fine woman, Missus Wilson," he began. "I've had my eye on you since I arrived in these parts. I lost my wife some years ago, and you're a widow woman. Your young 'uns are all grown now, and I expect you may be as lonely as I am sometimes. I'd like to court you and consider a wedding next fall. Are you willing?"

"To court or marry?" Jemima asked. His declaration didn't surprise her. She had a keen eye for human nature, and she'd figured he had been a little smitten. She also thought perhaps he didn't want to marry so much for a second love but for convenience. He had no one to cook his daily meals, or darn his socks, or keep him comfortable.

"Either one," he answered with a hopeful glint in his eye.

"I'm willing for neither," she said without hesitation. "If I'm lonely, it's never for long, and there's always my Lord Jesus. I've no wish to marry, not you, sir, or any other. I thank you for your offer, though, and wish you well."

After that, he didn't linger, and after he departed, she figured he would move on to another widow, maybe Elizabeth Dickens or Rosie Lassiter, and still be wed come autumn.

When she told Jacob about the proposal over supper, he cracked a rare smile.

"Did you say no because you still love my father?"

She shook her head. "That's not the reason. Oh, I'll have love in my heart for Robert Wilson till they lay me in the black grave, but he's gone, dead as the rocks that cover his grave. I never thought to marry again and if I did, I'd have to have the right feeling for the man. I respect the Reverend Coffey, but there was no spark like there ought to be between a man and woman."

"Ma, you are a caution," Jacob said. "I've no thought to marry again neither, but I'd feel the same, I reckon. Do you think you broke his heart?"

"I don't," she said. "I expect he'll find another bride before summer and get wed in the fall. He wasn't favoring me so much as he just wanted a wife, a woman to tend him. He'll find that easy enough. Besides, I do mean to go to Texas one day, maybe when a train travels close enough to that ranch or when I come into a fortune so I can take ship to Galveston and go from there."

Jacob looked up from his plate. "You're serious about that, aren't you?"

"I am," she replied. "I know you children figure I'm getting too old, and maybe I'm soft in the head, but I ain't addled at all. I'd like to see my other three sons again."

"You're stubborn as a mule, so you might very well do it,"

he said. "You know I mean to head for Texas myself soon, don't you?"

He'd mentioned it more than once. Jemima could see he needed a change of scenery. Garrett had little time to spend comforting his brother. The girls, all married with children, were building their own lives. Jacob sought the companionship of his other three brothers. The lure of adventure might be an antidote to his grief.

"I do, son, and I'll miss you when you go," she told him. "I'll just have four sons to visit in Texas instead of three."

"Garrett won't leave Kentucky."

She shrugged. "He might or might not. But I will."

And in that moment, she made up her mind beyond any doubt. She didn't know when or exactly how, but she would one day find her way to Texas.

CHAPTER TWENTY-ONE

Marriage suited Moses. It grounded and enriched him. Mattie provided something he hadn't had since leaving Kentucky – a home. Until now, he'd bunked where he could, usually with his brothers or the other hands, but in a short time, she had transformed the humble cabin into their home. Her tender attentions and nourishing food helped speed his convalescence despite a small setback after Hammerschmidt's visit. By the time young Rob celebrated his third birthday on January 27th, Moses could once again sit in a chair for a good part of each day. By the end of the first week in February, he could walk a few steps if he went slow and didn't push it. On the Sunday before he turned 24, Moses was able to shuffle from one cabin to the other.

Although Rachel was great with child, she invited him and Mattie to join them for Sunday dinner. Since Moses' birthday was the next day, the meal was also a celebration. Ezekiel joined them in time to sit down to ham slices, fried potatoes with onion, biscuits, and a dried apple pie. Zeke turned up just as they sat down to table, back that very morning from Laredo.

"Come eat a bite," Boone told him. "What's the news from town?"

"Nothing much," he said. "But I brought a letter from Ma."

Although the news would be old, that brightened Moses' day. A letter from home was usually a grand occasion, and he thought they all liked the contact. As was their custom, Boone read the letter first, and then he'd read it aloud. He opened it, but in no more than a few lines, his pleasant expression turned grim.

"What is it, Boone?" Rachel asked, her belly so large she couldn't sit close to the table.

He sighed before he answered. "Sad news. Jacob's wife Sally Ann died."

Moses' mood darkened. He liked Sally Ann. She'd never been anything but kind to him, and now, having a wife of his own, he could better understand how hard the loss would hit his brother. "What happened?"

Boone's forehead creased with concern. "She had a stillborn child in late November, Ma writes, then had the childbed fever and died of it."

Rachel gasped but said nothing, just glanced down at her protruding stomach. Mattie reached over and took her hand.

Moses hurt for Jacob but also for Boone. With Rachel so near her time, Boone was already worried, and this would just give him something more to be concerned about. Thinking about what Mattie had said, that she expected Rachel would deliver sooner than anticipated, he said nothing because it would only increase Boone's anxiety.

"What about the three little gals?" Ezekiel asked. "Faith, Hope and Charity."

"Gone to live with their ma's folks," Boone said. "Let me just read the letter to all of you."

When he'd finished, they sat in silence for a few moments.

"She knew," Moses said with surprise. "Ma knew somehow when I was so bad sick."

"And she prayed," Boone said. "I imagine it helped, and then Mattie came. I'll have to write her back right soon and let her know you're well."

Moses nodded. "I'll write her a few lines, too. Maybe write a letter to Jacob, too."

"What do you reckon he'll do?" Zeke asked. "Stay there with Ma?"

"I doubt it. If he's like me at all, he'll run from his trouble," Boone said. "He might come here, or he might head for California or Oregon or some other place. He won't stay at the homeplace long."

"If he comes here, he's a fair hand with horses, and we could use him," Ezekiel said.

"We could. Liam wouldn't object, but since we own shares of the place, it wouldn't be a problem at all."

"Let's eat before it gets cold," Rachel said. "And let's not forget it's Moses' birthday tomorrow. You got sorrowful news, but let's not forget the happy."

The food was delicious and after the meal, his brothers presented him with a new canteen to replace his old one that leaked. The new style one boasted a canvas strap and a woolen cover around the canteen designed to keep the water cooler. It would prove handy as he made his rounds and did work on the ranch or out on the trail.

"Thank you," he told them.

After the meal, Mattie stayed to help Rachel wash dishes and clean up. Boone excused himself to smoke outside. Moses followed, and so did Ezekiel.

Zeke had never taken up the habit, but for the first time since his illness, Moses borrowed fixings from Boone and smoked. Boone said little until he'd finished two cigarettes, then he said,

"It's sad news from home, and my heart hurts for Jacob," he said. "But it worries me too. The same could happen to Rachel. I've worried myself near sick about her giving birth. I won't rest easy until the baby is here and she's all right. If anything happened to her or one of the children, I doubt I could bear it."

Moses figured Boone could. He was tougher than that, but he'd suffer, and Moses would do anything to keep that from happening. "I don't figure you'll have to, Boone," he said. "She'll do fine."

"I hope so. I guess I'd better start a letter back to Ma so she can rest her mind about you," Boone told Moses. "Not that she'll get it till March at the earliest."

"I'll write Jacob, too."

"You can if you want but I'm thinking he'll be gone before a letter could get to Kentucky," Boone said. "Starting tomorrow, Liam wants me to ride the perimeter of the ranch with him, the old boundaries and the new with what we've filed a claim on. He plans to survey it. I hope the weather holds, and I ain't fond that we'll be gone for several days, maybe most of the week. If it were closer to Rachel's time, I'd flat say no but that's not for a month or more. You'll look after her, the both of you, while I'm gone?"

"You know we will," Ezekiel said. "Moses'll be right here, and I'll look in every day."

"I know I can count on you both," Boone said. "Once we've done that, Liam said he'll file and get a deed with all our names on it, so it's worth doing."

The next morning, he saddled up Sprat and left with Liam. Mattie presented Moses with several pairs of socks she'd knitted him, but first, they idled in bed.

"If you're well enough to walk over to Boone's," Mattie said with a mischievous grin. "You're healthy enough to make me your wife in every way. Love me, Moses."

Three weeks married, he didn't need any further encouragement. If he'd had his way, they would have been joined that first night, although he knew well that he hadn't been physically able. He likely would have fainted during the act and suffered a setback worse than he'd had after confronting Hammerschmidt.

Now, on the day he turned twenty-four, Moses kissed her slow and lingering, his mouth cherishing hers. He set fire to her lips with his, and when a sweet heat roared through his body, he thought it consumed her, too. He used care, his motions tender as he caressed her, taking his time. When they came together, there was a moment when her virginity slowed things, then they came together, man and wife, in a way as old as time. Now their love was complete, he thought, and he hoped a child might come from their union soon. He knew the risks of pregnancy and childbirth, but he still longed for children with his beautiful, wonderful wife.

He made his way over to see Rachel. She greeted him with a smile, but he could see she was tired. He played with the children for a long time, then swept the floor for her. That taxed his strength a little, but he didn't mind. Moses came each morning and afternoon for a little bit. Mattie visited, too, offering her help with chores and the children.

On Wednesday morning, the third day after Boone left, Moses came over to find a frazzled Rachel trying to soothe Rob, who cried and held his belly.

"What's wrong?" he asked. "Is he sick?"

"He's got the bellyache," she said. "He got into the raisins and ate a bunch, so it's hurting his stomach. It'll pass, but he'll fuss till it does."

"Will it help if I rock him a spell?"

She sent him a smile. "I imagine it would, Moses. Thank you. I'm feeling a bit funny myself."

He took the boy in his arms and carried him to the rocker. "I hope you're not taking sick, Rachel. Boone'd have my hide if you do while he's gone."

"It'll pass, I'm sure. It's just being in the family way."

Moses rocked the boy and sang to him the old song about the Irish rover, then others. After the first few, Rob stopped crying and holding his stomach. Mima stood beside the rocking chair, adding her voice to his. "I think he's falling asleep," she told Moses. "He's fine. He ought not to have eaten those raisins, and I told him so."

"He should've listened."

She nodded. "Then Mama's belly was griping her too, but she ain't ate no raisins at all."

Alarm rocketed through him. "What do you mean, Mima?"

"She's been having pains in her belly all morning," the little girl said. "I don't think it's a bellyache, not like Rob had, but every once in a while, she'll groan and put her hand on her belly."

It sounded a lot like labor pains to him, but he was no expert. Moses watched his sister-in-law as she worked around the cabin. It wasn't long now that he paid attention that he saw her pause, grimace, and grab her belly. After a few moments, it seemed to ease because she straightened up and went back to the task at hand.

"Mima," he said in a quiet voice. "Could you go fetch your Aunt Mattie?"

She skipped from the room, and when the door closed behind her, Moses said, "Rachel, tell me true – are you having pains?"

He knew the moment she hesitated that she was. Boone should be here but wasn't. Mattie came in with the child and glanced at Moses, then at Rachel. When Rachel bent and moaned, Mattie rushed to her side.

"When did your water break?" she asked.

"Last night, I think," Rachel replied. "I got up to make water, but there was a big gush. My belly's been paining me on and off, but since Rob had a bellyache too, I thought maybe it wasn't the baby."

"Unless you ate a lot of raisins, too, I think it's the child," Mattie said. Mima must have explained. "Let's get you into the bedroom, then I'll fetch Ezekiel."

"I'll go," Moses said.

His wife shot him a look. "You won't. You've not been farther than across the dog trot. It won't help anything if you get down sick. You'll mind the babies and help Rachel if she needs anything, and I'll go. Is that boy asleep? Let me lay him down."

Mattie moved the trundle bed into the main room and put Rob on it, then she wrapped her shawl close and left. Ezekiel, flat running, beat her back and burst into the cabin.

"She's having the kid?"

"Looks like," Moses said.

Within the hour, it became evident Rachel was in labor. Her pains came hard and fast. Mattie managed to slide a clean sheet beneath her on the bed. She emerged from the bedroom and glanced from one brother to another.

"One of you is going to mind the children," she said. "The other one will catch this baby when it comes."

Moses felt weak, and his stomach flipped. "I reckoned you'd bring the baby."

"I've helped at many births, but I've never caught the baby. Boone's done it, so has Liam but they're not here. There's no midwife, so it's got to be one of you."

The brothers debated it for several minutes. Ezekiel suggested they settle it by playing odds and evens, but Moses rejected it. Finally, Zeke settled it by taking both kids over to Moses' cabin.

An hour later, the labor intensified, and Mattie told him the baby would come soon. Moses scrubbed his hands with lye soap and rolled up his sleeves. Terror made him more than a little shaky, and he wished Boone was there. Since he wasn't, though, Moses determined to do the best he could and not let Rachel die. What happened to Jacob's wife floated through his mind.

When the baby came, it happened fast. Rachel groaned the most she had all day, then Mattie had her spread her knees wide. Moses saw the top of the child's head and tensed. He got into position and waited. When the baby emerged, he caught it despite the fact the tiny body was covered with a waxy substance and a little blood. He'd always heard you had to slap a baby on the bottom or tap its feet so it would cry, but that wasn't true in this case.

He saw right off it was a boy, and then the baby yowled. His cry was both loud and powerful. Mattie handed him a blanket and said, "Keep him warm. I have to help Rachel pass the afterbirth, then I'll clean him up. Rachel, you have a fine boy. I'd guess he weighs ten pounds or so."

Rachel's face lit with joy. "No wonder he's had me worn down," she said. "Boone's been looking out for a boy, though he said he didn't care."

Moses looked down at the tiny face, bawling, and smiled. "He favors Boone a good bit, I'd say. What are you callin' him?"

"Benjamin Moses," Rachel told him. "Boone chose it, and I like it."

Once young Benjamin had been washed and then wrapped again in a clean blanket, Mattie handed him to his mama to nurse. She directed Moses to help her remove the stained sheets, and he winced at the sight of blood.

"She ain't bleeding bad, is she?" he asked.

"Not much. This is normal, Moses," his wife said.

His knees threatened to buckle, so he headed for the rocking chair. Mattie brought the baby to him. "Rachel will sleep now," she said. "Rock the baby, Uncle Moses."

He did, singing softly, his heart brimming full.

On Friday, Boone returned. Moses had been minding the children, but when he heard his brother's voice, he went out on the dog trot to wait. When Boone mounted the steps, Moses put out a hand to halt him.

"Rachel's got someone for you to meet," he told his brother. "I reckon you'll want to go and say howdy."

Boone frowned. "Who's here? This close to her time, she don't need to be entertaining much of anyone."

Moses watched as the possibility dawned, and Boone's face changed. "Moses, what are you sayin'?"

"I was telling you that you'd best make tracks in there and meet your son," he replied. "He's got all his fingers and toes, weighed ten pounds when he was born two days ago. He's doin' just fine, and so is Rachel."

Boone paled. "The baby came whilst I was gone?"

"He did."

"Glory," Boone said. "I think I might need to sit a minute first. I didn't think it would be until next month, and here he is. She's well, though, my wife?"

"Yeah, Boone. Mattie's with her now, and your other children are at my cabin with Zeke."

Mima popped through the door. "Daddy! I heard you talking! We got a new baby."

Boone opened his arms to hug the girl. "That's what I hear."

Rob came out, followed by Ezekiel. "Daddy's back!"

"I sure am," Boone said. He gathered his children to him. "I think I'd best go meet your new brother. Come with me, Moses. He's named for you."

"That's what I heard, and I'm honored."

Zeke rounded the kids back into the other cabin, so Moses trailed Boone into his home. Mattie was stirring something over the fire and smiled. "Rachel's got the baby. She's been looking out for you."

Although Moses held back so that his brother could have a private moment when he met his son, there was little privacy in the small cabin. He saw Boone approach the bed where his wife rested against pillows and kneel. Although he couldn't hear what Boone said, he knew his emotion was high. Then Boone kissed Rachel and lifted his son into his arms.

Once Rachel had gone to sleep for a nap, Boone brought the baby out into the main room.

"I think the little fellow looks like you, Moses."

Moses laughed. "I said he favors you."

"Well, there is plenty of a resemblance," Boone said. "I reckon then he looks like us both."

When Boone wrote to their mother, he had plenty of news.

Dear Ma,

All is well here, including Moses and my new son, Benjamin Moses Wilson, born two days after Moses' birthday. We were sorrowed to hear about Sally Ann. Tell Jacob my heart breaks for him with this loss.

You asked about Moses, so I will tell you true. Moses was taken bad with pneumonia right before Christmas, and I feared we would lose him. But the lady who is now his wife came from San Antonio, and she doctored him with an onion poultice. She brought him through Ma, and he is recovering well. In fact, he delivered my son because I was out on the range.

That's more news, and it is good. The three of us are now partners in the ranch with Liam Rafferty. Right now, it's still the Double B – short for Bonnie Blue like the late Confederate flag, but that may change. We are men of property now. Moses wed in January to Mattie, and she is a good wife to him. Soon as he has a chance, he and Mattie will have a picture made, and I will send it to you.

If you make it to Texas, we will always have a place for you to visit or to stay. I miss you, Ma, and send all my love. My brothers send the same, and our families, too.

Your loving son, Boone Benjamin Wilson

PS You might be pleased to know that my new son favors me or Moses or both. He says the child looks like me, I say he looks like Moses. Either way, he is a handsome little fellow.

The next time Ezekiel headed up to Laredo, he took the letter along and put it in the mail.

In time, it would reach Kentucky where Boone hoped it would ease his mother's heart and her worries, that she would find a measure of joy within the lines.

CHAPTER TWENTY-TWO

On the day that Jacob Wilson mounted his horse, Biscuit, and rode away from the homeplace where he'd been raised, he had no notion where he was headed. Away was enough for the moment, he thought. Biscuit was a rare horse, a pinto-colored Morgan, one of the horses that they raised or had when there were enough brothers to make it viable. Now, Garrett was the only Wilson brother remaining in Kentucky, and he still raised the horses. He trained them and sold them, still living on the homeplace with Ma. Jacob had been, too, right up until his wife died of childbed fever after bringing a stillborn child into the world.

He considered California because it would be a far distance, maybe enough to leave his grief and troubles behind. For the same reason, he thought about Oregon or Montana. Stories about St. Louis and Saint Jo, both in Missouri, intrigued him, but he shied away from towns if they were very large and both were growing. Heading East had no appeal, so it would be west or south.

After traveling aimlessly for a week, he realized he'd known all along where he was headed – Texas and his brothers. It was true he'd told his mother he meant to go to Texas, but he hadn't really decided. He had just named a place to relieve her mind.

Now Jacob knew it was where he'd been drawn from the start. Although he hadn't seen Boone for near ten years, he wanted to see him. They'd been close growing up, always vying to see who could throw a rock the farthest or who could shoot the most squirrels for the cook pot. They'd fussed and feuded but always with affection, and if they needed one another, there was no doubt – the other was there. Young Ezekiel had lit out for Texas at the age of fifteen, and he would now be twenty come March. Moses had been gone almost as long.

It wasn't until he reached Shreveport, Louisiana, and was about to cross into Texas that it dawned on him that he didn't know the exact location of the ranch. He knew it was near Laredo, in far southwest Texas, but also somewhere south of San Antonio. Jacob's plan had been to go straight to the ranch, but now he realized that wasn't possible, not unless he met up with someone who could provide directions.

He consulted a map, then asked around. Once he had, he headed first for Fort Worth, skirting around Dallas, then trekked south toward San Antonio. By the time he reached that city, he'd been on his journey for a good six weeks. Jacob left Kentucky a week after New Year's Day, but he'd dawdled. If he'd ridden hard and fast, it could have been less, but he didn't care.

Jacob had planned to spend no more than a night, maybe two, in San Antonio, but his money dwindled, and so he decided to stop long enough to earn a few dollars. He'd rather not arrive destitute, not when he wasn't completely sure how he would be received once he made it to the ranch.

In his search for short-term employment, he made the rounds of the livery stables, then the sale barns, and then the mercantile stores. Jacob came across one called Dawson's Emporium that seemed like a going concern, so he entered. Although it turned out to sell more notions than general merchandise, it was clean, with neat aisles brimming with wares. It was also warm and dry, both inducements since the wind had turned cold. Rain had been falling all day, and Jacob was more than a little damp.

The proprietor, one Phineas Dawson, greeted him and when he asked for work, he gave his name.

"Wilson?" the man said, his face brightening. "You wouldn't happen to be kin to either Boone or Moses Wilson by any chance?"

"I would," he said. "That's two of my brothers."

"Splendid, splendid," the man said, transformed. He shook Jacob's hand with such enthusiasm he might be pumping water and slapped him on the back. "Your brother Boone and I served in the war together, with Liam as well. If it wasn't for Boone, I'd not have my leg. I got to know Moses last fall when he came courting one of the Baumann gals. Then, of course, I got right in the middle of all that to-do with the German banker when I took her to the ranch because she feared for Moses' life. Turned out she was right about that, but oh, the results!"

Jacob had no idea what the man spoke about, but he did get two facts – one, this Dawson knew the way to the ranch, and two, Ma must have been spot on when she worried for Moses' sake.

"I've just come from Kentucky," he told the storekeeper. "I don't know about any of that. We hadn't had a letter for a spell."

As garrulous as a grandmother, as full of gossip as a housewife, Phineas Dawson proceeded to sketch the recent events for Jacob. If what the man said was so, his brother Moses had come to court a young lady from a German family. Not only did they object to his suit, but a German banker named Gunther Hammerschmidt had also been smitten. He was the preferred suitor, but the young woman, Matilde by name, had eyes only for Moses. After he'd gone back to the ranch, she had some premonition or something that he was in mortal danger, that he needed her, and she'd persuaded Dawson to take her on a six-day journey to the ranch.

They'd found Moses near dead, but she'd brought him back from the edge with her love and some remedy, Dawson didn't know what. The story didn't end there, however, for with her family's blessing, the banker set out to bring Mathilde home as his bride. According to Phineas, her mother had a dressmaker sewing a fancy wedding dress and was making plans.

The hitch came when the German found her at the ranch, married to Moses. She had refused to come back to San Antonio. Although her reputation had been in tatters, Hammerschmidt tried to bring her by force. He'd been stopped by Boone as well as Moses, who had come from his sickbed to stop it. Once back in town, Hammerschmidt and this woman's folks had tried to set the law on the Wilson brothers, but they'd done nothing wrong.

"And they tried to hurt my business with their talk," Dawson said. "But he's not a likeable fellow, Gunther, and no one listened. I have more business now than ever."

Jacob had taken a seat midway through the story, his mind reeling as he imagined the events that had taken place. He'd known Texas was a wild place, but the story sounded more like legend than fact. As he tried to sort it all out, he asked, "So, my brother Moses did recover?"

"He did, he did, and married the girl to boot. And I've heard now your brothers, all three of them, are partners in the ranch with Liam."

"And you know the way to this ranch? That's where I'm bound, but I've no notion where to find it."

"I do, and I can tell you how to get there."

His plan to stay in San Antonio and earn some money faded. He had enough to make the remaining six-day journey. Since he was that close to his brothers, Jacob would rather go on than not. If they were part owners of the spread, then surely, they could find work for him.

"I'd like to get headed that way as soon as I can."

"You're welcome to bunk at my home if you like. You can have the room where Moses stayed last fall. I'd recommend you wait until the rain stops – it's likely to rain for a few days straight, and it will make for a miserable ride. Just steer clear of Hammerschmidt and Mattie's family while you're here. I doubt they would take kindly to another Wilson."

Jacob accepted the hospitality. He was saddle weary, and the thought he could sleep in a bed for a night or two was inviting. He never meant to tangle with the banker or anyone else, but when he strolled down to the nearest saloon, not to drink but for a few hands of cards, someone spotted him. Although he'd never thought his resemblance to Moses was that great, he'd been pegged for him, and when he exited the saloon, his pockets lined with cash from a few wins, he'd been jumped.

Two thick-set men jumped him as he stepped into the street. He wasn't sure if they meant to intimidate him, rob him, or hurt him, but he fought back, which they hadn't expected. If he'd worn a pistol on his hip the way he saw most men here did, Jacob probably would have used it, but instead, he relied on his fists to best them. He did, but not without gaining a black eye and a bloody nose in the process. As he stood above his attackers, jubilant but more than a little winded, a man dressed in a fine suit strode up.

"How dare you come to San Antonio," the man said. "I will have you arrested and put under the jail. Have you jilted her so soon? If my men didn't convince you, then I shall. I've already spoken to the sheriff and he will be here momentarily."

"Mister, I don't know who you think you're addressing, but you've never met me before this day. I'm Jacob Wilson, late of Perry County, Kentucky. Since you set your thugs on me, I'll have a word for the sheriff myself. I'm guessing you're this Hammerschmidt character."

Gunther's expression wilted when he realized this wasn't

Moses Wilson. And, when the sheriff, who had no particular fondness for the banker, arrived, he wasn't pleased to find the German's hired men had jumped an unarmed man. Still, Hammerschmidt was an important man in the community, so the confrontation ended in a draw, and no one was arrested.

Jacob, with detailed directions and a hand-drawn map, departed the next morning despite the rain and headed toward his brothers. Because of the poor weather, the six days became seven, but he arrived at the ranch before dawn one morning. He stopped the first cowboy he encountered and asked where he could find Boone.

"I'd not rouse him this early," the hand said. "Not if you don't want a tongue lashing. But he lives over yonder, on one side of the dog trot cabin, and his brother Moses lives on the other. The other Wilson boy lays his head in the bunkhouse these days, but they're all partners in the ranch. If you're looking for work, I'd say go up to the main house and ask Liam Rafferty. He's the man who founded the place."

"I'll take my chances with the Wilsons," he said. His black eye had faded, but faint bruises remained, and after more than two months in the saddle, Jacob figured he looked like a vagabond.

He tied Biscuit to the nearest corral and walked to the cabins. Both remained dark, not surprising since it had to be a good two hours, maybe more until dawn. Jacob considered pounding on one of the doors but imagined the hullabaloo that would result. Boone did have a bit of temper, and he'd rather not be met with a loaded pistol, so he spread out his bedroll on the porch to wait. Although he hadn't planned to, he fell asleep.

Jacob roused to daylight, a cool wind, and a crick in his neck. For a moment, he forgot where he was and why he was there. He sat up, and a little girl stood, staring at him with Boone's eyes.

"Jemima Ann, what in tarnation are you doing?"

The voice came from a cowboy striding across the yard. He mounted the steps to the dog trot like he owned it, and when Jacob recognized him, he realized he did. Ezekiel was no longer the scrawny fifteen-year-old kid who hauled out of Kentucky. He'd grown several inches taller and had filled out. He was lanky and lean, but he was not a boy any longer.

Before he could call out a greeting, Ezekiel swept the little girl into his arms.

"You know better than to be talking to some saddle tramp," he chided her. "Your daddy'll spank you if he sees you. One of the hands told me there was a stranger lurking about, so I made tracks over here. I didn't expect to find you out here staring at the man."

He set the child down. "Go rouse your daddy," he told her, then directed his attention to Jacob. "Best tell me your name and what you want. My brother's particular about his family, and if he's in a bad mood, he's likely to shoot you first and ask questions later."

"Ezekiel, I wasn't expecting a fatted calf, although since it's a ranch, I thought it might be a possibility," Jacob said. He kicked aside his bedroll and stood. "I know it's been a long while now, near six years or so, but I thought you'd recollect your brother."

His youngest brother stared at him, mouth slack and eyes round.

"Jacob?"

"Yeah, it's me, kid."

Boone charged out of the door onto the dog trot. He had his big Griswold pistol in one hand and wore a battle face. He looked fierce until he caught sight of the stranger.

"I'll be," he said and lowered the pistol. "You look like you've been rode hard and put up wet, brother. Let's get you inside where you can get fed, bathed if you want, and get better sleeping than out here in the air. It's good to see you, Jacob."

Boone had aged but then he hadn't seen him since he headed to Texas after coming home from the war. He had to be just past thirty now. His face wore a few more lines, and there were a few touches of gray dusting his brown hair. "I'm glad to be here, Boone. It's been too long."

His oldest brother grabbed him in a bear hug. When he released him, he became practical.

"Where's your horse?"

"Tied to one of the corrals. It's one of ours from back home, a Morgan but a pinto."

Ezekiel patted Jacob on the back. "I'll go tend to him."

"I appreciate that."

Boone took his arm as if Jacob were feeble and steered him toward his cabin. "Zeke, holler at Moses, will you? Tell him the prodigal has come."

The little girl who'd first seen him peered through the open door, and Boone paused to tug on her braid. "Can you say howdy-do to your Uncle Jacob?" he asked. "He's come a long way."

"I have another uncle?" she said with a grin. "I thought it was just Mo Mo and Z!"

"Tell your mama there'll be an extra one for breakfast."

For a tired man, the whirlwind of family made his head spin. Before he could walk into Boone's home, Moses appeared. He grinned and hugged him, too.

"I'm as dirty as the devil," Jacob said, but he was smiling, too. "Ain't had much chance to wash in my travels. I might have had the chance in San Antonio if I hadn't tangled with some banker, Hammerschmidt."

"Gesundheit," Boone said, although Jacob thought the man's name had been Gunther and spat. "He's not worth the bread he eats. Come meet my wife and the other babies."

He introduced Jacob to a sweet-faced woman with light brown hair, a little boy of about three who was playing with a wooden horse, and a baby that couldn't be more than a month old who looked like Boone in miniature.

"He's our uncle," the little girl with his ma's name told the little boy. "He's Jay 'cause his name is Jacob."

Another woman walked into the cabin, as pretty as a porcelain doll with blonde braids wrapped around her head like a crown. Moses put an arm around her and drew her forward, "Mattie, this is my brother, Jacob Wilson. Jacob, this is my wife, Mattie."

"I'm pleased to meet you," Jacob said. This, then, was the woman whose family preferred a German banker over Moses, which had led to a confrontation at the ranch. If Dawson had it right, she'd also saved Moses' life.

Boone's wife served biscuits baked in a Dutch oven, milk gravy, and peach preserves.

"If I'd known you'd be here, I would have got some bacon from the smokehouse," she said. "At noon, we'll have frijoles and cornbread because we eat our big meal in the evening when Boone's home. We'll have beefsteak and fried potatoes."

Jacob nodded. Despite sleeping on the porch, the warm food made him sleepy. He had a thousand questions he wanted to ask, hundreds of things he'd like to tell, but weariness hung over him, heavy and thick. He required sleep but craved a wash first. And there was one question he had to ask. "Did you get Ma's letter about Sally Ann?"

Boone's grin faltered. "We did, and I'm sorry, Jacob. She was a good woman, and I liked her fine. Whatever I can do to help, I'll do."

"Don't talk about her," Jacob said. "Don't even say her name. I can't bear to think about her, so I do my best not to, Boone. I just had to know if you all knew."

"Fair enough," his brother said. "So, how's Ma?"

Grateful that they weren't going to pry, Jacob grinned. "Feisty as ever. She swears she's coming here to Texas one fine day, soon as they have train service within spitting distance."

"I wish she would," Ezekiel said. He'd returned from stabling Biscuit. "I miss Ma."

"Her letter said she was fretting over me right before Christmas," Moses stated. "Around that time, I near died of pneumonia."

"That's what I heard when I was in San Antonio," Jacob returned.

"Seems you were busy up to San Antone," Boone stated. "Heard all the gossip, tangled with Griping Guts, and met Phineas. Is that where you got the shiner?"

Jacob touched his eye. "I thought it was near about gone, but yeah. I likely wouldn't have found the ranch, though, with help from your buddy Dawson."

He wanted to shoot the breeze with his brothers and would, but right now, if he talked much longer, he'd probably put his head down on the table and go to sleep. Boone's wife seemed to be the only one aware.

"You look tired, Jacob," she said. "The rest of you let him go get washed up and sleep for a spell. He's here now, so there's no hurry to talk."

Once they had realized it was him, they couldn't be more hospitable.

"You can sleep in Zeke's old bed. It's still set up in the bedroom," Moses told him. "You can get a bath, too. We have a fair-sized tub, and I'll heat the water for you. I reckon my duds will fit you fair enough until yours get washed."

"Nothing ever sounded better," he said. Though they made him welcome, Jacob had an odd sense of disconnection. His brothers were familiar and yet they weren't. So many years had passed, he thought, so much they'd missed in one another's lives.

He'd arrived early in the morning, and by ten a.m., he'd had a warm bath in a tub that looked like it could water cattle and probably had at one time. He shaved and felt renewed. Jacob put on a calico shirt and some wool trousers that belonged to Moses and crawled into the only bed in the separate room. The main room held not only another bed but a table and chairs. Moses stayed until he got into bed.

"I'll let you sleep," he told him. "When you wake up, if you're hungry, come over to Boone's."

"I'll do that."

Jacob was almost asleep when Moses paused.

"Hey, Jake," he said, using the boyhood nickname that only the brothers had ever used.

"What?"

"I'm glad you're here."

"So am I," he replied and meant it. Then he did sleep without dreams.

CHAPTER TWENTY-THREE

Moses had not made it to the other cabin yet when Liam arrived, galloping up on his horse, eyes wild. He dismounted in a rush and tied the animal to the porch post.

"Is anything amiss?" he asked as he rushed up the steps. "One of the hands told me that some drifter was seeking Boone, and then neither he nor Zeke has shown up to work this morning. I came to see if there's trouble."

"No trouble," Moses replied, unable to keep from grinning. "Just the arrival of the prodigal brother."

Liam halted and stared. "Are you fevered again, Moses? What are you talking about? It's son, not brother in the Bible."

"I know that well, but our brother Jacob turned up from Kentucky," Moses explained. "I reckon he's the saddle tramp you heard about. It's a long journey, and he's been sleepin' rough. We weren't expecting him, so it's addled us a fair bit, although we're glad."

"Well, I'll be blessed," Liam said. "I would think so. Where's Boone? I wanted a word."

"Inside," Moses said and gestured for Liam to enter. Rafferty, however, knocked first.

As he came into the cabin, he removed his hat. "Miss Rachel, I apologize for my intrusion," he told her. "Might I speak with Boone?"

Moses edged around Liam and moved to where Mattie

sat, his niece at her knee.

"I'm right here, Liam," Boone said.

"I hear another brother has arrived."

"He has. I lost track of time, or I'd been on the job by now."

Liam waved a hand in dismissal. "Never fear, take today off. It's not every day a brother arrives. Does he plan to stay? He's more than welcome, all the more so if he knows horses."

"Back home, we raised Morgans," Boone said. "He's well-versed. I reckon he may need a few days to get settled, though. He came a long way and before he left Kentucky, he lost his wife, but I've no doubt he'll want to work if you'll have him."

"You should know I would, Boone. We'll be trailing cattle in six months. I imagine he's as good as you other three Wilsons," he said and glanced around the cabin. "Where is this prodigal? I'd like to meet him."

"Sleeping," Moses replied. "He's fair tuckered out."

"Tomorrow, then, or the next day. Zeke, you can have the day as well."

As quick as he'd come, Liam departed.

"Did Jacob get settled?" Boone asked.

"He did, got a good wash, a shave, clean clothes and was sound asleep when I left," Moses replied.

"I should've asked Liam if there's a place in the bunkhouse for him."

"He can stay with us for now if Mattie don't mind."

She spoke up. "You know I won't, Moses. He's welcome."

"You're barely a month married," Boone said. "I figured you'd want a bit of time alone."

"You sure didn't have it," Ezekiel said. "It didn't seem to hinder you and Rachel much."

Boone cocked his head as if remembering, then laughed. "I reckon not," he said. "I suppose he may be glad to have some company at that. Did he have more gear than just a bedroll?"

"He did," Zeke said. "I'll go fetch it, so it'll be here when he wakes."

Once the young man had left, Moses said, "Boone, reckon Jacob remembers it's the kid's birthday on Sunday?"

"I doubt he knows what day it is. Did you figure out how to make those tamales?"

Rachel nodded. "I have, Boone, with Mattie's help. I couldn't quite get them before but every time Ezekiel's brought some home, I've studied them. I remember most of what Graciela taught me back in Laredo. We'll have a batch of tamales with frijoles, and I'll make that apple cake he favors."

"I bought him a cheap pocket watch last time I went to town," Boone said.

"I still think we should have got him the Sharps rifle," Moses replied.

"After buying into the ranch, I don't know about you, but I'm a bit tight on cash. I figure we'll get one for him next year when he turns 21. I wouldn't mind having one myself, and I know you would too."

"It would be a fine thing to own, but I'll make do with what I have."

"Ezekiel's the best shot of us all. He's been using my old Springfield rifle since he got here. It'll serve him well for another year."

"Unless you need it," Moses said.

"My Griswold does me well," Boone replied. "I don't do much hunting, so a long gun isn't something I need. If I do, I'll borrow it back."

"He'll like the watch just fine," Rachel said. "Since you're men of leisure today, could one of you fetch water for me? And bring in a bit more wood, too."

"I'll go," Boone told his wife. "Wind's a bit cool for Moses yet. Then we'll go sit over at his place for a spell instead of being stacked in here like cordwood."

Rachel bussed her husband on the lips. "That would be helpful for your youngest son smells like he needs a diaper change and fed, then a nap."

The three brothers gathered before Moses' hearth and waited for the fourth to rouse. They spoke in low voices so as not to wake him, but from the volume of the snores from the bedroom, it wouldn't be a problem.

"He rode hard to get here," Boone said. "He's still grieving, too."

He lit a smoke, and so did Moses, the first since he'd been so ill. After the first couple of puffs, though, it made him cough, and he started to put it out.

"Give it to me," Ezekiel said and took the cigarette. He inhaled.

"Since when did you take up smokin'?" Boone asked.

"I smoke once in a while over to Laredo while I'm in the saloon – playing cards, not drinking," he replied.

"I'm here to say card playing can be dangerous too, Zeke."

"I watch my back."

"So did I," Boone said with a rough laugh. "Still nearly got killed."

"We thought you had," Jacob said, coming out of the bedroom with his hair sticking out in six directions. "We had the letter from your boss man saying you were gonna die for sure, then we got a letter from you saying otherwise. I was glad to hear you weren't dead and buried, Boone."

"If it hadn't been for Rachel, I likely would have been," he said.

"Then you escaped the hangman after Moses lit out for Texas, then from what I heard in town, he near died from the fever a few months ago."

Moses pulled a chair from the table for Jacob and listened.

Boone answered. "I feared he was a goner. Never tended anyone so sick as he was."

Thinking perhaps this wasn't the best conversation for a man mourning his wife, Moses asked, "Garrett's the only brother left back there. Reckon he'd ever come out to join us?"

"I doubt it," Jacob replied. "He's the one who took up the horse work and the farming. You never know, though."

"Do you think Garrett might travel?" Boone asked.

Jacob shook his head. "I don't reckon. He's set in his ways."

"I wonder if Garrett gets lonesome," Ezekiel said. "I would, I think if I was the only one of us here or there."

"I don't rightly know," Jacob replied. "But I don't think I'll be so lonely now I'm here. Gonna miss Ma, though, and she's missing all four of us. I think she's serious when she says she'll come down here one day."

"She'll be welcome if she does," Boone said. "I'd like my children to know her."

"That little gal of yours favors her," Jacob told him. "Though she has your eyes."

They spent the remainder of the day until supper time swapping stories and memories. Just before they headed for Boone's, Jacob said, "Yesterday, I felt like a poor wayfaring stranger, a little bit lost even with y'all, but now I feel about as at home as I reckon I'll ever be."

"That's what being brothers is," Boone said. To Moses, he sounded more than a little emotional. "Family is for always."

Those words reminded Moses of a verse he'd learned in church long ago. It niggled at the back of his mind until he could recall it all and spoke it aloud, "Two *are* better than one; because they have a good reward for their labor. For if they fall, the one will lift up his fellow: but woe to him *that is* alone when he falleth; for *he hath* not another to help him up. Again, if two lie together, then they have heat, but how can one be warm *alone*? And if one prevails against him, two shall withstand him; and a threefold cord is not quickly broken."

"Ecclesiastes Chapter 4," Jacob said in a quiet tone. "I recollect Ma reading that out to us after we'd quarreled over something stupid."

A rush of love for his brothers filled Moses' heart. He thought of their unity, their closeness, their caring while they dined on tender beef steak as they laughed and talked. The fact that they seldom said the words or admitted that they loved each other didn't matter, not when they demonstrated it in many ways.

They'd been raised with love, he thought, and it showed. Moses gazed across the table at his wife. Mattie laughed as she played with young Rob, bouncing him on her knee. Love came in many flavors, he thought, and kinds, but it all had a power that he could see but not explain.

Love was Mattie, cradled close to him in the deep of night. Love was Boone, his big hands clumsy and uncertain, tending to him when he burned with fever. Love was Ma back home in Kentucky, knowing somehow that he lay in mortal danger. It could uplift and strength, Moses mused, but it could also rip out your guts. Love was Jacob laying his wife to eternal rest, too.

At 24 years of age, Moses realized he had endured. He'd survived in unlikely circumstances, and so had Boone. They thrived and lived despite the obstacles fate cast in their direction.

That night before the fire, he sat with Mattie. Jacob had already retired, and judging by his snores, he was deep asleep. Moses banked the fire for the night, his thoughts still philosophical and deep. Mattie had some bit of knitting in her hands, the needles clicking out a quiet rhythm as she worked. He hadn't thought anything about her work. She'd made him socks before and knitted scarves, even a little wool hat for Jemima.

She glanced up at him and said his name. "Moses."

There was something in her tone that told him she had something meaningful to say.

"What is it, my heart?"

Mattie lifted her work so that he could see it. It was not a sock or a scarf but something that resembled a miniature boot. Her stitches were fine and even. He wasn't sure what reaction she sought, but he smiled, "It's nice."

"Do you know what it is?"

Moses shook his head, and she smiled, her expression as bright as dawn and as sweet as an angel. "It's for the baby," she said.

For a moment, he thought she meant young Benjamin Moses and then realized. His heart raced with such force he'd swear it bounced up into his throat. He had trouble finding his voice, and when he did, it sounded hoarse. "Mattie?"

"We're going to have a baby, Moses," she said with serenity. "As far as I can guess, it'll be born around Thanksgiving time."

He stood and reached to take her hands in his. Then he lifted her to her feet and pulled her close. Moses kissed her, his mouth slow and tender against her lips. He cherished her through that kiss, and when he released her, he folded her tight into his arms.

"Was I too rough?" he asked, worried.

Mattie shook his head. "Not at all, my beloved Moses. In fact, I'd like it if you'd kiss me again."

He did, and then again.

Moses was married. He would be a daddy before the year was out, and he tasted happiness in a way he'd never known until now.

He had lived for this, Moses thought, this, and more. They would live and love and raise a family.

Moses would love her forever and beyond, steadfast and

strong, part of the endurance of Moses Robert Wilson.

Lee Ann Sontheimer Murphy is a former newspaper editor and reporter who makes her home in the Ozarks. As a widow with three grown children, her focus is on writing romance novels that range from sweet to heat, from contemporary to historical. She has written more than twenty-five novels and novellas, along with a variety of non-fiction and freelance works. A native of St. Joseph, Missouri, where the Pony Express began and outlaw Jesse James met his end, she is a graduate of Crowder College and Missouri Southern State University. She lives in what passes for the suburbs in far southwestern Missouri, a little north of Arkansas and just east of Oklahoma.